Vaughn Collar

The Rift

Beginnings

The Rift
Beginnings

Vaughn Collar

© Copyright 2024 Vaughn Collar
First Edition

ISBN 978-1-953278-42-5 Hard Back
ISBN 978-1-953278-43-2 Soft Back
ISBN 978-1-953278-44-9 E-Book

All rights reserved. No part of this publication may be reproduced, stored in a retrieval system, or transmitted in any form or by any means – electronic, mechanical, photocopy, recording, or any other – except for brief quotations in printed reviews, without the prior written permission of the author.

This is a work of fiction. The characters are both actual and fictitious. With the exception of verified historical events and persons, all incidents, descriptions, dialogue and opinions expressed are the products of the author's imagination and are not to be construed as real.

Published by

Chesapeake, VA 23322

The Rift - *Beginnings*

CHAPTER 1

May 2, 2076
Scotland

It was a new day and a new age for energy. Peter McCormak stood at the site of the world's first commercial, full-scale fusion reactor and watched as the sun rose across the distant North Sea. A light breeze blew, carrying the salty aroma of the ocean, and only a few wispy clouds were visible, a dull orange from the rising sun.

A perfect day for a new beginning. Peter entered the building and made his way to his office.

No longer would the world be scarred by the search for fossil fuel or the atmosphere polluted with greenhouse gas. The promise of clean, almost unlimited energy had fueled the imagination of just about everyone – well, almost everyone. Various investment groups were still highly opposed to the reactor, especially anyone who had invested in gas or oil, for they stood to lose billions. Several times, their political attacks to disprove the science had failed, however, this didn't mean they were giving up.

Peter wasn't reflecting on the political atmosphere of the time. His concern was with the operation of the plant and the chiming from his phone – it was the Minister of Energy.

Vaughn Collar

Probably better if he chose visual feed. He used his best smile, practiced in front of a mirror countless times, and pressed *answer*. "Good morning, Minister."

"And good morning to you, Peter. This is the day!"

"Yes, it is, sir." Peter hummed. "Um ... I do have a busy schedule."

"Of course. And I'm guessing calls from political figures are nae high on that list. Very well ..." – the minister paused – "... I presume it's a *go?*"

"Yes, sir. We should be operational in about an hour," Peter replied. "And before I forget, thank you for your help with the press."

"Aye, I know what they can be like. Bloody vampires lookin' for the next juicy story."

Both men laughed.

Peter watched through the glass wall as the last member of his team walked through the door. "Minister, sir ... I have to go. Hope you have your speech ready ... including why you didn't tell the press."

The minister laughed and smiled and disconnected the call.

Peter was alone again with his thoughts. Recalling what had brought him to this point caused him to wonder. He was proud of his work – proud of the team he had working with him. The project, over twenty years in the making, was his life's goal. Ever since what happened to the environment, with the impacts of global warming and recovering from the recent nuclear war, he had dedicated himself to finding a different source of energy – a cleaner source. All past attempts were lessons of what *not* to do, and his team *would* succeed.

As he walked the short distance from his office to the control room, Peter glanced at his team. His pride swelled just knowing what they were about to accomplish. He strode to his workstation,

The Rift - *Beginnings*

ready to review the lengthy checklist. Multitudes of safety precautions were essential. The proper functioning of the magnetic containment chamber was his main priority. He looked over the readings and felt somewhat relieved. The instruments displayed the generators were operating at peak proficiency. He ran through the checklist again and then again for good measure. His hands shook with the magnitude of the moment. He took a deep breath to calm himself. Making his crew nervous was the last thing he wanted to do.

He cleared his throat. "Everyone! This is it. Just do your jobs, and we'll be generating power soon." One last glance at his team gave him reason to pause. A few were studying him, but most were focused on their work.

It was time. Peter sighed. "Ready the lasers."

"Ready," a technician replied. "Reading nominal."

The energy flow increased, raising the overall tension in the room, and a low background hum vibrated across the floor. A few techs glanced up with slight grins.

Peter nodded at the lead technician. "Begin the hydrogen boost."

"Boost phase startup," the man replied.

Peter watched the dials as the pressure rose. It needed to reach four atmospheres before firing. He stepped over to Carolyn's station – his assistant.

"Pressure's nominal for laser engagement," Carolyn said.

"Power up the lasers ... one through sixteen, ten-second lapse. Engage ... now!" Peter almost yelled. The excitement of the moment was affecting him.

One by one, the lasers fired. After the twelfth, a faint tremor rumbled through the building. Carolyn glanced at Peter and frowned.

Vaughn Collar

Peter studied her instruments and those of a nearby station. He felt reassured as he gave Carolyn a quick smile and nod. "So far, so good."

The thirteenth and fourteenth lasers fired. The tremor subsided and with it, the palpable tension that was filling the room. The pressure inside the chamber caused the plasma to increase temperatures. Sensors showed a microscopic ball of pure energy was forming. The degree skyrocketed, hotter than the inside of the sun, steadily increasing.

Carolyn kept her focus on her panel. "Sensors show everything is still in the green."

Peter nodded.

Another rumble coursed through the building. A few nervous looks accompanied the subharmonic sound that was felt more than heard. The atoms inside the chamber were almost at the correct density and temperature needed to initiate fusion.

"Carolyn?" Peter frowned. "Still good?"

She shrugged, pointing at the readings.

The fifteenth laser fired, and a loud beeping sounded. Peter glanced at the containment chamber and froze. Inside was a shimmering light resembling rolling ocean waves, and with a sudden crack in the outer shell, a blinding light blasted directly into the room.

"Sir?" a technician stated. "We might want to –"

The sixteenth laser fired. A sensor blew, shooting a shower of sparks. Plasma-like heat erupted from a nearby electrical panel. Smoke billowed with an acrid odor of burning metal. The feed controlling the lasers spiked. The matter condensed to a pointed source almost a singularity. A strong and rogue gravitational force erupted, causing the vessel to implode.

The sudden burst of protons ripped apart the room, growing and accelerating the gravitational wave. The excited particles

The Rift - *Beginnings*

soared faster than any human sense could register. The energy rebounded, mimicking a hydrogen bomb.

The blast blew through the reinforced concrete as if it were nothing more than paper, searing the countryside, and destroying everything. The pressure condensed into something almost solid with the rubble following behind. Nothing remained of the smaller towns north of Edinburgh. Edinburgh itself was just a smoking ruin - no one could or would survive.

The singularity ejected straight up as an invisible trail of thickened vapors blistered the upper atmosphere. Satellites would not track the path as it soared toward the moon, the speed was nearly ten percent of the speed of light.

The passage of the singularity phased across an unusual disturbance floating freely in space. Visible light bent as subatomic particles of electromagnetic waves condensed before expanding. The dark continuum was below normal detection thresholds. Invisible to Earth's sensors. Invisible to the human eye.

The strong magnetic field shimmered only briefly before the waves intensified, thickening the inner structure, and reallocating the basic characteristic of light. Now, influenced by an unknown reality, the ambient condition dispersed into an awakening vibration, saturating the dielectric field in a consciousness not experienced on Earth for billions of years. Contributing to and expanding the inner matter, fleeting electrical sparks now swarmed from the invisible field. Stray atoms emitting random particles only added to the phenomena. The polarized radiation gave, only briefly, as the split between realities merged. Light shards sprinkled across the darkened expanse as the singularity passed across the moon's orbit.

Earth spun as it slowly entered the shimmering rift. A slight warble echoed into the core's essence similar to how spring's early breath awakens a flower's bloom. But the influence on Earth was

Vaughn Collar

only just beginning. The beginning of a new time, a new era for mankind, and his inevitable search for a replaceable energy source.

The Rift - *Beginnings*

CHAPTER 2

cool breeze flowed from the mountains high above Petroșani in Romania. Spring had not yet arrived in the Carpathians as snow still clung to the peaks, collecting in the shadows. Fresh footprints, leading to a worn path, descended into a small glen. A temple, largely forgotten and surrounded by steep, rock cliffs was embraced by a dense grove of trees. Centuries of exposure to snow and rain had reduced two of the temple walls to rubble, with lichen now clinging to the stone.

Lucian Ciobanu, slightly overweight, a little gray running through his dark hair, and entering middle age, dug through the ancient temple, unaware of the events unfolding in Scotland. Reaching a good stopping point, he stood and arched his back to ease a cramp. His knees cracked. Sometimes, the dust made it hard to catch his breath. But the cold kept his joints stiff, despite the hard work, and a headache was slowly developing. Taking a sip of water, he realized a couple of hours had passed since starting his day. He sat on an old bench and dug through his pack for a bite to eat. Maybe a brief rest would help to rejuvenate him – a little.

Time for some fresh air.

Vaughn Collar

Stepping out of the small room, he paused. A strange flickering light was now emanating through the chamber.

Did I leave a lantern on?

The main chamber was brighter than it should be. His curiosity grew as he peeked into the larger room. A glowing, amorphous ribbon hung precariously in the air. It shimmered as if being waved back and forth, and small sparks glittered as they bounced off the temple walls. The hair on Lucian's arms stood.

Static electricity?

No sound and that seemed strange. Lucian took a step, and a small spark bounced off the floor, landing on his boot. The light fascinated him. It resembled a river of essence floating through the air.

Impossible.

He held out his hand and took another cautious step. A flash grazed his fingertips and he hesitated. He stared at the hypnotic glow, enthralled by the various colors coursing through the ribbons. His fascination begged, and he stepped closer. He reached out, and the sparks made contact.

The light covered his hands, curling around his fingers. Lucian felt neither heat nor cold. Slowly, sinuously, the light circled up his arms. An electrical surge swept through his skin and coursed deep into his soul. His eyes widened as the light pulsed. The tingling intensified only momentarily before stopping. The light pulled away, condensing as it faded. Lucian stood quietly in the now-darkened room.

He reached for the flashlight hanging on his belt. His shaking hands fumbled with the switch before it flipped on. A slight stinging remained as his mind tried to comprehend.

"What the ...?"

Pink blotches stood out against his pale skin, wrapping up his arm in a fractal pattern. He flexed his fingers.

The Rift - *Beginnings*

"They still work ... what was that?"

Lucian walked outside and studied the surrounding trees. Their outstretched limbs remained motionless – no wind, no noise from small animals, and no chirping birds. The silence made him shiver.

Strange. It's May ... there should be much more activity.

A pile of leaves stirred, and a squirrel's head popped up. A few moments passed before it went back to searching for nuts. Other small animals were now becoming more active. Before long, the sparse woods had returned to normal.

But what happened?

No signs of anything untoward. Lucian walked over to the nearest tree. He stared into the higher branches. Nothing looked or felt out of place.

He limped back to the monastery and picked up his pack. Standing inside the large chamber, he sighed. Tomorrow, he would return and continue clearing out the rubble covering what looked like an ancient altar. He felt certain there was much more to be discovered. Walking under the remnants of an old arch, Lucian stopped – markings?

I could have sworn those weren't there ...

He stepped closer and lightly ran his fingers over the symbols. The surface felt smooth, not carved as expected. He didn't recognize the language. Reaching for his phone to take a picture, he noticed motion. The script seemed to be reshaping into letters. Letters he recognized. They described some type of a protection glyph, but the last few words were missing.

Lucian reached again for his flashlight. Flicking it on, he scanned up the column and across to where the arch had crumbled. The darkness absorbed the light. He walked over to the pile of rubble. A few blocks on the floor showed the same texture as the standing columns. He crouched and searched for any signs

Vaughn Collar

of the script. He slowly examined each brick. A growing mound grew behind him as he moved the stones. The main column was deeply buried, and Lucian would need heavier tools than those he had with him.

"Without the other half of the glyph, the protection won't work!" Lucian shone his light around the room. Then it struck him. "Wait a minute ... how could I possibly know that?!"

He held three master's degrees in ancient European cultures. Perhaps some hidden knowledge was buried deep within the folds of his memory. Something he had once seen in his studies perhaps? But why would the lettering of this arch change?

Still feeling puzzled, he shone his light around the room to see if there was anything he hadn't noticed before. He gasped. A small door was now visible at the base of one of the square columns.

"I *know* you weren't there earlier!" Lucian scratched his head, taking a deeper breath. *This day is getting stranger by the minute.*

He picked his way through the rubble and knelt in front of the small door. He brushed his fingers around the vague outline. *No visible latches or handles?* All was smooth, except for a faint bump almost flush with the column. A darkened line along one side reflected when he brought the light closer. Over time, the wooden door must have shrunk and the hinges warped. He dug into his pack and pulled out a couple of small pry bars. One bar he inserted into the slight opening. After using his weight to make the opening big enough for the second, he repositioned the first. Lucian pushed and the door gave way with a loud crack. A shower of wood splattered his face, and he lost his grip. He yelled as his hand smacked into the cracked wood.

"Damn!"

A large splinter sunk into his palm. Pain shot up his arm and into his neck. Clamping his jaw, he pulled out the slender and aged wood, silently cursing the whole time. A wave of nausea and

The Rift - *Beginnings*

dizziness hit, and he sat back on the dirty floor. His vision narrowed. He waited for the sensation to pass. When his vision cleared, he fumbled through his pack for his bandana and wrapped his hand.

Shining his light into the darkness, Lucian peered into a small cabinet. Something brown grabbed his attention, and he used the pry bar to carefully lift up what looked like old leather. Two ancient books greeted him. He slowly pulled out the tomes, using the leather covering for protection. His hands shook as he tried to hold back his excitement.

He pulled out his nitrile gloves and a pair of tongs. With his dirty and bloody hands now covered, he cautiously opened one of the old books. The writing was ancient.

"What have we here?"

A page crumbled.

He sat back and sighed. *Slow down, prostule!*

Lucian needed to gain control of his environment. He could easily damage his precious find. After wrapping the tomes back in the leather, he placed them inside a weatherproof bag. He looked for anything else of interest. It was well after lunch before Lucian stopped searching. Heavier equipment was definitely needed to lift some of the blocks out of the way. He shrugged, deciding it was time to leave. As he walked past the glyph, he paused and snapped a few more pictures. He would need to examine this area more closely. Maybe he could find similar scripts on his computer to compare them to.

It was a three-hour hike down the mountainside to his hotel. He arrived with enough time to clean up before dinner. The hotel's restaurant was the only place offering American food. Most of Lucian's education was earned while living in the United States where he'd developed a liking for burgers.

Vaughn Collar

After his dinner, he worked well into the evening until his eyelids became too heavy. Sleep threatened but his mind refused to stop thinking about the strange, glowing glyphs. How could he have understood something in a language he had never seen before?

What have I found?

Ian McGregor – tall, blonde, handsome, well trimmed beard, and not quite fortyish – busied himself with his research in the Scottish Highlands. He had returned to his ancestral homeland courtesy of a grant from Boston University. His dig would help him finish his doctorate.

His research had led him through a maze, starting with the Norse in Scandinavia and ending in Scotland. It took him the better part of a month before he found traces of an old god house or temple. Ian had tried using ground radar and overhead imaging before reverting to plain old digging. The site was small but rich in artifacts. He had opened a passage into a new room, but the thought of crawling into it was unappealing. Tomorrow would be better.

The following morning, he opened the passage just enough to gain access. The room held the desiccated remains of a few leather bags and decaying shelves that formed a pile of rocks and roughhewn wood.

Oh great, an old root cellar. Adjusting his weight, he sighed. "I'm getting a little old for this."

A pain shot through his knee, and as he lifted himself off the rock, he banged his head into a beam. Dirt rained down the back of his shirt. The room was too small for him to stand properly. He reached out to balance himself but still fell over.

Ian, next time find a taller ...

The Rift - *Beginnings*

As he fumed, he noticed an opening behind a rock that moved when he had tripped. He shone his light into the opening and it disappeared into the darkness.

Another room?

He pushed and pulled on the rock until he revealed a small but carefully hidden chamber deep enough to scoot into. Ian repositioned himself on the floor to see better into the darkness. His light fell on several rods leaning against a far wall, where vague shadows had hidden the presence of carvings. As he panned the light around the small room, something metallic reflected.

I've got to get in there!

He crawled out of the root cellar and jogged back to his campsite.

"Now where are ... ah hah!"

He grabbed a small shovel along with a pick and a hand broom. The pain in his knee throbbed, reminding him to also grab a foam pad. He shoved several pairs of nitrile gloves into his back pocket.

Back inside the temple, Ian placed the pad on the floor. He studied the fragile wall and sighed. One wrong hit and the room could collapse. With a makeshift chisel and mallet in hand, he carefully picked out the loose rocks and dirt. With the opening now large enough to crawl through, he smiled as he shone his flashlight around the room.

Four rods covered in ancient symbols leaned against one corner. Several others were resting on the floor. A cache of animal bones sat on a ledge with more in a pile below. A slender cord hung from a peg in the wall with a miniature hammer, the symbol of Mjolnir, Thor's hammer, dangling at the end. The reflected flash from his first look turned out to be a shield. The bronze center boss and bands were in good shape, though the wood was pitted and cracked. He knelt and carefully brushed away the accumulated years of dirt. An intricate Aegishjalmr was revealed.

Vaughn Collar

This is a jarl's shield! No one but a jarl or maybe his favored second could bear such a symbol!

The rune was inscribed to ensure victory for its bearer. Ian's heart raced and his hands felt wet inside the gloves. He had to control his excitement at what he had just found.

He examined several rods, intricately etched with runes. Picking one up, he slowly turned it over. The rod felt light, probably dry from many years of being buried.

Well, this is odd ...

The rod appeared pristine, much more than it should, considering its age. Ian had never seen a rod like this before. Usually, Norse runes were on stones or weapons, such as shields or bones. Ian felt almost giddy, for this was the find of a lifetime and it was all his.

Over the course of the week, Ian worked alone inside the chamber, minimizing the artifacts' exposure to the elements. Sunlight, wind, and humidity could irreparably damage the cache. Every bagged piece, he carefully placed into containers lined with foam. The process was long and arduous. As he closed the last container, the ground rumbled. A trickle of dirt sprinkled from the ceiling tickling his neck.

"What was –"

Ian slowly crawled out of the chamber and stared into the sky. Birds screeched and swarmed from somewhere deep in the forest. Another rumble and pebbles danced on the ground. The sky brightened and a luminescent wave crested the mountain's ridge. Rocks, dirt, and dead trees tumbled toward Ian and his camp. A small boulder rolled past his tent, knocking out a light he had set on a pole. A blast of energy hit, sending an electric shock sizzling into his nerves. Pain surged through his fingers and up his arms.

The Rift - *Beginnings*

He screamed as he crumpled to the ground. His body tingled for only a moment before everything fell quiet. But the ground heaved sending Ian into the air. He rolled as if nothing more than a toy thrown by a petulant child.

Then, all became quiet. He opened his eyes and stared into a bright blue sky. A few puffy clouds drifted past. He sat up and glanced around as a cloud of dust floated down from the hillside. The aroma of flint and fresh dirt filled the air. Moving slowly, he tested his arms and then his legs. *Nothing broken* – but there would be bruises by tomorrow. He rested on his knees before standing.

He swayed. No real damage to his campsite except for the light pole. *Where is that water bottle?* Grit and dirt stung his mouth and eyes. The bottle was near his pack, and he splashed water into his face before taking a few sips to rinse out his mouth. As his vision cleared, Ian froze.

The surrounding trees looked as if they had been cut about halfway to the ground with dull clippers. The treetops were scattered along the mountainside with thick tendrils of smoke rising into the still air. Taking in a deep breath, he gasped as a million leaves spiraled down, adding to the green blanket that had already fallen. Feeling more puzzled than afraid, Ian stumbled to the top of the hill. He glared at the terrifying sight. The south face had been scraped clean. No trees remained as far as he could see. The valley, however, seemed undamaged. Although, the shadows cast by the peaks farther south made it difficult to be certain.

"My god!"

Ian sat on a nearby rock as his adrenaline rush slowly waned. Far to the south, nothing remained except for a clear path of destruction. His hands shook as he cupped them behind his head. The shadowy fingers of death had come looking for him and barely missed. *Not by much, though.* His stomach knotted as he contemplated what could have just happened. No movie could ever match this reality.

Ian walked back to his camp and his head felt a little clearer. But a tingling sensation in his hands and arms grabbed his attention. Pink blotches now covered his skin, running from his fingers to his elbows. He wiggled his fingers and moved his arms. *No loss of motion or pain.* As he stared at the blotches, the markings deepened and a fractal pattern glittered.

"What the ...?"

Ian flew his aircar over the affected region. The damage seemed to be widespread and not focused on any specific area. Slopes facing south seemed more heavily damaged. Numerous fires dotted the countryside. Fiery graves marked where several aircars had fallen from the sky.

He climbed to six thousand feet and hovered. Not a smart thing to do in this aircar, but his curiosity was overpowering. The path of destruction stretched as far as he could see to the south. The ground was razed as if a gigantic bulldozer had been driven across Scotland.

"My god! No one could've survived this."

With a pair of binoculars, he scanned the area. He could see Balmoral Castle. Rather, what was left of it. Smoke was still rising from the destruction.

"Wasn't the royal family supposed to be there? This is nae real!"

Ian muttered out his words as his eyes passed over Inverness. The destruction was horrendous. The harbor bounced with wood and fiberglass from dozens of destroyed boats. A few were in clusters, their graves marked by pools of burning oil. Masts sheared from impaled boats filled the water. A few were stuck into

The Rift - *Beginnings*

buildings or scattered along the seaside. About a quarter of the city was on fire, centered mainly in the south. Some of the skyscrapers on the north side were still standing.

It looked as if Castle Inverness had taken some damage, but its sheer bulk had created somewhat of a protective shadow – and that shadow was where Ian's hotel was located.

Hovering behind the building, Ian searched for a spot to land. An opening between a truck and a bright, red car caught his attention. Dust billowed out from under his vehicle, covering the red car as he came to a stop.

"Oops! Hope it rains soon."

Entering through a back door, Ian inched his way into the main lobby. Cots and blankets were strewn about with injured people begging for help. Their cries and screams, along with the rusty odor of blood mixed with a flinty taste, now filled the air. One woman seemed to be the center of attention, tossing out orders. Nurses handed her the charts before tending to patients. A man in a lab coat reached down and closed a dead woman's eyes. He shook his head.

Ian's heart reached out to the injured.

"Sir, step aside!" a loud voice echoed from behind.

He jumped as a pair of emergency technicians brought in another injured individual. Ian couldn't tell if it was a man or a woman, but he knew he was in the way. He climbed the stairs to the second floor, glancing out a window and sighing. Damaged and burning buildings now dotted the landscape, damage which seemed to lessen toward the horizon.

Wait a minute ... isn't the museum around here?

Ian focused his gaze on the downtown core and spotted the building. The museum did not appear to be damaged. He took in a long, slow breath and whispered a short prayer of gratitude. He

Vaughn Collar

stepped up to the elevators and sighed – the power was out. With a long whine, he climbed the five floors to his room.

He entered and paused to catch his breath. After opening his tablet, he pulled up Sky News. The main story was about the explosion. It was the fusion reactor near Ballingray. The photos told a tale of mass destruction. What had once been a hillside now resembled a burned-out circle. Most of the nearby buildings were nothing more than rubble. It was clear there would be no survivors. Edinburgh was devastated. To Ian, it looked as if a nuclear bomb had been dropped. Other news sites were providing the same coverage.

Ian sat back in his chair and shook his head. *So many people ... wow.* The stress and shock of the day was wearing on him. Incongruously, his stomach growled. *Oh well, lad ... might as well grab a pint and some food, then get started on my find.*

After pulling out the makings for sandwiches, he opened a bottle of Guinness. The first sandwich was finished, and most of the next, when an odd rumble echoed through his window. He paused as the lights flickered and came back on.

The hotel must have an old generator handy. Good ... the medics won't have to work by lanterns and candles. His glance centered on the shield he had brought back from the dig.

"Let's have a look at you ..." he said, donning the protective gloves.

The shield looked Norse – but not exactly. The runes embossed on the bronze bands were not familiar. *Maybe older?* He frowned. *I'll deal with you once I'm home.*

He opened a protective case and examined a staff. It looked to be nothing more than an ordinary piece of wood. Oil stains and years of handling had darkened it in two places. The wood had separated a little from age, and the staff felt light. The runes, however, were a different story. He had never seen such markings.

The Rift - *Beginnings*

Strange ... He knew the words. He could pronounce them – no – he could *feel* them – no – that wasn't quite right either. *I know I've never seen this lettering before ... but I can read it.*

The lettering somehow beckoned to him. Little by little, Ian worked his way along the staff. One line did not translate very well. As he rested his head on his hand, his arm shadowed the runes. He reached for the lamp and through tired, dry eyes, stared at the sunrise shining into the window.

Oh wow, no wonder I'm so tired. Another sleepless night.

Ian crawled into bed, his thoughts on the lobby and the victims of the explosion.

CHAPTER 3

The rift traveled in all directions. The worst flew north before dissipating over the Atlantic Ocean. In England, Ireland, and a little of Europe, only a clap of thunder rumbled. A few citizens had wondered if someone was walking on their graves. Animals felt the sensation with their acute senses but ignored it, returning to their normal activities.

Across the globe, bands of ghostly energy had flickered into existence before fading. In most places, the effects lasted only a few seconds. But in some areas, the rift lasted several minutes, leaving behind a legacy of changes. How much change wouldn't be apparent for generations.

For the human population, transformations were minuscule compared to the horrors of World War III. The war had begun in 2032, though signs in retrospect would be noted as early as the 2010s and maybe even as early as 2001, such as the attack in New York eventually named, 911.

Civil unrest had rocked the world. Riots protesting race, sexuality, religion, and political ideologies were commonplace, tensing and maturing from decade to decade. Small encounters flared in the beginning as emotional cracks deepened within

The Rift - *Beginnings*

society. Under the turmoil and chaos, plans were made – but by who?

Millions of laundered dollars had been funneled into the U.S. to fund civil unrest with hate groups enriched by anonymous benefactors, providing guns and ammo. Gangs across the southern states were fed larger and larger sums with the intent of distracting the citizens from spotting the evolution in laws and regulations to control and not govern.

Violent flares enabled the invasion of Australia – the citizens were unaware, too busy with the unrest. China, with support from North Korea, landed two specialized detachments on South Goulburn Island. By capturing the small town of Warruwi, they had found the perfect place to hide additional troops. Over the first few months in 2032, smaller units secured landing sites for the larger forces.

A frigate of the Indian navy had a flotilla of landing craft through the islands of Indonesia. The frigates were the newest in India's fleet and outfitted with a new technology – stealth. Therefore, they were difficult to locate.

When the invasion was brought to the attention of the United Nations, China fired missiles at the Indian ships. A series of strikes between the countries followed. The Australian military forced the Chinese out and it seemed like the fighting would cease – until a nuclear bomb was detonated in Guangzhou. India denied any knowledge, decrying the action. But the damage was done. Another nuke was detonated over Baleshwar, erasing it from the map.

The world was in shock, but the citizens were too busy with their civil unrest and could not respond. The Middle East erupted each side understanding that no *superpower* would be coming. Throughout Europe, scattered spats flared into major fights, sides being drawn along religious and political lines. The U.S. was unable to help, despite pleas from numerous nations, as its government was invested in its own civil unrest along racial and political lines, in combination with a border war incited by drug cartels.

Civil wars had erupted throughout Africa and South America. Indonesia and Asia were used as steppingstones for the ever-increasing tension between India and China. Additional nukes were launched – Beijing destroyed and New Delhi flattened.

By the end of 2034, conflicts drew to a standstill, mostly resulting from a lack of material rather than a negotiated peace. The damage was horrendous and many lives were lost. China ceased to exist, except in the westernmost provinces, where the population was reduced to less than twenty million.

Fallout across India pushed life to mostly a memory. Europe was in shambles. Africa was quarantined due to the spread of Aids, Ebola, and other infectious diseases. The southern U.S. was depopulated by over ninety percent.

The world's population quickly fell to less than two billion.

Brazil still held most of the unaffected, but controlled by a ruthless military, which installed a socialist government.

It would be decades before the world would or could recover in population or technology. Satellites were destroyed and the world's communication had fallen silent. Manufacturing facilities were favorite targets. Technology was reduced to pre-1960 levels with rural areas being tossed into the dark ages.

Humans had been thrown into a serious dilemma of their own making as if God's judgment had been rendered.

Now, decades later at a campsite in southern Virginia, the Asher family was awakened early by their dog barking and whining. The dog seemed focused on an area just behind the tent.

The Rift - *Beginnings*

Lance peeked out. "Hush it, Abby!"

Abby stopped barking and sat down. Lance noticed her attention remained on something in the woods, but at least she wasn't barking.

"What is it, Lance?" Pam asked.

"Oh, it's just Abby," Lance said. "Something probably spooked her ... maybe a raccoon."

A sleepy David sat up and rubbed his eyes. "Daddy, what's wrong?"

Lance smiled at his five-year-old son. "Nothing, little man. Go back to sleep." He reached down and ruffled his son's hair. "I'm going to see if there's anything out there."

Lance unzipped the tent and shuffled out. Looking around, he noticed nothing out of the ordinary - although everything seemed way too quiet.

Why aren't there any birds or crickets?

As if on cue, one by one the birds started chirping.

Lance looked down at Abby and shrugged. "I guess you scared them with your barking. Whatever it was, it's gone now." He gave the dog an affectionate shake. "Good girl."

Lance thought about crawling back inside his sleeping bag, but no - he was awake now. A few sparks rose into the air as he stirred the coals from last night's fire. He placed more wood on the hot embers and soon heard a little cheery crackling.

Pam could hear Lance fixing breakfast. The thought of food this morning -

No, don't think about it.

She remembered the morning sickness with David, but this one didn't feel quite the same. And - she hadn't even told Lance yet.

Vaughn Collar

Time to tell him. Oh, I do hope it's a girl ...

"Hey, babe?" Lance whispered into the tent. "Is David up yet? There's something out here he might want to see."

David rubbed his eyes, perking up when he heard his name. "Wait up, Daddy." Forgetting he was in his pajamas, David scurried out of the tent. "What is it?"

"Look at where I'm pointing," Lance said. "See the little, white pebbles? Those are eggs. I think I saw the mama lizard."

"Cool!" David said.

There were well over a dozen.

"Why are some bigger, Daddy?"

Lance took a closer look. Two of the newly hatched eggs were easily twice as large as the rest. "I don't know. Let's leave 'em alone, okay?"

Pam smiled, listening to her two *men* outside. Lance was good with David.

Another spasm hit and she stifled a gasp. It was centered in her abdomen and not her stomach. It wasn't painful – more so as if her unborn child was moving, but that couldn't be. It had only been five or six weeks. Whatever it was, it didn't last.

Pam poked her head out of the tent. "What have you two discovered?"

Lucian woke with his head pounding. Glancing at his watch gave him a clue.

It's 2 p.m.? No wonder I've got a headache.

Popping a couple of ibuprofen, he looked around for some clothes.

Preferably clean.

After a quick shower and dressing, he made his way to a local café. Still bleary-eyed and with his head throbbing, he scanned the

The Rift - *Beginnings*

menu. He ordered and sat back. A couple nearby was talking just loud enough for him to eavesdrop.

"Amanda, you know that reactor incident in Scotland?"

From hearing the accent, Lucian knew they were Americans.

"You mean where the bomb went off?" Amanda asked.

"Don't think it was a bomb," the man replied.

The waiter arrived with Lucian's order. He thanked him and returned to listening to the conversation.

"Bloody reactor blew up in Scotland, did you hear?" asked another voice, with an English accent this time.

The café was soon buzzing with discussions about the incident in Scotland.

Lucian leaned over to the Englishman. "Um, sir ... I haven't had a chance to catch the news. What happened in Scotland?"

"Not entirely sure," the man replied. "The news keeps saying it was an accident, but ... bloody hell, Edinburgh is all but erased from what I've seen."

Eyes widening, Lucian dug into his pack and pulled out his tablet. He loaded a satellite image of Edinburgh.

Oh my god!

Edinburgh resembled Beijing after it was nuked. Only the farthest reaches of the city remained.

"Look!" he said, showing the image to the Englishman.

"Oh my god!" the Englishman replied.

Lucian could tell someone was peering over his shoulder. The American was almost breathing in his ear. The odor of coffee and stale breath rubbed raw against Lucian's nerves.

"Excuse me, but ... can you look it up yourself?" Lucian asked, his voice cold.

The American backed off and returned to his table. "C'mon, Amanda. Damn Europeans." The man and his wife left without leaving a tip.

Vaughn Collar

Lucian watched them walk out. "Good riddance," he muttered, returning to his screen and scrolling through the pages.

"Sir, your tab." The waiter nodded. "Will there be anything else?"

"No, thank you." Lucian returned to scanning through the news.

Lucian entered his room.

Some tea would be nice. That damn American. No manners whatsoever.

As the water boiled, Lucian hung up his jacket and cleared off the desk for his laptop. He wanted to compare the pictures taken of the old script to various known writings. Lucian expected he would need to research ancient languages. The sound of boiling water prompted him to fix his tea. With a full cup in hand, he sat to scroll through the photos.

"What? Where are the images?"

The photos were blank. He reached for the tome but yanked away his hands. *First things first, Luce ... gloves!* He opened the case to find that the text was still intact in the tomes.

"Ah, good. Still there. But why are some of the photos blank? They weren't last night."

Lucian kept searching the internet. He soon found a few pictures of ancient script written about daily life.

"Hmm, only a few of my pictures didn't work. How odd ..."

He shook his head and sighed. *Maybe a reboot?* As his computer screen flashed off and back on, Lucian took a couple of sips. He loaded up his photos of the arch again and sighed. They were still blank. *But why?*

Thinking back, he remembered a few words. His memory seemed fuzzy and not at all like his normal memory. He could

The Rift - *Beginnings*

remember a portion of a few sentences – a few words then a gap – almost like poor reception on an old-fashioned radio.

Biting his lip, he thought about what tomes he had taken pictures of. He opened the first book and turned to the page where his photos had turned blank.

Pinch of sand ... Lucian shook his head. "What does that ...?" He kept reading. *Lubricant ... slippery surface ...*

The passage seemed to have been written by various people. The handwriting looked different, and even the way the words were used was distinct. He placed the tome aside and reached for another. The second tome was the same. The handwriting looked different in certain sections. The segments that blurred his vision seemed to be more carefully written from what he could tell.

Glancing out the window, Lucian studied the gray sky, clouds building up on the peaks of the nearby mountains. He thought about climbing back to the site where he had found the ruins to take another good look at that arch. However, the pending storm wasn't going to allow that.

"Maybe another day."

With his frustration building, Lucian opened the first tome and returned to the section with a list of items – powdered silver, a glass lens, and an oil he'd never heard of. The remainder of the section wasn't legible.

Muttering a few choice words in his native Romanian tongue, Lucian closed the tome. His eyes stung and the tension in his neck was returning. He thought about calling it a night, but sheer stubbornness moved his hands to the second tome. Opening it, he scanned over the odd script. A sharp pain seared through his brain as if needles were being shoved into his eyes. He resisted the temptation to toss the tome aside and carefully closed it instead. He sat back, rubbing his temples.

Enough of this ... no, not yet Luce.

Vaughn Collar

He stood and stretched out his legs. The window faced the mountain where the old temple stood. His gaze rested on the mountaintop.

What other mysteries do you harbor, I wonder?

He glanced over his shoulder and stared at the tomes. A few steps brought him back to the table. He opened the first one and read.

"Translate ... means ... use ..." The letters blurred with the same continued fatigue. *I need a break.*

Not far from Highwood, Montana, Steve Mansford searched for a couple of his lost mares. A rancher with a small herd, losing two would be a sore blow if truly lost. Not to mention they were carrying foals. His family needed them for the coming auction.

The wind piercing through his jacket chilled him. He followed the trail to the creek that ran through his property. More than once he'd tracked wayward horses to this small area. The tracks were recent and not yet washed away by the rain. He felt a little promise since the high water had receded, and there was a good chance the horses were simply stuck, unable to climb out of the muddy creek.

Nearing the stream, Steve's horse, Tartar, raised his head and sniffed the breeze. It neighed loudly and two calls returned.

"Uh, hmm. Just what I thought."

The path took a hard right, where a couple of large boulders blocked his view. As he passed the first, the distinct odor of ozone filled him with apprehension. The hair on his arms stood. He glanced up - no clouds, at least no thunderclouds.

"What in the ...?"

The world lit as a bright light pierced through the dense brush. Steve closed his eyes. It was as if he were looking directly into a

The Rift - *Beginnings*

searchlight. One of the horses screamed, and a loud *thud* echoed through the valley.

Just as fast as the light lit, it darkened. A horse screamed again and the sound tore through the air. A loud crashing as if branches were breaking filled Steve with dread. He hurried around the last boulder and prepared for the worst. Daisy, the light brown quarter, was on the ground and not moving. Star, a black Morgan, was tangled in a large bramble, thrashing and kicking with the whites of her eyes reflecting her panic.

Steve dismounted and approached, pulling Tartar behind him. Speaking softly, he stepped up to Star and rubbed her neck. Tartar nosed Daisy, and Steve feared the worst but was rewarded with the mare lifting her head.

"Good boy, Tartar," he said.

He checked Daisy for injuries and found none aside from a few scratches. Star looked at him, her eyes seeming shallow as if surrendering.

Steve nodded, thankful for the lack of injuries. *But what the hell was that light?*

They arrived back at the corral and his daughter, Stacy, darted from the house. Her dog barked, running across the yard.

"Dad? Are they okay?" Stacy asked.

"Yes," Steve replied. "Star was a little spooked. She was stuck in a briar. Seems fine now."

Stacy hugged Daisy's neck and was rewarded with a soft nicker. "You scared me. I'm glad you're fine now." She took the ropes from her father, leading Daisy and Star to the barn.

Steve watched with a soft smile. His little girl wasn't quite so little anymore.

Her dog's attitude differed somehow. The dog pranced around his horse as if to play. Tartar tossed his head at the dog.

Steve frowned. "What's gotten into you two?"

Vaughn Collar

Lucian left the hotel and headed to his favorite café. His footsteps echoed along the mostly empty streets. People walked by with their gazes lowered. A sense of malaise hung over the town like a thick fog. Lucian heard only a few faint whispers. *Ce este ...?*

He arrived at the café, and the sounds from various videos were a distracting contrast to the silence outside. All TVs were on programs discussing the recent destruction. He found a corner table where only one screen faced him.

A waitress arrived with a menu. "May I help you?"

"Yes, thank you," Lucian replied. "I'd like a cup of chamomilla bohemica, and ... um, a plate of GoGoși."

The waitress nodded, smiled, and aimed for the kitchen.

Lucian kept his eyes on the coverage, struggling to hear the newscaster over the cacophony of other videos. The explosion in Scotland now dominated the world news. He listened with morbid fascination. As a college professor, Lucian held the education and background to understand this was a huge setback. He idly wondered if anyone would attempt to rebuild.

The waitress arrived with his order. Lucian smelled the aroma of the GoGoși.

"Is there anything else I can get you?" she asked.

"No, thank you." Lucian smiled at the waitress. "This looks great."

He attacked his order with a barely restrained gusto. Finishing his food, *which was excellent*, Lucian sat back and thought about his next stop. *Just tell her the minimum, Luce.*

Lucian flipped through his wallet and left a nice tip before setting off to his destination. A sign that hung over an old, wooden door had faded into a uniform, dull blue, with the words, *Cărțile și Artefactele Nadei,* 'Nadia's Books and Artifacts.' The store

The Rift - *Beginnings*

specialized in antiquities, books and scrolls, and was family-owned and operated. Established by her grandparents, much of Nadia's stock was over a hundred years old. Her little store was as much a part of the mountain surrounding the town as the town surrounding her, well known, and visited by historians across Europe. The backdrop of the tall peaks to the east of Petroșani was in line with the store, drawing the attention of tourists and locals.

The old sheep's bell dinged as Lucian pushed on the door. As always, the aroma of leather, decaying paper, and tangy copper combined gave him the feeling of being home. Various old books and bound scrolls lined the numerous shelves. Glass cases held the rarest of carvings, statuettes, and jewelry. One case was held up with iron sides, the contents slightly distorted from the Lexan walls. Lucian spotted a newer display behind the counter, an ancient shield and sword, engraved with the crest of a house or lord who had long since passed.

An older-looking lady standing near the counter glanced up. "Lucian ... you have returned?"

"Hello, Nadia. I have something for you." He stepped up to the counter and smiled. "Found this at the site. The print ..." – he shook his head – "... I've not seen it before. Could you take a look?"

She peered over her glasses and frowned. "Certainly. You have it with you?"

He reached into his backpack. "I do. The book's old ... how old, I'm not sure." He placed the book still inside the leather wrapper on the counter.

Nadia donned rubber gloves and turned a small fan toward the book.

"Is there someplace more private where we can talk?"

She nodded, stood, picked up the leather-covered tomb, and strode to the back of her office, Lucian close behind. Rows of old

Vaughn Collar

books, scrolls, and numerous other items that look enticing were sealed inside plexiglass containers. Frames of various scripts hung on the walls. An old-fashioned microscope sat on a table next to a dagger with intricate carvings on the handle. The stench of various chemicals and years upon years of aging scrolls seemed stronger back here, filling him with a longing to stay in the room forever.

Nadia stopped at a blank wall and slid her hand up the paneling. A door swung open.

Lucian's eyes widened. He held back his excitement as he cautiously entered.

The room was filled with easels and desks with magnifying glasses. There were tables covered with containers of what looked like various chemicals. The scent of preservatives filled the air, giving him a feeling of familiarity. He'd never been in her private workspace before and had to push down his enthusiasm. If only he could spend a day and night in this room – *Oh well, I can only dream.* He was a little startled when Nadia interrupted his reverie.

"What have you brought that requires such privacy?"

Lucian pointed to the tome in her hand. "I have no true idea how old it is ... but most of the writing I don't recognize."

Nadia frowned and cautiously perused the book. Tapping her lips with her gloved finger, she appeared lost in thought. Her gaze sailed around the room until she focused on a far shelf. She walked over and picked through the scrolls, pulling one out before putting it back. She reached for two others with a barely audible, "Yes ..." She carefully unfurled one of the scrolls and scanned through the lines.

Lucian glanced over her shoulder at the ancient writings. A few words were familiar but most looked foreign.

Nadia glanced up and frowned before returning to the material. She opened the book, setting it beside the scroll. Slowly, she traced her finger along the ancient writings. At times, she

The Rift - *Beginnings*

skipped over a few words almost as if they weren't there. Lucian watched, feeling a little concerned.

Why can't she see all the words?

"This writing," she whispered, "I've seen only once." She stepped over to a different wall. After touching a hidden spot, a small drawer opened, and she pulled out a sheet of parchment. With a glance, she handed it to Lucian.

His eyes widened. The script matched.

"Where did you ... oh, never mind," Nadia said. "I don't want to know."

"What is it?" Lucian asked.

"This language is old ... very old. It predates the time of Vlad Tepes. I thought I had the only example that was not sealed away by an old museum." She pointed at the parchment. "It's a little shocking to discover I was wrong. Everything from that period was destroyed or hidden away. The communists didn't like to acknowledge history other than their version. They took extreme measures to deny us our heritage." She turned a few more pages before closing the tome. "This is authentic? Not placed by someone as a joke?"

Lucian nodded, frowning. "You do recall what I do for a living, yes?"

Nadia sighed.

Dealing with Lucian was akin to dealing with a snake. Most times, he remained calm and was easy to get along with – but he was always ready to strike if he should feel the least bit slighted.

"Yes, I remember. Senior professor and assistant department head of history at Leiden University. Multiple advanced degrees in history, linguistics, and sociology. I know very well who you are, Dr. Ciobanu." She studied him with a frown. "What are we –"

Lucian held up his hand. "I understand. This is ... a state secret? Your husband won't be curious about this?"

Vaughn Collar

She shrugged and touched another place on the wall. A piece of the floor dropped and slid out of the way.

"When was this built?" Lucian asked, staring into the darkness.

"1960's." Nadia motioned for Lucian to wait a moment, allowing her to step down a set of stairs. She reached the bottom and flicked on the lights. She smiled at Lucian.

He rolled his eyes. *She's enjoying this. Fine.*

"A bunker ... used for hiding dissidents," she said. "We found it quite by accident. Comes in handy once in a while. Come."

Lucian stepped down into a room where bunks lined the walls. The place appeared to be huge. "Sleeps, what ... ten?"

Nadia nodded. She motioned to one of the cots and sat across from him. "If what you say is true ... and this is authentic ... then what you have found is priceless. There are only two documents known to trace to the Tepes era. Those letter variations ..." – Nadia shook her head – "... were used by one individual and one individual only. Tepes himself. It is written that he practiced black magic. Streaks of barbarity, absolutely no conscience. Many of the Dracula legends draw from his reign of terror. Even if only half the tales are true ... he makes Hitler look like Gandhi!" She sighed again. "Where did you find this?"

The coastal forest of British Columbia was still mostly wilderness and barely explored. Many animals had never set their eyes on a human before. Only those living near the coast were exposed to people.

A small fishing vessel pulled into one of the innumerable inlets, seeking protection from a summer storm. Usually, this time of year was a quiet time in British Columbia. However, the captain knew the ocean was a capricious place, even during calmer

The Rift - *Beginnings*

weather. A couple of deckhands were taking advantage of the downtime, repairing a few of the nets.

A shimmering light flashed from inside the forest not far from the beach. The deckhands stared, frozen in place.

"So pretty ..." one of the men whispered.

The other ran into the cabin. Fumbling in the dark, he found the ship's alarm and pulled the handle. As the horn blared, an eerie scream echoed out from the forest, loud enough to be heard over the alarm. It sounded like an animal or whatever it was in pain.

The captain ran up on deck. The strange light was now fading. The crew looked at each other, dumbfounded by what they had just seen. The captain glared at the two, not pleased at being disturbed by a mysterious light show.

"Next time," the captain grumbled, "figure out if there's a *real* threat before waking –"

The animal's cry charged through the air. It sounded as if it came from where the mysterious light had just faded. The cry was answered as a different call echoed out from much deeper inside the forest.

"Get the bloody guns!" the captain ordered, panic edging his voice.

The crew jumped, now holding rifles.

The first wave appeared in a small clearing of the forest. A tree had fallen long ago and left a large hole. Water had filled the depression, and mosquitoes had laid their eggs. Vegetation was growing in a circular pattern around the small pool.

The light washed over a huge creature still considered a myth and fable. It had been thrown across the glen and landed inside a patch of devil's club. It screamed out. It had hit its head on a log

Vaughn Collar

and acted dazed. Shaking, it rose onto one knee and grabbed the nearest plant. Another devil's club. Yowling, the creature scrambled out of the patch with only its dense fur protecting it from the sharp thorns. It stumbled over a fallen log and sat. A cry from the northeast told the creature its mate was nearby.

The strong odor of fish drifted across the water. Fish, mixed with another scent, a familiar stench the creature associated with danger. It had smelled both before. The strangers were now holding those sticks that spit flames and could kill from many paces.

Its mate called out again.

The creature left, its feet and hands throbbing from the embedded thorns. The night calmed as it disappeared into the denser brush.

The Rift - *Beginnings*

CHAPTER 4

Ian woke to the sound of sirens, which had haunted him throughout the night. He had finally fallen asleep sometime in the early morning. Still feeling groggy, he shuffled into the kitchenette. After filling a kettle with water, he placed it on a burner. He missed coffee, which was quite rare and expensive – another victim of the war. He turned to the small fridge and picked out the cream cheese, placing it next to a bag of bagels. A small basket held a few bagged utensils, and when he tore one open, they flew across the room.

Gonna be one of those days is it, Laddy?

He picked up the utensils and brushed them off. As he spread a thick layer of cream cheese onto a bagel, the water boiled. Ian preferred his tea with a little sugar, no milk. After dropping a teabag into the water, he reached for his tablet.

The disaster now occupied just about every streaming site. A satellite image showed the true extent of the destruction. Inverness was heavily damaged. Though few buildings were destroyed, it looked almost as if every window was shattered. Fires were widespread, especially on the western side. The destruction

Vaughn Collar

appeared to follow the main road connecting Inverness to Central Scotland.

He sat back, trying to digest everything. Scotland had taken a heavy beating. It could be decades before the country recovered. Even the Highlands were affected, with most of the southern-facing slopes stripped bare. Luckily, the northern slopes only showed damage at their peaks.

The programs continued to cycle through the same information, so Ian shut off his tablet. The water was still hot enough for another cup of tea, and he needed to focus on his work.

It was time to study the mysterious staffs. Most of the runes he could read but some were archaic and would require more research. The style of the carvings was noteworthy because the runes were not in the typical blocky style. They seemed to flow together. Something only a master carver would be capable of creating. Someone only a clan jarl would employ – *hmm*.

Turning the staff over revealed an odd pattern in the script. The placement of the runes was such they would only be visible with a two-handed grip. Turning the staff slowly showed that the design circled the rod. Carefully examining the markings, Ian's vision blurred, and a pounding flared inside his head, feeling like the worst brain freeze he'd ever suffered, centering just behind his eyes.

He winced and placed the staff on the table, resisting the urge to throw it across the room. Disoriented and dizzy from the headache, Ian reached out, feeling for his chair, and collapsing into it. The pounding stopped almost as quickly as it started. He sighed, shaking his head, still feeling disoriented from the pain.

That was strange. A quick check of the time showed it was almost noon. *Woah ... no wonder I'm getting headaches. I'm hungry!* As if needing a reminder, his stomach growled. *I wonder what's open? The dining area is ... well ... full of bodies.* He stood and strode over to

The Rift - *Beginnings*

the window, spotting an open bar and café about a block away. *One of the two should have something decent.*

The elevators were still not working. A glance into the dining area confirmed it wasn't open. A few victims were still being cared for, although most were up, sporting a variety of casts and splints. The kitchen looked operational, serving small meals to the patients.

A soft drizzle greeted Ian as he walked outside. Though the streets were now slick, Ian guessed the firefighters were rejoicing. Numerous fires were still smoldering and therefore, the rain was a true blessing.

Ian walked into the café and scanned the menu. The daily special was steak and Guinness pie. *Perfect!*

A harried hostess greeted him and showed him to a window seat. The waitress was right behind her.

"I'd like the daily special, lass. It's been a while and that sounds good."

She nodded. "And to drink?"

"Hmm ... Earl Grey, please. Too early for anything stronger."

She smiled and headed to the kitchen.

Ian looked past his reflection, studying the foot traffic. People seemed to stride to their destinations now with a purpose. Very few acknowledged others.

The misty rain had helped to further dampen the mood. But the freshwater was a godsend. The sky looked smoky, and the air redolent with the pungent odor of burning material. Little trails of ash collected by the rain coursed murky water down the buildings and streets.

Ian jumped when the waitress arrived with his food. He thanked her and dug in with gusto. Too many campfire dinners had left him with a deep yearning for a good, hearty meal. *This is hitting the spot, for sure.* The taste was so good that Ian didn't

Vaughn Collar

consciously notice how fast he ate for his plate was now empty. *Do I want a beer? No, too much to do, Laddy.*

He looked for the waitress and spotted a line forming at the front door. Instead of waiting on her, he approached the hostess, asked for his bill, and paid. He left a considerable tip for the overworked young ladies.

It was only a few minutes' walk back to the hotel. The activity level still hadn't diminished, though the aroma of baking bread signified the restaurant would likely be serving everyone soon enough. A *ding* from behind alerted him that the elevators were working again. *Thank you!* Now back in his room, he was ready for a few hours of intense research.

He picked up the nearest staff and sat down. The translation was proceeding well until he reached a certain script. The headache returned just as quickly as before. He sat back and closed his eyes. *Damn it, damn it, damn ...* Placing the staff back on the table, the pounding stopped ... *and it's gone?* He shook his head.

"I must be losing it!" He glanced around. "What's wrong with me?"

He picked up the next staff. His vision blurred and it felt as if the pain would explode through his eyes. He sat back and waited for the headache to dim. Just looking at the staves did not seem to bother him. It was only when he tried to decipher the actual markings that the pain would start.

"Okay, maybe third time's the charm?"

He picked up another staff and closed his eyes. Slowly, he opened one. His vision did not immediately blur, and the headache did not return. Whispering a quick, *"Thanks."* He opened both eyes and set about deciphering the markings.

He traced a finger along the runes. The script looked old – very old Norse runes, associated with Seidhr, an ancient magic that

The Rift - *Beginnings*

could tell and shape the future. The staffs predated Christianity. One rune in particular drew his interest.

"This is the rune for sleep ... no, wait ... it's different."

He knew the rune for restful sleep – *Svefnthorn*. However, this marking was slightly different. The verbal casting was there, but it was worn from age. Ian ran his fingers over the script.

"Now, what's this?"

The markings after the sleep rune were not Nordic. Then again, they were somewhat familiar. It was as if he were trying to grasp a wisp of smoke between his fingers. He watched as the markings faded in and out.

Two other runes appeared somewhat altered. One was a minor protection ward, the other represented light. The same sense of vagueness surrounded them. The longer he stared at the markings, the farther he felt he was from understanding them. It was as if a light fog prevented a clear understanding.

He sat back and clasped his hands together. Pressing his fingers to his lips, he remained deep in thought. Leaning back, he stared at the ceiling.

Maybe if I can figure out how old these markings are ...

A wave of fatigue rushed over him. He stood and walked to the sink. He placed a cup of water into the microwave. Soon, he was sipping tea. *Why am I so tired only a few hours after lunch!*

Perhaps a visit to the local museum would shed some light on the subject. He had heard a former student of his had landed an assistant curator position. He hadn't seen her in a few years, and the museum housed a fairly large collection from various digs in northern Scotland.

Hmm ...

Ian wrapped one of the staves, protecting it under his arm. The sun was shining, drying the streets from the earlier rain. The mood of the city seemed somewhat lighter. Even the dense aroma from

Vaughn Collar

the dust and smoke had somewhat washed away. Thankfully, the downtown district was largely spared from the destruction. He smiled, he always enjoyed this small city. One more road to cross and the museum would be in sight.

Oh great ...

The museum was closed.

Ian, duh ...

He peered through the glass and smiled. A light was on in the office. After he pounded on the door, a young woman glanced out with an expression of disdain.

"We're closed!" she yelled.

"I know, but I need to speak with Shelly Lang. Is she here?"

"Is this an emergen- You're Ian McGregor?!!"

Ian smiled. "Yes."

The woman nodded and opened the door. "Of course, Mr. McGregor. Yes, Ms. Lang is in. Let me page her for you." She walked over to the intercom and stated, "Ms. Lang to the lobby." She looked at Ian, blushing a little.

The speaker buzzed. "Yes?" a soft voice replied.

"Um, M ... Mr. McGregor is at our front door. He's asking for you."

"I'll be right there." Her voice sounded excited.

Ian chuckled. "You recognized me. Study history?"

"Yes, sir, I am. Ms. Lang speaks very highly of you." She looked away briefly before shyly meeting his gaze. "I've purchased your book on the Norse and Celtic people."

"A major battle to complete." He laughed. "It needed to be written. Much of early U.K. history was tied within that merger, including a bit of your Scottish brogue."

The sound of heels clacking on the tiles grew louder. Shelly smiled as she walked into the foyer. "Ian!" They hugged. "It is so good to see you again."

The Rift - *Beginnings*

He smiled. "Scottish climate hasn't hurt you in the slightest. You look well."

"Thank you. So ... what brings you here?"

The smile on his face waned. Glancing at the receptionist, Ian guided Shelly away from the door. "Can we speak in your office?"

Shelly studied Ian and nodded. "Certainly. Sue ... for the time being, neither of us is here. In fact ... why don't you take the rest of the day off?"

Looking surprised, Sue nodded. "Thank you, mum."

The elevator ride was quiet. But the long hallway echoed their steps to her office. Shelly opened the door and they entered.

"It's not like you to be so secretive, Ian."

Ian sat. "I've seen what most sites are saying about the reactor incident. Are you hearing anything?"

She paused and glanced out the window. "Mostly second-hand stuff. They're keeping the press away from the site. I've heard everything from terrorists to religious miracles. If anyone knows, they're keeping it quiet."

Ian nodded. "No terrorist group on Earth could pull that off. The damage looks to be in line with a nuke ... concussive waves rolling out for thousands of miles, and something else I can't quite place." He paused, realizing he opened his mouth prematurely. "To be honest, I haven't felt ... *normal* since."

"Normal?"

"Something just out of reach. Almost as if ... I'm more aware of things."

"Were you on a dig ... out in the open? Are you okay?"

"I'm fine, but yes. I was at the site when it happened."

"Let's go see a doctor."

Ian shook his head, glancing outside, motioning at the people cleaning up the debris. "I'd imagine just about every M.D. in

Vaughn Collar

Inverness is overworked right now. Maybe later. The only thing wrong is these headaches."

Shelly placed her hands on her hips and glared at him. "Exposure to a shockwave can cause serious damage. Did you hit your head?"

"I fell but didn't hit anything." Ian chuckled. "Just my pride. The headaches only happen when I try to read ..." – he held up the wrapped staff – "... these runes."

He pulled out the staff and handed it to her. She stared at the long, dark rod.

"There's nothing on this. There may have been engravings centuries ago, but nothing now."

Ian looked at the staff and frowned. The writing was clearly visible. He pointed to a place on the staff. As he read off the symbols, his head pounded. He grabbed a chair and sat.

"If you didn't hit your head, then it's something else. You're coming with me." Shelly motioned for him to follow. "Leave that here. I'll lock up. I have friends at the hospital. We're going to pull a few strings and get you an MRI."

Shelly did have a point. With the headache fading, he followed her out the door.

The Rift - *Beginnings*

CHAPTER 5

Nadia and Lucian pulled out several scrolls from inside a tall safe. Nadia read over the file numbers and selected one in Lucian's hand. She placed it on an easel with Lucian's copy next to it. The lettering, minus a few stylistic differences, was clearly the same.

"Can you read this?" Lucian asked.

Nadia shook her head. "No. I doubt if anyone can." She pointed at a word, then another. "This one and this ... they look Slavic, ancient at that."

Lucian picked up a magnifying glass to examine the finer details. The writing appeared to match ancient Slavic, for the most part. He could just make out the words *light* and *truth*. Strangely, reading the words was not bringing on a headache. There was also a vague sense of something missing, something he had felt when reading the actual tome.

"There's a vague sense of something missing, something ... I can't quite ... the best I can think of is ... it *feels* less complete. But I do see similarities," Lucian stated softly. "Wouldn't surprise me if there were dialects only spoken in certain places. Maybe this scroll represents one of those, and not directly translatable into old Slavic."

"You may be right. I've met a few old timers who spoke in an ancient tongue only they could understand. I tried talking to a few, but all I received was a glare, except for one guy. He said there were many valleys with different tongues, and his group were their descendants. To the rest ... I might as well have been an alien. No one said a word to me."

Lucian knew of several valleys that held one or two smaller villages that barely changed since medieval times. He was a little intrigued to hear they claimed to be descendants. "Okay, Nadia. Thank you for your time. I can see I have a little work to do." He climbed the stairs and made his way to the front. As he walked by Nadia's desk, he dropped a few bills.

He opened the door, and Nadia yelled out, "Thank you!"

Sitting in his hotel room, Lucian opened one tome and glanced over the script. Again, letters closely resembling old Slavic jumped out at him. He opened the other book and scanned down the pages. The words looked familiar. Before he could finish the first line, the headache returned. The pain was less severe, however, and felt different.

Curiosity prompted him to keep reading. As he proceeded, he felt a strange urge to continue. The lines were clearer and more of an instruction.

I'll need a spiderweb. But why? And why does a web need an anchor point?

Cautiously, he turned the page and the pain seared through his temples. He sat back and closed his eyes. The darkness helped and the pain receded.

"What in the *hell* is going on? Damn it!"

He considered the tomes that were out. A moment's thought and he chose one that appeared to be the most worn and

The Rift - *Beginnings*

tarnished. Oils from countless fingers had dyed the leather, wearing it smooth. He opened it slowly, a little leery of another headache. The writing did not immediately affect him. He read down the page, puzzled by the rhyming scheme. He turned the page and the words blurred – the headache had returned. He stumbled back, blindly feeling for his chair. He collapsed, waiting for the pain to diminish.

It finally receded and his vision cleared. Lucian glanced at the clock and was surprised. Hunger pangs were reminding him of the passage of time. After ensuring his room was locked, Lucian left the hotel.

A cool breeze filtered down from the mountains as night approached, helping to clear his mind as the last shreds of dizziness vanished. Voices echoed out around him. Deep shadows hid a couple of girls who just walked out from between two buildings. Close behind followed several younger men. The girls seemed uncomfortable and hurried their pace.

It's not any of your business, Luce ... just keep walking. A stray thought of the boy embarrassing himself crossed his mind. He absently made a hand motion.

A loud thump echoed out from the street, followed by the young ladies' laughter. Lucian glanced over. One of the boys was kneeling next to a car, holding his head. The others were trying to help him to his feet. One slipped, falling directly on his face.

The girls glanced at each other and laughed again.

Lucian chuckled. *Serves them right, harassing people like ... wait a minute. I was just thinking about that happening, and hmm ... oh well.* Lucian shrugged.

The deli was just around the corner, and the aroma of fresh baked bread wafted by.

Vaughn Collar

CHAPTER 6

The first snow frosted the highest peaks in the Highlands, and Ian spent his time breaking down his camp. It was time to return to the states. The staves he'd found proved to be the most difficult to pack.

After arriving in Boston, Ian felt almost like a stranger – a foreigner. The air full of grinding equipment hurt his ears, and the acrid odor of welding burnt his nose. The cacophony of noise from the city now felt overwhelming. It seemed to Ian that the largest project was a new bridge over the Muddy River as it flowed out of the Fens. With adjusting sea levels, it had become more of a seaside marsh than a river. The bars and taverns of Boston were mostly filled with talk of having to abandon historic Fenway Park and the university.

Ian's concerns focused on the incoming juniors transitioning into their majors. The seniors, however, seemed worried about their last year. He always hoped to hear that the graduating students had enjoyed his classes. Perhaps at least one junior would declare history as their major.

Ian sat on his deck, absorbing a fresh breeze floating off the bay. It was just enough to wash away the summer's heat and humidity. The day was too pleasant to spend staring at a computer

The Rift - *Beginnings*

screen, reviewing lesson plans. His phone chimed, interrupting his reverie. He grinned when he saw Shelly's number.

"Hello, Shelly. This is unexpected." His heart warmed to see her beautiful smile on his phone.

"Hello, yourself. How was the trip back?"

"Normal. Boring over the Atlantic. Glad they've modernized the old Concorde. Makes the trip twice as fast."

Shelly laughed. "I know, right? I've made that trip too many times. Nothing beats arriving fast."

"So ... how's Scotland? Still picking up the pieces?"

"Yes, and will be for a while. The U.K. will take years to get over this. Edinburgh is basically gone. Most of the royal family is too. Balmoral Castle was right in the path of the blast. They've only just released that information."

Ian gasped. "The king? His family?"

"And the duke. They're not saying who is next in succession ... I think Scotland Yard fears this was terrorism."

"There's some talk of that over here too," Ian replied. "The news is filled with various theories about what happened. Don't know if we'll ever know."

"I agree with that. Look, reason I called ... well, one of the reasons is ... I was wondering how you're doing? Any more headaches?"

"None, at least not like what I was getting."

A smile lit Shelly's face. "Good to hear."

"You said one of the reasons. What's the other?" Ian raised a 'brow.

"I did, didn't I?" she replied with a smirk. "Have you had a chance to look into those runes?"

"Unfortunately, no. Classes just started."

"Oh, that's right." She sat back in her chair. "I got a little bored and had a few minutes and dug deeper into what you gave me."

"And ...?"

"And ... I found a reference to a stone tablet discovered many years ago. The runes are in Old Norse. I can't read them. Could you take a look?"

"Of course," Ian replied.

"Great ... email just sent."

A chime sounded as he grabbed his tablet. The runes matched. The stone was obviously ancient, worn smooth from centuries of handling. Ian knew of this stone but had never seen it.

"Shelly, this is fantastic! How did you get this? This stone is damn-near more rumor than truth." He paused, staring into his phone. "More importantly ... can anyone read it?"

"Not to my knowledge. Maybe a few of the runes, but not the whole thing."

"Do you still have it?"

"Yes, it's here at the museum."

"Wait ... *your* museum? Oh, this is wonderful! How long have ... never mind. Not important." He stared at the stone. "Try looking at it under a UV light. Many ancient cultures used dyes that faded over time. Occasionally, UV can bring 'em out."

"Have you done that with the pieces you have?"

Feeling embarrassed, he smiled. "Not yet. Actually, it just occurred to me."

Shelly laughed. "Well, don't let me stop you. But don't forget to sleep tonight."

"I won't ... *Mom*." They both chuckled. "Good night, Shelly."

After arriving at the university, he walked directly to his private lab. Over the years, Ian had subjected many of his finds to numerous tests ranging from airbrushing to acid baths and different lighting. After his conversation with Shelly, he was

The Rift - *Beginnings*

anxious to try it on his finds. Choosing one of the smaller rods, he turned off the overhead light.

Under UV, several runes appeared that were not previously visible, and there seemed to be a pattern. They were somewhat connected, similar to cursive, not at all typical of Norse culture.

One at a time, he pulled each staff to check them under the UV light. Those that were blank, he set aside. Grabbing a magnifying glass, he concentrated on the fainter marks. For all his knowledge of old Norse history, he couldn't recall seeing these runes before.

He sat back, chewing on his lip in thought. *Ah ...*

He retrieved a book from the shelf, flipping through the pages until he found the section he was thinking about. He then compared the runes on the staff to the runes in his book.

Very close to a match ... just slight variations.

The rest of the items would also need to be checked. Three of the five staves revealed script under the UV light. Turning the regular lights back on, he glanced at the remaining items in the storage box. There were a couple of bone-handle dirks, the shield, and several pieces of silver jewelry along with a few bars of silver bullion. After examining each, nothing else was revealed under the UV. All in all, it was still a pretty good find.

So, why am I disappointed? Why just the staves? What's so important about them?

The script in the reference book was from the oldest runes found in Iceland. The Norse had settled there sometime in the eighth or ninth century. He looked back over at the nearest staff, trying to read the runes. A faint headache waved from behind his forehead. Then his vision blurred. After rubbing his eyes, he looked again. The headache worsened. Leaning back, the pounding stopped.

What in the hell is going on?

Vaughn Collar

He stood and paced, mostly to convince himself to stop for the day. But no, he wanted answers. He flipped back on the UV and picked up another rod. He had looked at this one before but not under the UV. One glance brought the headache back. He switched on the overhead lights, fighting the temptation to throw the rod across the room.

Maybe this is enough for ... no – no, Ian. Don't give up that easily. I got a little farther this time.

Gritting his teeth in anticipation of another headache, he examined a rod that hadn't revealed anything under the regular light. This time, several runes looked familiar – *fire, light, cold, hot,* and *wet.* Typical runes for the Norse – but no headache.

Hmm ...

He gave the box a long look. If anything was stamped or written on the bullion, it would be easy to identify.

The dirks ... yeah, those look like fun.

He had nothing on his calendar for tomorrow. Glancing over at a shelf, he understood – he had a decision to make.

Tea or the last of my coffee?

Caffeine was needed and lots of it. He poured in the water, added a coffee pod, and waited.

Wait a minute. How old is that bloody rod?

Carbon dating would help – it certainly couldn't hurt. He looked at the finished brew and reached for his cup. It was cold.

Oh yeah ... cold coffee. Hot would've been nice ...

An odd sensation washed over him, and the background headache vanished. His fingers tingled as a tendril of steam drifted up from the now-hot brew.

"How ... what the ...?"

Ian stared at the cup, idly scratching his beard. This wasn't the first odd occurrence to happen around these rods. Incongruously,

The Rift - *Beginnings*

his stomach growled. A nearby leftover cinnamon roll made for a quick treat.

With his hunger appeased and the caffeine energizing his system, he risked the UV lights again. He selected a rod he'd been able to read while still in Scotland. Now, the hidden script was visible. And – no headache. But not all of the words looked familiar.

____ is heat, but ___ through the hands of the ____ read (?) this seidhr.

"This is a power rod? Woah!"

The rod likely belonged to an old Norse clan skald or bard, a poet. The skalds were not well known. Very few names were ever documented in the old tales Ian was familiar with. Even so, if this rod was as old as he suspected, it would be a very rare and valuable find.

The great majority of preserved Norse writings were poetry or tales from pre-Christian times. The skalds recording them were purveyors of knowledge, keeping the Norse folklore alive. It was somewhat unusual to find actual written tales. Most were passed down orally, skald to skald. One of Ian's master's theses had been on the works of the oldest known, a Braggi Boddason. What was not known was from whom Braggi had learned his craft. Ian had just confirmed that the rods in his possession were definitely ancient.

About ten years earlier, Ian had uncovered a rod dating at least a century prior to Braggi Boddason. Tree rings inside the wood matched up to several stumps known to exist from around 775-790 ADE. Wars in Northern Europe had caused widespread fires, limiting forest growth across the continent. Ian had surmised that the smoke was one of the reasons the Norse had left their homelands. And that piece now formed the centerpiece of a display in the Smithsonian.

Vaughn Collar

Carbon dating would be key to this research. If these rods were as ancient as he believed, then the carvings were likely the life's work of an unknown skald. Possibly one accompanying the raiders looking for fresh territory in the British Isles. There very well could be something else on the rod in the Smithsonian – something he had missed.

Now, how could I get it back?

The Rift - *Beginnings*

CHAPTER 7

Across the globe, changes were taking place. The energy wave seemed capricious wherever it left an imprint. Some affected areas were as insignificant as a nest of slightly larger lizards. For others, the imprints were more forthcoming.

Kyle Richards was a typical eight-year-old. Catching bugs and placing them in jars made up a good part of his day. As a result, he developed a sense of what bugs should look like. In the waning days of summer, Kyle didn't look forward to school. He'd much rather be in his little patch of woods behind his house. He knew every bush and every tree by heart. He knew where their den was and had been around enough for the rabbits to become comfortable with his presence.

A few months earlier, strange lights had emanated from the woods. Kyle had ventured out the following morning to explore. He'd found a few scorch marks on a couple of trees and a curious pattern burnt into a patch of grass. It'd looked as if someone had waved a blowtorch over the area, close enough to burn but not enough to affect the grass outside the path.

Vaughn Collar

Today, Kyle wanted to explore the small clearing. Nothing remained of the burn marks, and even the trees seemed to have recovered. The only sign of the event was the grass. Most of the plants were withered and brown from a lack of water due to the dry summer. A few isolated thunderstorms had provided some moisture, but the grass still crunched under his feet, stirring up the dust in little puffy clouds. However, the grass where the burn marks were was as green as it would have been in the spring – a visible trail of healthy growth inside the brown, dry vegetation.

Grass didn't interest Kyle – except when it held the bugs he wanted to find. He paced slowly around the edge of the green patch and looked for his next catch. He spotted a large grasshopper on a particularly tall blade of grass. Kyle froze, his eyes never leaving the insect. There wasn't much wind. Slowly, Kyle's hands worked the lid from his jar.

"Stay there, little one, stay there ..."

Kyle traced a path to the grasshopper. No sticks or holes in the ground to trip over. A slow step, then another. His pulse quickened as he drew closer. Two more steps and Kyle was within striking distance. He slowly raised the jar above the insect. Sweat ran into Kyle's eyes and off his nose. But his focus was tight, no distractions now. One last breath and he held it. The insect moved its back legs. Kyle let out his breath slowly before taking another. His hands shook in anticipation.

The grasshopper pulled a leaf away from the stem and ate. The jar was placed perfectly over the insect just as it jumped. Slapping on the lid, Kyle stared into the jar.

The insect hopped around crazily before settling down. Kyle knew several dozen species by heart. Looking closely at this one – there were some differences. The eyes were not the same – not as many facets. The smaller simple eyes seemed to be missing. The front legs ended in two small claws facing forward and just

The Rift - *Beginnings*

one facing back, not the normal spacing. The head – it was shaped a little different too – not quite as triangular.

"Wow! I've got to show Dad!"

Kyle ran for home. He didn't notice that several other grasshoppers had climbed the stalks, almost as if they were watching one of their kind being taken away.

Stacy Mansford burst from her house and ran to the stables. Her favorite mare was in labor. No matter how much she pleaded and begged, her father refused to allow her inside the barn. Since Daisy seemed to be having difficulty with this colt, Steve had called a vet from Great Falls to assist with the delivery.

Throughout the night, Daisy struggled. When she finally delivered, the colt was white and slightly larger than normal. Stacy was captivated by the youngster. She watched as it lay there, looking confused by the new sounds and smells. Several times, the colt fell over as it attempted to stand. When it was finally successful, Stacy clapped her hands. The colt glanced over at her before walking to the mare to suckle.

"Steve, you don't have any white stallions, do you?" the vet asked.

"No ... and the closest one I can think of ..." – he ran his hand across his beard – "... is the Crooked Z near Raynesford."

"Well, it's not entirely unknown for an off-color colt to be born. The stud must've been big. That colt looks to follow suit."

"Hmm. A white stallion." Steve glanced over at his daughter who looked up at him.

"Please, Daddy!" she begged.

"Alright. Just go slow. The colt doesn't really know anything yet except its ..." He stopped.

Vaughn Collar

The colt had walked over to Stacy without prompting. Carefully, she held out her hand. The animal stretched and touched Stacy's fingers with its nose. It pulled its head back and snorted. Without hesitation, the colt gently head-butted the girl before prancing backward.

Stacy squealed and followed.

Her father watched with amusement.

"Can I name him?" Stacy asked.

"Sure looks like he's gonna like you."

Stacy glanced back at the colt. It had returned to its mother and was nuzzling again. She touched her lips with one finger and said, "I want to call him Ghost. Can I?"

"Ghost it is."

Stacy gave her father a hug. "I'm gonna tell Mom!" She darted out of the stable with her ponytail bouncing off her shoulders.

"Steve, you're gonna need a shotgun here in a few years," the vet said with a chuckle.

"Yeah, I know," Steve replied with a slight smirk.

Hohiro Oshida viewed his work as important, though somewhat boring. The rhesus of Jigokudani Monkey Park were well known and studied as the troop made active use of the hot springs of the valley. Hohiro felt there was little left to learn. Day in and day out, he recorded the troop's movements and habits.

Over a century ago, a smaller population of rhesus were relocated to Texas. While completing his master's thesis, Hohiro discovered he too would be moving to Texas since his research application had been approved. He was anxious to see the monkeys under far different conditions. Now, with the weather cooling off and the days shortening, Hohiro arrived at the park early. He

The Rift - *Beginnings*

neared the blind and noted the lack of noise. Only the sounds of a nearby waterfall tickled his ears.

The troop should be around the springs. Strange ...

He stood in the thicket shielding him from the troop, feeling intrigued and a little worried. The monkeys always seemed aware of his presence, but as long as he was out of sight, they never reacted. He stepped around the last bush, and the pools were in sight.

Only a few monkeys were active near the water. The troop normally consisted of twenty-five to thirty individuals. Hohiro counted and when he reached fifteen, he paused.

Maybe they're still in the mountains? Not that unusual ...

A charred area a little way downstream drew his attention. The trees looked burnt through their bark and the ground was barren of the normal leaf covering. New vegetation was sprouting but in odd patterns.

Interesting ... a lightning strike?

Something white and curved rested near a tree. He pulled a spotting scope from his pack and scanned the area.

A bone? Looks like a rib.

Hohiro entered this notation into his journal. Upon returning to his campsite, he used his tablet to check on past weather patterns. Much to his surprise, it had been dry and cool. No thunderstorms since the prior year.

Odd. I wonder what caused the burnt ground ...?

He knew this area was far from the casual hiking trails.

What else would explain the burns and the much smaller troop size?

Over the next few weeks, Hohiro readied his camp for the oncoming winter. The weather had cooled rather dramatically along the mountains. Frost now appeared in the mornings, and

Vaughn Collar

more of the troop were visiting the warm springs since temperatures were cooling. Soon, the snow would fall.

Hohiro woke, shivering from the cold. He draped a pair of socks over the heater, reluctant to place his feet into his ice-cold boots without some warmth. Dressing was an exercise in tolerating being chilled to the bone.

He stepped out of his tent, knowing he had chosen the correct site. The trees provided protection from the wind and the worst of the snow. Only a light frost speckled the forest around him. Outside the tree cover, over three fresh feet had fallen. Though he yearned for the warmth of Texas, he couldn't deny the beauty of the area. The snow muffled the sound with a hush consuming the valley. The sun's rays provided a multitude of miniature rainbows and sparkled amidst the snow and ice crystals.

Hohiro headed to his blind, treading carefully to not make noise. He spread out a blanket on the bench and turned on a portable heater. The blind was made of local bamboo to blend with the vegetation. When he was sure his skin wouldn't stick to it, he adjusted his tripod-mounted scope and watched.

The small troop was in a relaxed mood, and as usual, the alpha male was hogging the best spot. A lead female groomed him from behind. Two other females were across the spring, soaking in the warm water with their eyes closed. Three youngsters scampered around in an endless game of chase, taking advantage of having their mothers' constant attention diverted. Two others were combing through a pile of rocks.

Probably looking for a frozen grub.

One of the youngsters tossed a rock aside. It bounced off another rock and a spark flew out. Another young member stared at the rock. He glanced back at his mother and held her gaze. No response. He approached the area where the rock had hit. He picked up several and sniffed until finding the correct one. There

The Rift - *Beginnings*

was a look of consternation on his face. He tapped the rock against another. Nothing happened. He tapped harder and harder until a spark flew and landed on a dry leaf. A momentary puff of smoke curled into the air.

"Maji ka!" *Oh my god* ... "And I'm going to Texas *now?*"

Despite his hands stiffening from the cold, Hohiro set up both cameras in the blind.

This has to be recorded.

Vaughn Collar

CHAPTER 8

Lucian sat in his university office, reading through his assigned fall courses. After teaching for close to thirty years, he felt Leiden University of the Netherlands should be treating him a little more fairly.

All because a few students think I'm too tough on them. Bah ...

Over the last ten years, his courses had been the fundamental first-year's introduction to archaeology. This year looked to be no different. He scrolled through his assigned list and smiled. He'd actually been given a senior level class in early Celtic culture. The basis for one of his master's thesis.

He laughed. "Perhaps there is a god after all!"

Lucian glanced at his accompanying social calendar and frowned. Several get-togethers were listed as mandatory. He considered these meetings torture. He'd much prefer working on the newest pieces he just uncovered. If not that, then enjoying a cold ale at a local pub. Even grading papers was preferrable. He leaned back, thinking about the upcoming classes.

An easy semester, I think.

Scrolling down, he studied the attendance rosters. No names looked familiar, which didn't mean much. A couple of transfer

The Rift - *Beginnings*

students from Moscow and one from a small town in Pennsylvania, U.S. seemed to be the highlights.

After shutting his tablet, he headed for home, but his thoughts strayed to his finds in Romania. As such, he lost track of where he was walking. He looked up to discover he was almost halfway to his favorite pub.

He chuckled. "A drink doesn't sound like such a bad idea."

Lucian entered and stopped briefly to let his eyes adjust to the dark interior. His favorite table was available. He sat and a waitress approached, holding a menu.

He held up his hand. "I know what I want. A Bittberg and a plate of perogies, please. Knockwurst with onions and sour cream."

The waitress smiled. "Right away, sir." She left to place his order with the kitchen.

Lucian looked at his reflection in the window. His face was weathered from numerous years in the sun, making him appear several years older than his true age. A scar on the left side of his face ran from just above his eye down to his jawline, courtesy of a run-in with a gang. His hair, still full, was a nondescript dark brown, streaked with gray. He looked every bit of his fifty-four years. His dark brown eyes resembled that of a tired and worn-out man. At least he could still fit in his clothes from his youth. He sat back to reflect on the day.

I find interesting and rare books and other items almost every other year ... and they still have me teaching intro courses. Is it worth it anymore?

The waitress arrived with his beer. "Your food should be out in a few minutes, sir," she said.

Taking a couple of sips, Lucian idled his thoughts. His dinner arrived and was excellent, as always. Never one to indulge, Lucian paid his tab and left. He walked along the darkened streets, deep in thought. His footsteps dimly echoed off the empty buildings and sounded as if a metronome were measuring his pace.

Vaughn Collar

How much longer will I wait until I'm appointed the department chair?

He knew he was more qualified than anyone else on staff.

Fine, so I don't cut an impressive figure. Is that enough to keep me out of the position?

These thoughts reverberated through his mind. Finally, he looked at his watch. It was one in the morning.

Luce, you will regret this tomorrow if you don't get some sleep.

Shaking his head, he made his way home, hoping to fall asleep quickly.

Unfortunately, morning came all too soon. A bagel and a cup of tea was all he had time for. He left his apartment and proceeded across the campus to the history building. It was a cool morning for a late summer day. Many students were taking advantage of the glorious weather.

They look so ... young.

He stopped at his office to check on paperwork. Nothing seemed urgent. His classroom was only a few paces down the hall, and when he walked in and looked around, the familiarity comforted him. Rows of old books and faded maps gave the room character. It even smelled like a bookstore from the aged leather and parchment. He stepped over to his pedestal as the first students trickled in.

Taking roll seems so ... useless. Half of these kids will drop by next week.

He glanced around and sighed. After pulling his reading glasses from his pocket, he slipped them on. His eyes roamed over a small group of boys laughing about something. Another young man looked as if he were asleep. A girl up front was filing her nails. Several others looked either bored or scared.

I guess my reputation precedes me.

The Rift - *Beginnings*

He softly snorted a little chuckle and glanced at the clock. After rapping his gavel for attention, he stated, "It's a little after the hour. When I call your name, please answer with *here*. I will be reading so I will not see a hand or hear you nod your head." He looked up at the students.

No one said anything.

"Bakker, Johann."

"Here."

"Banfield, Sarah."

"Here," a soft, hesitant voice said from the front of the room. She must have been the one working on her nails.

"De Jong, Stefan."

"Here, sir."

"Gerbrandy, Benjamin."

"Here. And sir, could you use Ben?"

"Alright, Ben it is." Lucian made a notation next to the boy's name. "Goldobin, Natalya Ivanova." This must be one of the students from Moscow. He lowered his glasses and looked up.

"Here, sir." A beautiful blonde smiled at him from the middle of the room. "Please, Nat or Nat'cha is fine."

Lucian knew he gaped for just a moment and hoped no one noticed. The young lady's hair fell across her shoulders in gentle waves. She must have spent time at a beach or someplace warmer than most of Russia, so deep was her tan. Even from where he stood, Lucian could admire her sea-blue eyes.

"Nat'cha it is." Lucian found himself a little charmed, and he made the appropriate note on the roster. "From Moscow, yes?"

"Da."

Lucian nodded.

He continued through the remaining names before walking out from behind the podium and leaning against the table.

Vaughn Collar

"You are seniors. As such, I will not discuss the rules, and I will not review the syllabus. Those are all available on the campus intranet." He paused while looking at the students. "I will be guiding you through the earliest-known developments of Celtic culture. For starters ... does anyone have any family in the Brittany peninsula of France?"

No hands showed.

"Okay, how about southern Belgium?"

Two hands raised.

Lucian pointed at one of them. "How long have they lived there?"

The student thought about it. "Um ... I think since the 1700's, sir."

Lucian smiled. "That was an ancestral area for the Celts, dating back to the Roman Empire ... and not the Holy Roman, either. Back to the Caesars." He paused. "For that matter, the mere name *Belgium* is descendant from the tribe inhabiting that area, the Belgae." He looked around. "Don't doubt most of you, genetically, have roots in the Celtic peoples. That likely includes you, Ms. Banfield ... and Ms. Goldobin probably has the strongest claim to *not* being a descendant. That is, if your ancestors were always in Russia."

She smiled. "Actually, we're descended from the Finnish on my mother's side."

Lucian raised a 'brow. "Just makes it a stronger case of not having Celtic genes."

He paced the room, meeting individual gazes. He didn't intend to keep the class long on the first day. After about twenty minutes, he felt he had reached a few. Some he knew would drop, searching for an easier grade.

The Rift - *Beginnings*

Still, this class looks a little more promising than most. If only they would give me more seniors. "Alright. Let's call it a day. Please remember to at least glance at the syllabus. Good day."

He picked up his tablet and circled back to his seat.

As the students filed out, Lucian felt more than saw a shadow fall across his desk. Looking up, he found himself staring at the set of sea-blue eyes, deep and soulful.

"Excuse me, sir. Might I have a word?" Ms. Goldobin stood before him with a faint smile.

"Yes, certainly. How may I help you?"

"I know I met the curriculum requirements for this class, but ... are there any papers or books you could recommend to help me?"

Smiling, he replied, "Yes. I would recommend ..." Lucian listed a few sources, ones he would be drawing on occasionally. "Is there anything else?"

"Oh, that should do. Thank you, so much." She gave him a slight curtesy.

Intelligence, looks, and old-world manners? "Dasvidaniya, Ms. Goldobin," he replied with a nod. He was rewarded with a beaming smile.

The next few weeks were a bit of a blur. His classes were not abandoned by half of the students after all, and the distractions of the finds from Petroşani along with the Celtic culture kept him from being his normal, acerbic self. Even the staff events were not the normal bore. There was a definite change overcoming him. He now looked forward to Tuesday and Thursday afternoons for it was on those days he saw Ms. Goldobin.

As a transfer student from Moscow, Natalya brought in a different perspective. Her ancestry had no relationship to the Celtic culture. She constantly questioned Lucian about the importance of the Celts to early Europe, especially from a cultural standpoint. Normally, this would have enraged him. But she was

Vaughn Collar

prepared to discuss the subject. By the end of the semester, Lucian grudgingly acknowledged Natalya was an intelligent woman, and very close to his own level. Possibly on par with him. Not that he cared if she were male or female. Lucian wasn't the slightest bit of a sexist or one to hold any prejudice. He was just more intelligent than ninety-nine percent of the population, and genuinely felt he had few peers. But privately, he recognized that maybe a little humility might have served him well.

Semester break soon arrived. After his last office day, he swung by the campus café and grabbed a pizza. He arrived home shortly after dark, unlocked the door and entered. A practiced throw landed his coat on the rack. The pizza was still fairly warm as he placed a few slices onto a plate. He grabbed a beer from his fridge, walked into the living room, and collapsed into his favorite chair.

Ah, three weeks off!

After turning on his TV, he mindlessly watched some replays from the European soccer league. When the news transitioned to the weather, he stood and took his plate to the kitchen.

Three full weeks with the Petroşani tomes.

In the small room he used as a home office and lab, he set out the books. Donning gloves and setting up the UV light, he opened the first one. The first couple of pages did not seem to react. He placed it aside and opened the second. Strange lettering glowed. He reached for his tweezers to flip the brittle pages. The old script, so closely resembling Romanian, seemed easier to read. Almost as if this were his natural language.

Turning another page, pain lanced through his brain and his vison blurred. He leaned back, both hands covering his eyes. It felt as if an icepick had just been poked inside his head, probing the back of his eyes.

"Damn it!"

The Rift – *Beginnings*

The pain resolved quickly. Too fast to be a normal headache. His vision cleared.

"Ce ...?"

He adjusted the light. The first paragraph looked – strange. Priding himself on being logical, he read slowly, trying to take in every word. The pain struck again.

"Ach! This is worthless."

He stood, knocking over his chair. The loud clatter was followed by a string of muffled words from the apartment below. Lucian raised his voice to let them know what he thought in his native Romanian. Shaking his head, he walked outside to his patio.

"I brought back nothing but journals and old tales ... spells ... strange oils!"

He walked back to his office, closed the books, and placed them in his safe.

"Nothing but wasted time. I lugged this crap down a mountain just to find the fictional meanderings of some frustrated monk?" He thought for a moment. "Maybe I could let it be known I've acquired some books from the time of Vlad Tepes?"

He knew that any museum or school would bid on the books and with that thought, he aimed for the shower. An image of the beautiful Russian transfer student ran through his mind.

Hmm ... someone I could respect intellectually ... get serious, Luce. You're old enough to be her father.

Christmas break ended and Lucian was ready for his afternoon Early Celtic II class. He set his notes – just so – on the pedestal. A penchant for organization extending to his everyday life. Lucian had arrived eager to begin. He glanced at the clock and smiled.

"Hello, Professor."

Vaughn Collar

"Ms. Goldobin. I saw your name on the roster. Did you have a good holiday break?"

"Oh, yes. I was able to see my parents and little brother. I missed them so much. And you?"

"I stayed busy, so the time passed swiftly." After losing his parents as a teen, the concept of a family felt foreign. On the rare occasion he did remember his mother, chills would course through him.

The days flew by as the students settled in. Their questions were well thought out and challenging. It was rewarding to instruct such a class.

This is why I wanted to teach. This is nice!

Lucian watched as his students left for the day. He was mentally tired and more than a little hungry. His fatigue grew, just knowing that the outside was cold and rainy. The winter was wetter than the previous year with local flooding playing havoc with the tram routes. Making sure his laptop was secure, he pulled his coat tighter and stepped out. A quick glance ascertained the tram wasn't running on time as people were shuffling around.

Walking would take longer, but it beat waiting on a tram that may not arrive. The rain, cold and dreary, muffled his steps. Fog curling around the trees in small clouds seemed to make everything eerie and dark. A group of students walked by without noticing him, deep in conversation. They were comparing notes about who was the most attractive in their classes.

Lucian chuckled. *Typical youths ... hormones going crazy.*

The roaring of an engine grabbed his attention as he neared the intersection. The rain and fog made it difficult to pinpoint. Looking both ways, he found the source. He gasped. Water sprayed from an approaching vehicle. The rain was heavier now and Lucian doubted the driver could see much. The group of young men were still deep in conversation as they stepped into the street.

The Rift - *Beginnings*

Lucian extended his hands as if to push the small group out of the way. "Look out!"

One of the men took a wider step, and his foot slid on the wet grass. He fell awkwardly into a puddle. The rest managed to reach the curb. The car did not slow.

Lucian sprinted across the street once the car was gone. "Are you okay?"

The young man looked dazed as his friends helped him to his feet. "Yes, sir. That was close." He was soaked and covered with mud and grass, his pants torn.

"Professor, thank you for the warning." One of the young men seemed to recognize Lucian. "We didn't hear him at all."

"You're welcome. Have a good evening, gentlemen." Lucian resumed his walk, staring down the dark and empty street. *Stupid driver.*

Lucian slogged his way home in the gloom. His attention was on looking and listening for approaching vehicles, and he arrived at his apartment without further incident. A practiced motion placed his coat on a hanger. He took one step and paused, a thought echoing. This was the second time he had thought about an action and it happened.

What is going on?

The incident ran through his mind while the water heated for his tea. It was time to settle down for the night. Each time was after he had tried to read the tomes. He could remember the act of reading but not exactly what he had read.

This last time ... wasn't it something about force?

Steam rose from his cup in soft swirls, almost hypnotizing him. A wave of fatigue rolled, and he shook himself before he fell asleep in his chair. He woke feeling disoriented.

Whew ... time for bed.

Vaughn Collar

CHAPTER 9

Ian opened his email and scanned through the first few. Nothing important. A few students had questions – and of course, the electric bill. He started to close his tablet when a soft chime sounded. It was the lab. A few weeks prior, he had carved off samples from the bottom of a staff and sent it for carbon dating. This was the second test. The first was difficult to believe. He had purchased another to confirm the results.

The findings showed the wood was not from the United Kingdom or Scandinavia – not even Northern Europe. The wood traced to an area now in Croatia – an ancient pine. Dating back to –

"1600 BCE?! What?"

Ian took a second read and sat back to reflect. The date placed it around the time of the Minoan eruption. Much older than Ian had ever suspected. The second analysis only confirmed the findings.

What would a wooden rod from Croatia be doing in a cache in the Scottish Highlands? A Norse cache at that.

He idly rubbed the stubble on his jaw.

I wonder ...

The Rift - *Beginnings*

His personal library, collected over the years from a multitude of places, might have some answers. He stood at his shelves, lightly brushing his fingers across the rows as he thought about each text. Two books garnered his attention. Placing them on the side table, he turned the light on and sat. He scanned through the pages, trying to match the runes. Nothing looked familiar until he flipped to a chapter of the earliest-known lettering in Europe. The runes resembled those from the Futhark script.

And ... the Futhark inhabited that area around that time ... hmm. That makes sense. A little.

Cupping his hands around his face, Ian thought about the script. "Who knows about Slavic? ... ah, Shelly. Her master's thesis was on early Slavic languages."

He glanced at the clock and smiled. *Nine here, so it's ... two there. Okay.* He listened as the phone rang. When her face flashed into view, he smiled.

"Ian! Hello, old friend."

"Shelly." Ian nodded. "Good to see you too."

"To what do I owe this unexpected call?"

"I need your help on something."

"Oh?"

"I have a lab report I'd like you to review. That is, if you have the time."

"For you, Ian, anything."

Ian emailed the report and waited. He watched her reaction as she read. Her expression changed from happy to serious and then to incredulous. She glanced up at him and then back at the report. Her hand reached up to tuck a lock of hair behind her ear, and her gaze returned to the screen.

"Ian? What in the world have you found?"

"Rods."

"Rods?" she repeated.

Vaughn Collar

"Very old rods ... with runes matching Futhark script."

"Send me some images?"

"Most definitely. And already sent."

Shelly's eyes were fixed on her screen. Her lips moved as she read through the text, her eyes widening at the end. She held a long stare at Ian before she looked at something off-screen. "This script is definitely Futhark ... and the report said the wood was dated to 1600 BCE?"

Ian nodded.

"What an incredible discovery. This is from the dig you were on this summer?"

"Yes. There's another from an earlier dig I need to retrieve, but –"

"Yeah, but ... like ... how did these rods end up in Scotland?"

"That's the unanswered question."

"I would love to see these rods."

"By all means, come on over." Ian laughed. "The best I can surmise is that a shaman or religious traveler carried them, then most likely a skald picked them up. They were the only people possessing such items at that time."

Shelly showed an impish grin. "Well ... I am flying to D.C. next week."

"Oh?"

"Interview with the Smithsonian. The museum here is shutting down. At least until the recovery efforts are finished. Anything that doesn't directly affect the economy is closing."

"The *Smith* can always use a good curator. If you need a reference –"

"You're already listed." She laughed.

Ian smiled. "Good. How long will you be staying, or do you even know yet?"

"Long enough so I can have a night or two with friends."

The Rift - *Beginnings*

"Nice! Um ... how 'bout we meet for dinner?" Ian was rewarded with seeing the happiness reflecting in her rich, brown eyes.

"I'd like that. I'll come to Boston, though. Not a lot of good restaurants in D.C."

"Great, I'll make reservations?"

She nodded. "My interview is the day after I arrive. I'll take the train to you. Not entirely comfortable driving in U.S. traffic ... not after a couple of years in Scotland."

"Gotcha. Call when you arrive. I'll meet you at the station."

"Most definitely."

"I have a spare room ..."

"I'll book a room at a B&B. A little confession ... I've already been checking. There's a nice one not far from you."

Ian couldn't hold back a wide smile. "If you should change your mind, the invitation stays."

"Thank you. I appreciate it."

"You're most definitely welcome. The *Smith* is going to hire a fabulous person. They would be foolish not to."

"We'll see." She laughed again.

Ian watched as her eyes changed, just for a brief moment, before her smile resumed. *Why the change?* He shrugged. "Any contacts in the Croatian area or Bosnia?"

"I believe so, but I'll have to check."

"Sounds good. Maybe someone there would know more about the local legends."

"Exactly. I'll get back with you tomorrow. Same time?"

Ian smiled. "Any excuse to see your pretty face is fine with me."

Shelly fluttered her eyes and giggled. "Why, sir, I do believe you're flirting with me."

Both laughed.

"Good night, Ian."

Vaughn Collar

The day crawled by. Ian's thoughts remained with Shelly and not his upcoming lectures. Even the rods couldn't hold all his interest.

Admit it, buddy. You're hooked.

He walked into his living room with another cup of tea. The Futhark writings were bugging him, for Norse runes were heavily influenced by this precursor script. Setting the cup down, Ian glanced over at his library.

Wait a minute. Croatia is just outside of Greece. And Futhark script drew influence from the Greeks. So ... connection?

He ran a hand over each title. "No ... no ... ah, nah ... yes!" He selected a book and continued to read the other titles. "No ... no ... *definitely*." He placed the second book on the table and turned back to his library. His phone chimed and he smiled. It was Shelly.

"You're early ... or should I say late. Nice surprise."

"Well, you surprised me yesterday, so ... my turn!"

"Hah! Any luck?" Ian asked.

Shelly's smile waned. "Actually, very little. I have one contact that might be of assistance. But he's proving to be hard to find. Does the name Jusuf Arbanas mean anything to you?"

"Nope, can't say that it does."

"Really? He works at the natural history museum in Zagreb. Specializes in ancient languages, especially in regional dialects."

Ian grinned. "Sounds like someone I should know. As always, Shelly, I knew I could count on you. Can you send me his contact info?"

"Should be in your email already." Shelly's voice radiated a little concern. "You look tired. When was the last time you slept?"

The Rift - *Beginnings*

"Not sure. It wasn't last night, too caught up with the rods. It's not often a new language shows up. Especially in an area as heavily explored as Scotland. Kinda makes one wonder what else is out there."

"Yeah, totally."

"Shelly, you've been so helpful. Hmm ... there's a great new restaurant in Boston. I made reservations. My treat."

She beamed. "Sounds good. Let me track down Jusuf. You get some sleep ... that's an order!"

Ian cracked up. "Yes, ma'am, I certainly will. And don't kill yourself trying to track this guy down. Those rods aren't going anywhere."

Shelly nodded, the smile still on her face. "Goodbye for now."

The screen darkened, but the afterimage of Shelly remained in Ian's mind. *You're hooked, bud ... admit it.*

The tea he had earlier, along with the second cup drained while talking with Shelly, was kicking in.

Just a little more work ...

He pulled up the Futhark script from his database and picked up a rod. The runes blurred, then cleared.

"No headache?"

He was surprised to fully understand the script. Almost as if the ancient language were now his own. He blinked, then re-read the last few lines aloud.

"*For thine enemies, this ...*" – a few of the words still eluded him – "*... should be of most ... as those who are sleeping are not a ... using a ... of sand, recite ... and use a sweeping motion, palm down ...*"

He stood, rubbing his eyes. Pacing the room, he noticed the clutter.

Gotta clean this place up.

He tossed a few pieces of clothing into his bedroom.

"Wait ... what am I thinking. Seriously?"

Vaughn Collar

The hum from the aerator for his fish tank distracted him. He stared at the water, then his focus fell to the bottom.

Sand ... hmm.

He knelt and pulled out the spare bag. He poured a small amount of sand into his hand, then crossed the room to his hamsters' cage. Feeling a little foolish, he took a pinch and waved it over them. Nothing. He repeated the words he just translated and again, nothing.

"Didn't think so."

He laughed, mostly at himself. He walked back to the bag, and a surge of electricity hit, centering in his mind. The text swirled. The missing words suddenly materialized, and he knew their meanings and pronunciation. He reached into the bag and withdrew a larger pinch. Focusing back on the hamsters, he repeated the sentence. It felt as if the words had just drifted away, as if they'd never existed. But the two hamsters fell over.

He stood back and gasped. He reached inside the cage and cradled one in his hands. He could see it was alive, its tiny chest moving with each breath. It seemed to be - *asleep?* He gently placed the hamster back in its cage. He tried to recall the words, but they were gone - vanished. He knew *what* he had done, but not *how* he had done it.

"This is nuts." He stared intently at the rods. "There is no such thing as ... magic!"

The Rift - *Beginnings*

CHAPTER 10

The sunset across the North Sea was backlit with waves of amber and gold. The air warmed with the approach of summer, losing some of the freshness of spring. Lucian glanced at the horizon and yawned. The sky was also losing its vivid blue, becoming more of a pastel. He yearned to delve into the tomes but his summer classes took precedence. The small office patio beckoned even louder for him to enjoy this most ideal of evenings.

A notice came to him earlier, announcing he and one other professor were the prime candidates for head of the history department. Maybe the long days of devoting himself to his work were paying off.

So many years. Hmm ... You ready to be in the spotlight?

Isolation felt comfortable – safe. He was more at home in the field, exploring ruins and dig sites. Dealing with people left him feeling out of place.

But ... teaching young minds is so rewarding.

The tomes beckoned to him. He wondered how old they were. How long it had been since anyone had read them. Now, they were for his eyes only. How much time could he devote to revealing their secrets?

Vaughn Collar

Over the past academic year, he had dodged questions about his whereabouts and findings. His answers were vague, such as, "Romania," or "old books." The tomes were *his* discovery. Funded on *his* money. Deciphered on *his* time.

So that makes it my business entirely, no?

He was willing to share some of the material, just not anything involving the strange script. He watched the foot traffic of students and teachers leaving for home or arriving for an evening lecture. Already, streetlights shone, revealing the clouds of insects.

Not me ... Not tonight ...

He turned on the soft, blue light to signal he was working with light-sensitive material and to not be disturbed. Donning protective gloves, he opened the top tome. As always, he smiled at the centuries-old books and their faint, musty-leather aroma, their secrets soon to be revealed.

"How old are you, I wonder?"

He started with the one he had read a few weeks prior. Again, it struck him how familiar the script looked. Lucian was familiar with most of the ancient writings catalogued as Celtic or Celtic-descendant, along with several other Eastern European works. Tonight promised to be long, for he firmly believed the script to be obscure, very old or most likely both.

As the computer worked, he sat back and reflected on his upcoming classes. Rare were the times he looked forward to teaching. Early Celtic ranked in that few. It was always a challenge to create lectures, so bright were the students. Several showed they were capable of thinking and drawing intelligent conclusions instead of just regurgitating facts. Lucian didn't reward students for simply memorizing things, and he was particularly interested in seeing Ms. Goldobin. She seemed to not only grasp the concepts of early Celtic formation, but easily led the class with her

The Rift - *Beginnings*

conclusions and rationales. Lucian figured she would lead the class without much effort on her part.

Lost in thought of Ms. Goldobin, Lucian stretched, knocking over his water. The liquid splashed across the table as the glass shattered on the floor. Lucian jumped and threw a pile of rags on the table before retrieving a broom. Grumbling under his breath, he cleaned the area. A quick glance reassured him the tomes were safe inside their waterproof bag.

"Damn it! Keep your mind on your work, not Natalya!"

A chime sounded, announcing the search was complete. He read the results and scratched his unshaven face.

Impossible. That alphabet hasn't been used in ... what, two millennia or more?

The program showed the match to be ninety percent-plus positive. It was Futhark script from the area now occupied by Croatia, which meant the runes most likely predated the Celts. Lucian had attended a couple of seminars where the age and origin of Futhark was hotly debated.

Tomes were usually written by a village elder or maybe a scribe answering to them. Almost invariably, ancient texts dealt with a battle or the life of an important person. The book on Lucian's desk was of no exception. The text was remarkably descriptive, enough to make even a jaded scientist like Lucian cringe. There were odd patterns to the text too. Certain places revealed by UV light appeared to have been written by someone else. Lucian scanned over the lines, reading what he could.

"*By use of a pinch ... no ... bit of grease ... no ... fat, maybe oil (?) ... and motion toward the intended, a slick ... that's not correct ... wet surface will form, causing a person to fall. The ... is ...*" And he could understand no more.

He read through the lines a few more times.

Vaughn Collar

This makes no sense. This is ... doing, not showing, what had been done.

He read through the lines a few more times, trying to connect the strange script with the known text. No matter how many times he read, the text would not mesh with the original. Yet, the message seemed important.

He stood and paced, deep in thought. *Slick ... oil? ... What? ... Wait a minute. I read the translation off the computer screen ... not the tome. No headaches ... hmm.*

He strode back to the table. Opening the tome, he flipped through the pages until he found the desired passage. As he read, he felt the words *etching* into his mind. Each word appeared with an incredible clarity. He noted a pressure building behind his eyes, as if he were holding back an absurd power. The pressure mounted, then peaked when he finished the passage. He felt a channel or a doorway open. Lucian knew exactly what to do, exactly what to expect.

He stepped over to a cabinet and selected a small can of oil he used for lubricating the lab equipment. He removed any possible contaminants from the end of the table and dried it with a towel. After placing a drop of oil on his fingertips and reciting the line, the words trickled and then flowed in quick succession. He felt the power build before releasing a single surge of energy. A wave of fatigue coursed through him, and he grabbed the table for support.

The area now shined as if freshly polished. He looked at his fingers – they were dry – no oil. He ran his hand over the top and it felt slick, as if someone had just wiped a fine layer of oil over the surface.

"*Imposibil!*"

He touched his fingertips again. Completely dry, as if he had never dripped oil on them.

Wait ... what?

The Rift - *Beginnings*

He could not recall what he had just said. The knowledge was concrete, but the actual words were - gone.

The teens ... in Petroşani.

He had thought it appropriate if one of the boys hassling the girls could do something foolish. Which happened. And - he had been eating a buttery pretzel from a local street vendor.

No ... it can't be ... can it?

He reached for the tome again, stopped, and donned his gloves. He scanned through the pages until he found another familiar passage. As he read, once again, he felt the words etch into his mind. The pressure was there and almost felt reassuring.

Now I need a little sand ...

He spotted the warming container full of hot sand used for bending plastics. Taking a large pinch, he walked out to a bench hidden within the trees from the sidewalk. A chorus of frogs and insects greeted him in the humid night air. Bats were swooping down, catching bugs attracted by the streetlights. The parking lot was almost empty.

Am I too la ... ah, good.

The sound of footsteps drew closer, muffled echoes from the wall behind him. A man walked past. Lucian dropped the sand and whispered the words, sweeping his hand at the stranger. The person sagged and collapsed as if a puppet with its strings cut. Lucian walked over and checked on him - lightly snoring. No indications of an injury. He had simply fallen asleep. Lucian glanced around and neither saw nor heard anyone nearby.

Well, since he's not hurt ... Lucian walked back inside. A few moments later he reentered his office. *Magic? Really?*

He pursed his lips, gently biting the inside of his mouth. His gaze fell upon the opened cabinet where a bottle of bourbon sat beckoning. Pouring himself a small glass, he reflected.

Vaughn Collar

Okay. Some strange words, a little oil, and it causes a grease slick? Some more strange words, a little sand, and someone falls asleep? How?

He read over the tome and the words blurred and a headache flared. He groped for his seat, collapsing into the chair. A wave of nausea hit. As quickly as it came, the ill feeling left along with the pain. Bracing himself for another jolt, he looked at the same passage. Same results, same pain.

"Damn it! Enough!" Lucian began to put the tomes away but stopped.

The surface of the table was now dry. Nothing remained of the oil. Lucian gulped down the last of the bourbon and left for home. The events of the evening were becoming most unusual.

The Rift - *Beginnings*

CHAPTER 11

A year had passed since the explosion rocked Scotland, and little changes were happening across the globe, though most remained unseen or unnoticed by humans. Despite the radical alterations, evolution was still a slow process.

Pam's labor had been swift and uneventful. In late January of 2077, their daughter, Hope, was born. Just like her parents, her hair was dark. However, her eyes drew a lot of attention. They were a deep purple, the color of amethysts. Her pediatrician assured them this was nothing more than an unusual color. Hope was able to track visual stimuli, clearly demonstrating that her vision was normal.

Deep in the Serengeti, the local tribes were discussing the drop in the monitor lizard population. With so many animal species being tracked, the native tribes were having problems locating any for black market trading. Monitor lizards, decidedly not endangered, were high on their list of desired animals to catch. But something was killing them. Tales of entire nests found destroyed were widespread.

A young Maasai tribesman was explaining the disappearances to one of the *businessmen* buying the illicit animals. "Sir, I tell you. This is the only one I found in a week. I did not mean to kill it, but ..." the young man stammered.

The poacher stared at the dead reptile. It was definitely a monitor, easily distinguished by the head shape and coloring. However, it didn't have a fringe of small spikes around the back of the skull, nor did it have spikes down its backbone to the tip of its tail.

"Well, I don't pay for dead lizards. Throw that thing away. Don't come back until you have something alive. Got it?" The poacher gave the young tribesman a look of disdain and stomped off.

Steve Mansford stared at the corral and the two white colts born a month apart. His daughter, Stacy, was enthralled with them. Steve knew he could make money with a quick sale but couldn't do that to his daughter.

He had to admit that he too felt something for the little ones. They were easily the brightest horses he had ever owned. They would respond to their names and several other vocal commands. They were also a head taller than a normal horse their age.

Hell, even the dogs like the damn things.

Amazon howler monkeys were suddenly having larger than normal infants. The younger ones were showing aggressive behaviors, fracturing their troop. They seemed oddly comfortable on the ground, highly unusual for them. Though it was far from rare for howlers to eat the occasional insect or small reptile, they

The Rift - *Beginnings*

mostly subsisted on fruits and berries. These younger individuals were not only eating more meat, they were actively hunting smaller animals such as ground rodents or younger monkeys of other species.

The Homathko River in British Columbia was the site of numerous legends. All that changed when the war hit. The local resort and small village had become a sudden ghost town. The unceasing rain all but destroyed the buildings, almost as fast as any person could.

As far as he was concerned, Matt Searls was the first to see the crumbled ruins. His interest, first and foremost, was to determine if it were financially feasible to rebuild. He flew in by pontoon plane as there was no other way to approach than by boat. What he found did not show promise.

Nothing remained standing, only a few high mounds of vegetation where the buildings once stood. Not wanting to sleep in a tent by himself, he powered up the plane and floated into the middle of the inlet. He had seen one-too-many grizzly bears and had no wish to end up becoming a midnight snack.

Matt was sitting on top of the plane when he heard a loud humming.

Mosquitoes? Great.

He reached out to swat a bug and his hand hit something solid. He looked but couldn't see what it was. The humming was growing louder. Matt looked down and gasped when he saw the mosquito. It was as long as his finger. And its bite was painful!

"Ouch! You little motherfucker!" Matt slapped the bug and blood splattered onto his pants.

The humming grew louder.

Vaughn Collar

The outline of larger mosquitoes formed an amorphous, black cloud. He fumbled for the latch and crawled inside the plane, double-checking the panel to ensure it was shut tight.

When did mosquitoes grow to the size of a bloody dragonfly? Damn!

Buzzing wings covered the plane.

Now I know what it sounds like inside a blender.

The constant humming and tapping stretched on for what seemed like hours ... before somewhat quieting. The moon finally peeked out from behind the dense clouds, revealing the blackened plane. Matt froze, afraid to move or breathe. Small, cleared patches soon reflected against the moonlight, and the horrific hum dissipated, leaving Matt visibly shaken. His heart pounded with the adrenaline surge.

Now, something large and dark moved along the beach at the forest's edge.

What the ... where are those night goggles?

Matt searched and found them in a small locker just behind the passenger seat. But the animal was gone. He scanned the shoreline again before spotting the huge, dark shape.

A tall, black, and furry figure slowly walked across the beach. There was no way to determine its true size, but it was obviously huge. The creature bent down and picked up a small log like it was a slender branch. It used the thing to dig in the ground. Then, it picked up something else.

Matt shifted in his seat and the airplane creaked.

The creature raised its head and looked directly in Matt's direction, its eyes reflecting the overhead aurora. A noise somewhere between a cough and a yell blasted from the creature with deafening volume.

Matt covered his ears but was transfixed by the creature's glare.

One last look from the creature and it turned, disappearing into the forest.

The Rift - *Beginnings*

Too late, Matt remembered where the camera was. *Damn it, damn it, DAMN it!*

Hohiro welcomed the oncoming summer. Though beautiful, the mountains of Japan could become quite cold when snow bound. The past year was no exception.

His time with the rhesus monkeys was coming to an end. His request to conduct research with similar primates in Texas had officially been approved, and he would be heading out in just a few weeks. Akiko Matsuma, his replacement from Kyoto, had already reported in at the park's administration center earlier that morning.

She should be arriving any minute. Hmm ... Let's see if anything is happening right now.

From inside his blind, he watched a group of one-year olds playing near a pile of rocks. The same pile where one had used rocks to cause a spark. His fascination with their reaction kept him motivated.

The approach of spring brought longer, warmer days, and the steep valley was prone to snow slides. Warm winds and sunshine had raised the temperature above freezing. By midday, a large mound of snow had careened down the slope and lodged in a pile of fallen trees. Most of the troop paid little to no attention.

Scanning the troop, Hohiro noted the younger ones had gathered. It was easy to differentiate the exceptional individuals. They were slightly larger and able to more easily escape their mother's probing eyes. They also seemed less adept in the trees. Plaster casts of a few footprints were now at the nearby Nagoya University. They showed differences that could help to explain why the newer monkeys seemed less comfortable in the overhead canopy.

Vaughn Collar

As he set up his cameras, a crunching sound announced someone was approaching. He stood and nodded. "Hello ... you must be Akiko-san."

"Hai ... and you are Hohiro-san. Anything interesting?"

Hohiro explained about the young members and what he had observed.

"So ... these actions are deliberate?" she asked.

"Yes. There have been no attempts to start a fire, but still ... it is only the younger ones with this behavior." He rubbed his hands together, trying to warm them.

Akiko saw this and smiled. "I brought a large thermos of cha. Would you care for some?"

"You're a savior! Yes, please."

The two enjoyed a cup and observed. When Hohiro could feel his hands again, he pointed at the wide-view binoculars. He used a smaller spotting scope. Together, they watched the younger group.

Two monkeys seemed interested in the snow slide. They shared a glance before scampering off. The rest soon followed. For a few minutes, youthful energy took over as the youngsters ran along the trees, hopping onto nearby branches or chasing each other in a massive game of *tag*.

Hohiro felt the gentle pressure of a hand on his shoulder.

"The first two ..." she whispered, "... they do not appear to be as agile as the others."

He smiled. "Good observation. Yes, I've seen the same thing. I've taken a cast of ..." – he looked for the right individual – "... the one that's perched on that fallen tree. His coat is somewhat darker than the rest."

"Hai. I see it."

Another youngster approached. The three hopped down and examined the pile of debris. Over the next half hour or so, the

The Rift - *Beginnings*

three monkeys dug through the snow, recreating a barrier resembling the fallen trees.

Hohiro and Akiko looked at each other, speechless.

The two monkeys crawled under this rough construction and groomed each other. The one that seemed to be the leader looked directly at the two humans. He issued a soft hoot before resuming to groom his friend.

A phenomenon was happening inside small populations of humans across the globe. Though not yet reported and still a long way from these events being correlated with each other, there were isolated genetic reports flagged for an anomalous gene change with the markers known to affect aging. These changes were being noted in Scotland - especially Inverness and the surrounding area - southern Romania - including Petroşani - and in the United States - within the Appalachian Mountains of North Carolina and Virginia.

Chapter 12

The town of Boone, North Carolina was large enough to support several OB-GYN specialists. But it wasn't so big that the five didn't know each other.

It was early spring and Leah Harrison was late for her appointment. She had been window-shopping for her new baby and had not noticed the time. She was in her second trimester with her first child and very nervous about her baby's health.

The night before, she and her husband decided they wanted to know their child's sex. They didn't have the money to decorate and be wrong. She had been through an amniocentesis the prior week, and her doctor asked her to come in to discuss the results.

"Hello, Leah. Good to see you again," Dr Raines said, glancing over a chart. "No Down's ... looks good to me."

"Great!" Leah, hugged herself.

"Your baby is going to be just fine. I don't see anything that would suggest developmental issues." She smiled. "I do have a few questions. Are there any unusual eye colorings in either you or your husband's family?"

The Rift - *Beginnings*

Leah frowned, trying to recall if she'd ever heard of anything. "No. I don't think so. Why?"

Dr. Raines continued reading through the chart. "Genetics show your daughter –"

"Daughter?" Leah's voice rose with excitement as tears rolled down her face. "I'm having a girl?"

Dr. Raines smiled. *This is why I chose to be an OB-GYN.* "Yes, your daughter. Her eyes will not be blue or brown, but beyond that, no issues were noted. No myopia ... uh, near sighted." She looked farther down the chart. Her eyes narrowed momentarily.

"What? What do you see?" Leah asked.

"Hmm? Oh, nothing. There might be a slight skin issue. May want to keep her out of intense sunlight until she grows a little older that's all." She put the chart down. "Now, let's get this over with so you can tell your husband the news, okay? The nurse will be in shortly to give you a gown."

Leah left that day, bubbling with excitement.

Dr. Raines, however, watched through the window as Leah walked to the parking lot. Once the woman was in her car, she paged the front desk. "How many more appointments do we have this afternoon?"

"None, ma'am. Do I need to schedule one?"

"No. In fact, unless there's an emergency, mark me as done for the day."

"Will do, ma'am."

Dr. Raines closed her door. She sat with the genetic report and the highlighted items she wanted to discuss. She had already researched one notation, and the results shocked her. Her contacts still contained a direct number to the lab in Baltimore. A male voice answered on the third ring.

"OB-GYNectics, Paul speaking."

Vaughn Collar

"Paul, this is Dr. Allison Raines in Boone, North Carolina. May I speak with Dr. Chandra?"

"Let me see if he's in ... yes, he is. Transferring you now."

"Allison? How are you?" Dr. Chandra's strong Indian accent identified him almost as readily as his name.

"I'm fine, Dr. Chandra. I'm calling because of the genetic report on one of my patients. A Leah Harrison, report number 2077C12."

"Give me a sec ... yes, found it. How can I help?"

"Could you explain the notation under the Hayflick limit?"

There was a moment of silence.

"Dr. Chandra?"

"Allison ... we've known each other a long time, so I'll be frank. When I noticed this genetic anomaly, I had to refresh my knowledge of what I was looking at. I contacted Johns Hopkins. Have you heard of a Dr. Richards? He's in their genetic research department."

"No, I can't say that I know him. Has he gotten back with you? Is this a serious mutation?"

"He has ... and it is potentially quite significant. Serious, mmm, wrong context. He found that the Hayflick limit is showing a cell division around three times less than the normal divide."

"Three times?" *Shocking ...* "That would mean ... a potential age of over 200?! That's impossible. Humans don't live that long."

"When is the mother due?"

"Just checked her. She's halfway through her second trimester."

"Allison ... I don't envy you trying to explain this one. But the results are clear. The gene in question shows extreme resistance to natural enzyme processes. It's crazy, no doubt ... but this child has the potential to live well into her hundreds ... maybe even two hundred."

The Rift - *Beginnings*

Dr. Raines sat back.

She and Dr. Chandra had attended medical school together. To her knowledge, he'd never shown any desire to treat actual patients. Instead, his talents led him to becoming a lab specialist. She had no reason to doubt him – *but damn! Two hundred?*

"You're talking biblical ages," Dr. Raines replied. "Does Dr. Richards know where the report came from?"

"No. I was careful to keep the origin unknown."

"Thank you. The last thing we need is the press. They would blow this little town up." She glanced at the antique clock, an anachronistic touch she loved. A glass of wine was going to be needed after this conversation.

"I understand, Allison. It will not pass my lips. Um, if there are any other developments or complications, you will let me know?"

"Yes, of course. I doubt there will be any ... problems. Both parents have clean bills of health, no substance abuse issues." She paused. "If you ever want to get away from the big city, come on down. That is, if you're still into fishing."

He laughed. "Oh, most definitely, and thank you! Have a good rest of your day, Allison."

The line disconnected.

In two other OB-GYN offices in Boone, several women were undergoing amniocentesis. The same lab would handle the genetic testing – OB-GYNetics.

From just north of Asheville, North Carolina and almost all the way to Roanoke, Virginia, several children were born with abnormal eye and hair colorings. The first family, the Ashers, were not far away. Hope was now several months old. She seemed to be a happy baby, frequently laughing and giggling. Her eyes and hair, however, showed no signs of changing. Pam had noticed that the

Vaughn Collar

family dog, so beloved by their son, now couldn't leave Hope alone. And she could have sworn she had noticed items move, seemingly on their own, and she was positive she had seen little, dancing lights above the baby's crib. Always when Hope was giggling.

The Rift - *Beginnings*

CHAPTER 13

Lucian's early college years were a blur, just vague memories of students and teachers he'd rather not remember. Only a few could be considered even near his level of specialization. Most of his PhD research was completed in the field. The highlight from those thirty-some years had been his participation in an archeological dig in Turkey when he was in his twenties.

Finally ... I get the chance to show my worth.

However upon arrival, he'd soon discovered he was just one of a number of research assistants. Ursel Mannheim, another assistant, had been his equal in every way. Privately, he admitted she was better in the field than him - but only privately.

Together, their brilliance was observed by the field supervisor. They worked on anything others found difficult, such as artifact identification. Lucian respected her intellect first, then admired her as an individual as an unfamiliar sensation slowly grew within him. He was soon looking forward to hearing her voice, seeing the obvious intelligence in her blue eyes. Spending much of their spare time together, they actually started finishing each other's sentences. Of course, these conversation hadn't been average.

Vaughn Collar

Their talks roamed over history and archeology in such depths as to need a doctoral degree to keep up.

And she is easy to get along with, to talk to.

Gossip around the camp buzzed as people watched the two interact. They seemed a little mismatched. Lucian had a reputation for coldness with a hint of street manners he had learned as a homeless teen. Ursel was quiet but warm and welcoming. She was marginally taller than Lucian and definitely thinner.

They'd been given a day off at the mid-point of the summer, and Lucian had no desire to visit the dusty, little town. The locals were observant Muslims with little tolerance for alcohol. The one tavern, dirty and with a bad reputation, was not officially within city limits and attracted the few non-Muslims – which meant the lower classes.

Lucian heard from another that Ursel was staying at camp. For the first time, he felt the stirring of an emotion, a feeling toward another person. Sure, he remembered he had loved his mother, but who hadn't loved their mother? This emotion was different. They often found themselves together during much of their spare time.

Lucian had asked Ursel earlier if she wanted to go for a walk that night. A front had warmed the temperatures to tolerable levels for a change. She told him she would be happy to share the evening. Since then, he had been unable to get her smile out of his mind.

Time played tricks on him all day. It seemed that the minutes were moving at alternating speeds – sometimes too slow, sometimes too fast. He found it impossible to concentrate on anything more than a minute at a time. Finally, he resigned to pacing the floor.

Luce, what do you know of romance? Odd thoughts ran through his mind. *You've never been kissed, much less anything else!*

The Rift - *Beginnings*

That night, the stars appeared to be sprinkled diamonds. The moon, even though just a crescent, provided more than enough light. The temperature wasn't too cold to enjoy, a rarity in this arid land.

"Lucian, I've been meaning to ask ..." Ursel looked down. "Is there anyone ... special ... in your life? Someone you look forward to seeing?"

"At home?" Lucian frowned. A spasm of pain crossed his face before he could control his emotions. Shrugging, he sighed. "I live alone. My mother passed some years ago. I was an only child."

Ursel smiled. "No, that's not what I was thinking. I mean ... is there anyone, umm, you plan to share your life with?"

Lucian gave her a long look before understanding. "Oh. Uh, no. No one. I've not really had time for a relationship." *Luce, you ass ... you've never even kissed a girl.*

She reached for his hand as their eyes met. She whispered, "Could you make time for me?"

His hands seemed sweaty inside hers. His heart raced and his chest felt as if bands of steel were tightening around it. He didn't know what to think. Affairs of the heart were foreign to him. But her eyes were luminous and with the reflection of the moon, full of emotion. He raised one hand gently to her cheek and leaned forward. Ursel pulled him toward her and their lips met.

After that night, their relationship grew more passionate. Days were spent with work. Nights were spent together, each one more intense than the last. Lucian often thought of their intertwined lives. Did they have an untold future together? *Was this – love?*

He stood at the edge of the camp, staring at the empty land around them. The heavy equipment sat mutely to one side, barely visible as the last of the afternoon sun set behind the mountains to the west. Actinic light revealed the outline of a dark hole in the side of the hill where ancient caves were finally giving up their secrets. A few tents remained lit, their occupants reviewing the prior day's findings. The dusty aroma of the arid countryside was laced with food from around the world and the somewhat sour odors of various lubricants for the equipment. Even though the dig was far from civilization and with few comforts, Lucian felt more at home there than anywhere else.

Lost in thought, he failed to hear the sound of steps until a voice spoke. He jumped and turned, staring into the face of the lead archeologist.

"Enjoying the sunset?" the lead asked.

Lucian nodded. "Yes. It is beautiful. I never knew the desert could be so ... picturesque."

"I'm happy you're enjoying it. Look, I've been on the phone. Our time here is being extended another two years. Evidently, several museums are contributing. So, if you want to stay ... I'd be thrilled to have you."

Lucian's 'brows raised. "Really? Oh ... most definitely!" Lucian reached for the man's hand, exuberantly shaking it.

"And by the way, I found Ursel first. She is also staying," the man said with a crooked smirk. He gripped Lucian's shoulder. "I'm happy to have the two of you here."

Lucian had to admit that recruiting the two together made sense. They complimented each other's skills, as Ursel was better at finding, and Lucian was better at determining what they had found, especially with understanding the artifact's timeline.

Well, full day tomorrow. Ursel will be going underground again ... I'll have time to prep a bunch of the pottery they found.

The next day dawned and heat waves rippled off the sand. Not long after breakfast, an eerie stillness had settled over the camp. Birds filled the sky with their calls mixing together to form a discordant cacophony. A long, low sound rumbled through the camp. The ground beneath Lucian trembled – then shook, turning

The Rift - *Beginnings*

over tables. As the waves continued, Lucian felt pottery shards slice through his clothing. Roaring sounds filled his ears and he listened to the faint cries echoing around him. Then – everything stilled. Only a few pebbles rolled down the slopes here or there. A fetid smell filled the air.

A sudden scream destroyed the silence. "The cave!"

Lucian looked at the opening. His heart stopped. His breath caught in his throat as the dust settled. Lucian could see that the entrance was now blocked with boulders and dirt.

"NO!" He ran to the cave-in and fell to his knees. Using his hands, he clawed at the rocks. Blood dripped from his fingers as his nails tore. Fear and rage flew thought him. He screamed again, "NO! Ursel!" Tear ran down his face and his lips quivered.

Two strong arms pulled Lucian from the mound. He struggled wildly, scratching and kicking to free himself.

"NO!" Lucian screamed again.

The field supervisor stood in front of him. "Lucian!" he yelled. "LUCIAN!"

Lucian glared at the man through red-rimmed eyes.

"Lucian! There's nothing you can do. Those boulders weigh tons. If you managed to move one, another would likely come down on you."

"But Ursel's in there! I've gotta find her!"

The supervisor nodded as the man holding him relaxed his grip and stepped back. They walked from the entrance and sat Lucian down.

"Lucian, we know. Ursel and three others are in there. They were in fairly deep. Hopefully, the cave-in didn't go back that far." The supervisor wiped sweat from his forehead, leaving a muddy streak. "We will notify you as soon as we find her. But for now ... stay here. We're bringing in heavier equipment."

Vaughn Collar

The rumble of diesels almost matched the sounds of the quake. Over the next few hours, men swarmed through the rubble, identifying the correct areas to move first. They soon cleared a path into the cave, and two of the most experienced diggers entered.

Lucian continued pacing as he had been for most of the day.

The men waved the dig supervisor over. A few words were exchanged, and when they motioned for Lucian, the supervisor nodded. "Lucian, it's time."

Lucian slowly approached the entrance. Someone handed him a lantern, and he entered past the rubble. Several dozen yards in, the bodies of three men were visible. Ursel lay a few feet away. Her face was at peace, but it was clear her neck and back had been crushed.

"Lucian," the supervisor whispered. "I've been a part of too many of these. I can assure you, she died instantly. There was no pain, no suffering."

Lucian fell to his knees. He was drained from feeling helpless. Ursel was gone. He had no words. No emotions. He was nothing more than an empty shell.

He resigned the next day.

The supervisor was not surprised. He knew Lucian and Ursel were close and didn't think Lucian would stick around – too many memories. He did give Lucian a package, asking him to open it once he returned to Europe.

Lucian opened the package two nights later. It was a letter of recommendation, stating that any university would be foolish to not hire him on the spot.

Leiden University reached out the next day. Within a week, Lucian had tendered a position in the history department. The chancellor had contacted the dig supervisor and was advised to hire Lucian before any of the British or American universities found him. Lucian turned out to be a good teacher. He developed

The Rift - *Beginnings*

a reputation for being cold, but this was simply a result from the lack of emotion. The only thing that ignited him was people treating others without respect or dignity. Lucian's passions were now devoted to his studies, both professionally and personally.

His single-minded desire now drove Lucian to researching the old tomes. Daily, he poured through the books. Daily, he tolerated the headaches. Daily, he spent hours challenging his boundaries.

The headaches were actually a sign that he had reached his limit. He could study no further without rest. The realization was a relief and a quandary. The relief was knowing he could avoid the teeth-grinding, eyeball-piercing pain. The quandary was knowing he had parameters – *and set by an old book?*

He spent days figuring out what he could do with each spell. As such, he found himself laughing for what seemed to be the first time in – *years?* He picked his targets – people who were making themselves a nuisance, usually. Someone talking a little too long? Sleep spells were a great cure. A guy unable to take *no* for an answer? A quick slip spell.

His repertoire increased over the summer. He added a spell to apply a *push* over longer distances. A spell with practical use allowed him to read and listen to languages he formerly couldn't. He now understood conversations in Gaelic. By the end of the summer, Lucian had deciphered a spell allowing him to cast a web just like a spider – but a *big* spider!

About a week prior to classes reconvening for the fall of 2077, Lucian took a rare few days off in downtown Amsterdam to recharge a little before the college year started. If he wasn't casting spells at unlucky targets, Lucian liked watching people.

He sat on a bench, enjoying the wind rustling through the leaves in the surrounding trees. It was an older section of town,

Vaughn Collar

and many buildings had been removed to adapt to adjusting sea levels. What was left was an accidental park where food cart vendors were doing their best to bring attention to their wares.

A body hit the ground, rather hard, accompanied by a splash. Lucian turned and smirked at a man in a suit, now dripping from what looked like a spilled soft drink. An older woman was on the ground, the contents of her shopping bag strewn about. Lucian had seen her talking with the cart owner just a few minutes before. As he watched, the man kicked the woman's groceries out of the way. A head of lettuce ended up at Lucian's feet.

"Watch what you're doing, old woman! Look what you've done to my suit!"

The woman sat with tears running down her face.

A younger woman screamed at the man. "Why don't *you* watch it yourself, asshole! You bumped into her!"

The man sneered and kept walking.

Lucian felt his blood boil. Holding the lettuce, he walked over to the old woman and helped her to her feet. He turned to see where the man was headed. He was now waiting at a crosswalk. Lucian could feel the pressure peaking as he prepped to release the spell.

Narrowing his eyes, Lucian muttered, "Ventilabrum," making a subtle motion with one hand.

The man took a step off the curb. But his next step was awkward. His eyes widened as he fell, face-first, into a parked car. Lucian had timed the push perfectly. It appeared that the man had stepped on a banana from the woman's shopping bag.

Lucian chuckled, turning his attention back to the woman.

"Oh, thank you, sir," she said.

Lucian gave her a second glance. She reminded him of his mother, for the woman was not well off, judging by her clothing. "Frau, I am so sorry. Here, let me help you." Lucian gave her the

The Rift - *Beginnings*

bills in his wallet. It was probably more than she paid for groceries in a month. But this was the one soft spot in Lucian's heart – people who life had mistreated.

As he walked back to the tram station, Lucian was giving his career some serious thought. He was enjoying teaching less and less. More than anything, he wanted to return to Petroşani, to the monastery in the mountains. He was sure there was more to discover.

Becoming a department head – just wasn't appealing anymore. But – Ms. Goldobin would be back. Lucian was going to be teaching a master's level course, and he was sure the class would be on her list of required courses.

Hmm ... maybe there is a reason to stick around, at least another year.

He passed a window and caught a peek at his reflection. He almost didn't recognize the skinny, haggard-looking man staring back at him. So deeply into studying the tomes, he had forgotten to eat – a lot, it looked like.

Luce, you're not going to attract anyone but a crow looking like this!

He snorted out a laugh and kept walking.

Vaughn Collar

CHAPTER 14

Shelly arrived at Reagan International and received her first surprise. Being greeted was usually reserved for important people. Not her.

What's going on?

Two men wearing basic black suits walked toward her. Both clearly looked to be government functionaries. Afterall, looks weren't deceiving.

"Ms. Shelly Lang?" the older of the two asked.

"Yes. Have I done something to warrant this?" She continued her walk to the escalator.

The man walking next to her smiled. "Shall we pick up your luggage? We can talk on the way."

Shelly stopped. "Am I being detained or arrested?"

The smile waned slightly as the man shook his head. "No, ma'am. Nothing like that. I'd rather not go into specifics, but ... there are a few who are interested in your expertise, not only in history and biology, but also ... and most especially ... organization."

Shelly nodded, mystified but curious.

The man motioned for her to walk next to him. Not an easy task – the man had a long stride.

"Are we in a hurry?" Shelly asked.

The Rift - *Beginnings*

"Hmm? Oh ..." The man slowed and the other matched. "What I'm allowed to say is that your upcoming interview with the Smithsonian is known. There is a confluence of interests between them ... us. You've already received the position by the way, and your interview has been changed, both the time and with whom."

Shelly glared at the man. *Talking point?* Stepping closer to the younger man, she noticed a faint scar just behind his ear – right where an implant could have been placed.

Coupled with the suit and their obvious athletic appearances, Shelly guessed them to be Secret Service. She was now curious, her tension building. She glanced at the older one. "I'm guessing no introductions until we're safely in a vehicle?"

He looked down at her, flashing his badge.

Shelly held his gaze. "One more adapted to silence?"

His response was just a blank stare, but a 'brow lifted, marginally. They continued walking in silence, their footsteps lost in the crowd. Her luggage was retrieved and soon she was being escorted to a government car. The two men sat in the front with the younger one driving.

The older man turned. "My name is William Moncrief. I work for the director of national security. He tasked us with greeting you and taking care of other little things like customs. He and a few others wish to speak with you about events we are closely monitoring ... in connection with the reactor incident last year."

Shelly eyes narrowed. "Okay, but ... why me? I'm a history specialist. I don't know anything about physics."

"Nothing about physics. The reasons might surprise you. Your work in history provides a convenient cover." He glanced out the window momentarily, then turned back. "Do you recall a paper you wrote about lack of organization in governments? Most notably ... the U.S. That paper has garnered attention at higher levels."

Vaughn Collar

Now, her 'brows raised. "But ... okay." She remembered the project, *but – what?* "Wait! That paper was more of a thought experiment than a cohesive argument. The director read it?"

Mr. Moncrief nodded, then shrugged. "Yes, he has. As did several others. They liked your processes. Now ... they want to talk with you about it, and how it may pertain to our current issue."

Shelly sat back, still feeling confused and somewhat concerned. *What have I gotten myself into? One minute, I'm going to an interview for an assistant curator position, and now ... what? I'm meeting with the director of national security? And ... who else am I meeting?*

Her thoughts bounced, unable to form a clear picture of just *what the hell* was going on. The vehicle slowing distracted her from her thoughts. She looked out and realized she had no idea where she was as they turned down a paved drive.

The drive ended at a tall hedge. The driver slowed but didn't stop as a large section rolled to one side. Beyond the hedge, the drive ended at an ordinary-looking, two-story house. A couple of government vehicles were parked in front. Several individuals were outside, one throwing a Frisbee at a dog. They all stopped what they were doing as the car pulled in and parked. One man approached and opened the door for her.

As they walked to the house, Shelly felt the intensity of the stares directed at her. Even the dog was at attention, its tail not moving.

Mr. Moncrief opened the front door.

Shelly was struck at how much the house looked like someone's home. Her senses fully alert, she noticed only slight incongruities with the furnishings and decorations. Some things seemed out of place or outside of time itself. And everything was clean, too clean. She doubted a white glove would reveal even the slightest trace of dust.

Someone has gone to a lot of effort to make this look ordinary.

The Rift - *Beginnings*

After crossing through the living room, the younger man opened a door and motioned for her to follow. A staircase led down. At the bottom, Shelly paused and glanced around. The walls were blank with a laundry room on one side. She wasn't overly surprised when Mr. Moncrief placed his hand on the wall and a light appeared behind it. The wall opened and the younger man motioned for her to enter the hidden room.

The hidden room could have been an alternate control center for NASA. Large screens dominated the walls. Computer terminals were stationed at every desk. Numerous workers were busy. Several grouped together were paying attention to a large screen showing orbital paths of - *satellites?* Any computer programmer would feel like they were in computing Disneyland.

A voice from behind grabbed her attention. "Ms. Lang, welcome. I'm sorry for the subterfuge, but ... well, you'll find out."

Turning around, she froze as her eyes locked onto the president of the United States.

Hayden Newman reached out to shake her hand. "It's nice to meet you. I've been listening to ..." - he motioned at a tall man standing near one of the terminals. The president laughed. "Okay, he's going to be rude. That is the director of national security and intelligence. It's on his advice this little pow-wow is taking place."

The director turned at the introduction. Shelly was struck by his appearance. She was a devoted fan of old movies and had inherited her father's collection that extended back to the mid-1900s. The director could have been a photo double for an actor from that period, Christopher Lee.

The director smiled. "Ms. Lang. It is good to meet you and put a person to the image." He even had the same deep, resonant voice.

The president cleared his throat, motioning to a small conference room in the back. They entered and found seats and spoke with a waiter who left with their orders.

Vaughn Collar

Shelly looked around the room.

The president and Mr. Moncrief were sharing a private joke. The director was scanning data on his laptop. Everyone seemed so casual.

But that's the president!

The waiter returned with their drinks. He left and the door shut. The director touched a place on the table and an electronic lock activated.

"Let's get rolling," the president said. "Ms. Lang, you are here to, hopefully, accept a position of potential importance. First, a little housekeeping. If you would sign the security clearance and NDA ..."

The table, which seemed to be clear plastic, changed into a screen displaying the documents. She read over the standard security clearance – with reference to a few bylaws she'd never heard of before. Each passage ended with *as directed by the president of the United States.* A stylus rose through the screen, and she used it to sign the forms. When she replaced it, the stylus and the screen disappeared. The table was again clear except for their drinks.

"Everything here on out is classified. Understood?" The president seemed relaxed, but no one mistook his seriousness. She met his gaze, and his eyes reflected his smile. He glanced over her shoulder, and she turned as cameras lowered from the ceiling. She nodded. Her hands felt clammy, and she didn't know what to do with them. Holding her drink would keep one hand busy, at least.

Smiling, the president said, "It all started with the reactor incident last year. Since then, there have been a number of ... interesting events. We are receiving word world-wide. Ms. Lang, you've been on our radar for quite some time. That paper was more than you think ... as was the moderator of that project." He paused. "We'd like you to head up a new department. Your organizational skills are self-evident. Working that little museum in Inverness ...

The Rift - *Beginnings*

not only getting it up and running despite prior incompetence, but actually helping it become well-known internationally ... well, that takes a special kind of competence." He was clearly trying to charm her and it was working. "Your academic qualifications speak for themselves. Out of curiosity ... no doctorate?"

"Not yet, sir. I was scheduled to start in Edinburgh last fall, but ... Edinburgh's not there anymore." She shrugged.

"Ah ... yes, having the city wiped out would put a damper on things. Okay, back to the subject. You've shown you can keep science and history separate but still have them correlate. Steve?"

The director stood and walked over to a blank wall. It turned opaque as a picture of the world was displayed. He pressed a place on the screen and bright spots appeared in various locations across the globe. The only continent not affected was Antarctica. The closest location was a cluster around the Virginia-North Carolina border.

"Ms. Lang," the director said, "each dot indicates a reported anomaly. And as you can see, each dot directly correlates with this."

Another picture of the globe appeared. Bright lights sparkled, much more numerous than the initial map. The one in Edinburgh was incredibly intense.

"This is a compilation of satellite captures from the time of the incident to about thirty minutes later."

The president joined in on the conversation. "We don't know exactly what happened. I've somewhat asked to stay out of the loop ... at least for now. For one, I have a rather full plate. The other is ... if I don't know about it, I can't say anything about it. Helps dealing with the press and all that."

Soft laughter filled the air, and Shelly felt her tension beginning to subside.

Vaughn Collar

"Alright," the president said with a chuckle, "they had to show me this much, at least so I would know why we are bringing in talent from outside the government. After this, unless Steve feels I need to know ... I don't need to know." He took a small sip of his drink. "What we are offering is for you to lead a new department. We don't even have a name for it yet. You choose your own people, within certain parameters ... being able to keep a secret paramount. They have to pass SAR."

She felt her tension ratchet up again as she met his stare. "SAR?"

The president chuckled. "Special access," he replied. "It's a level of clearance." He nodded. "Your mandate is this ... determine what is happening in these hot spots. Is there a security threat? Your title will be special assistant to national security. Your office will actually be attached to the Smithsonian, and you will have some duties there. That should keep the press off your back, at least initially. You will report directly to Steve."

She took a drink of water, noticing the ripples from her shaking hands. A drop of sweat ran down her back. She bit her lip to steady her nerves. "And funding?"

The director cleared his throat. "Funding is already committed. You have a more-or-less open budget. I should say I'm sorry to bring you in with only minimal information ... but ..." He looked around the room, as if to see if anyone had something to add.

No one moved.

"We go no further without this becoming official," the director stated.

The same area of the table lit again with another document.

"Additional forms for you to sign, both visible signature and voice analysis. But first ..."

The Rift - *Beginnings*

A rod extended from the table. At the end was a lens with a retinal scanner.

"Both eyes, please."

Shelly paused, but only for a second. She knew – *knew* – this opportunity would never cross her path again. With her parents deceased, her only concern was wondering if this would affect her potential relationship with Ian. True, she had a sister in Draper, Virginia but they had little in common. Her thoughts swirled before settling down. She looked at the director, then at the president. She bent over slightly and stared into the visual scanner. Several signatures later, she added her voice for recognition, and the table resumed its normal appearance.

She beamed. "Okay, when do I begin?"

CHAPTER 15

The discovery of magic and being able to manipulate it was just as exciting and overwhelming for Ian as it was for Lucian. Ian, however, did not have as much time to devote to it. He had a social life and intended to enjoy himself. As a senior professor at Boston University, he was not assigned summer classes – and with no aspirations for department head, there were no reasons to ask for them.

The idea that he could cast magic was unbelievable – but readily apparent. Even more apparent was the need to keep his abilities a closely guarded secret.

His free time was filled with experimenting with the spells he knew and expanding on them. His knowledge and skill grew daily. Initially, two spells were all he could manage before the headaches signaled his limits. Daily, Ian pushed those limits and eventually expanded to a third spell, and then a fourth. Within a few weeks, he was up to five.

His repertoire included the ability to cast a small ball of light he could control, a spell to put people and animals to sleep, one to apply force in the form of a solid push, one that could create an almost-frictionless surface, and the last could create a web resembling an average spider's – but much bigger.

The Rift - *Beginnings*

The spells were printed on one staff with more he hadn't yet mastered. *And the others?* His curiosity led him to examine each rod more closely. Some spells required a component, others simply required a thought or strong intent. Deciphering the runes on the second staff took the remainder of the summer. Despite working through many nights, he only gained one additional spell before the school term started.

Ah, but what a spell! I can think of a lot of uses for telepathy.

The third staff gave him the worst headache of all. He set it aside and decided not to try it again until the first two were mastered.

Ian searched for places to practice. Usually at parks where he could target animals that wouldn't be injured – such as putting a squirrel to sleep – but only if it was already on the ground. Inanimate objects were his preferred targets. Repeated uses of the push spell had moved a park bench several feet, much to the puzzlement of the park workers.

Late one afternoon, he was strolling along a tree-lined street as he returned home from shopping. A commotion started with loud voices, then a scream from farther down the block. A young man sprinted into view. Two older women were yelling.

"Stop!" one hollered out.

"My purse!" the other wailed.

Ian remembered he still had a slip spell and the required component on him. His aim was true. The spell landed, and the young man lost his footing, slamming into a tree, knocking himself out. The crunch of the man's nose caused Ian to wince. He waited until the police arrived before leaving quietly.

Yes! No one the wiser and a thief caught. It's been a good day.

Feeling a little regret over the injury, he rounded the corner and pumped his arm slightly, his grin wide.

It's his own damn fault – shouldn't be stealing.

Vaughn Collar

Ian had grown up rather sheltered. His parents came from wealthy families, which gave him every advantage he could ever want. Ian had not known what underprivileged felt like until he attended college and witnessed another side of life. Many of his classmates scraped by working part time, shopping at thrift stores, and eating the cheapest foods possible. These experiences had changed Ian. By the end of his sophomore year, he was helping others as best he could. *And now ... magic!* How could he help – without being seen or suspected? The recent incident was a prime example.

Everyone is going to say karma. Fine. Let them. I don't want to be judge and jury, but speeding up karma ... oh yeah, I can live with that.

The next few days passed swiftly. He was marking the time until Shelly was able to visit from Washington. With her new position at the Smithsonian, she was unable to come up as early as they had planned.

"Some problems with logistics," she had said.

Probably government red tape around an exhibit, he surmised.

But now, she would soon arrive. They had talked frequently on the phone. The more he thought about her, the more he realized he viewed her romantically and less as a friend. An unexpected complication. Ian yearned to share his experience with magic but knew it was an impossibility at this point in time.

But if I don't tell her ... am I lying? How do I balance this? Got some thinking to do there, don't yah?

Ian was at his school office working on assignment schedules when his phone buzzed. Shelly – he placed the call on *visual* before answering. "Hello there! In town yet?"

"About thirty minutes ago. I found the cutest B&B overlooking the harbor."

"Great! I'm almost done here ... or at least I can put it down. Have you worked up an appetite?"

The Rift - *Beginnings*

She paused, apparently thinking. His heart raced knowing she was only a few minutes away.

"Yes, very much so. Uh ... have you heard of Buon Rapporto? It's just around the corner, and the aroma is heavenly."

"Buon Rapporto? Yeah, I've heard of it. Not been there. Sounds Italian ... and I love Italian. I'll call for a reservation in about ... an hour or so?"

Again, a slight hesitation before she replied, "Sounds great. Want to meet there?"

His turn to think. "No, I'll bring my vehicle. Maybe we can find something to do after." He smiled. "We could walk there, but just in case."

Shelly nodded. "See you soon, bye." She winked as the screen faded.

Ian immediately put down his schedules and hurried home. A quick shower and fresh clothes, a glance in the mirror to touch up his beard, and he was out the door. He arrived at the B&B and was ready to greet her. As he reached out to knock, the door opened. Shelly was standing there – looking fantastic.

With just a bit of hesitation – mostly to get his breath back – Ian grinned. "Woah. You look great!"

Shelly blushed a little and curtsied. "Thank you. You look great yourself."

The two walked to the restaurant. Ian could just detect her perfume. The meal was wonderful. A small bottle of wine capped it off. They enjoyed the boardwalk around the harbor, a slight breeze from the ocean made the night pleasant. Deep in conversation about her new position with the Smithsonian and Ian's upcoming year at Boston University, they ended up at a coffee shop – one of the last in Boston. It had an outdoor seating area where they sat at an isolated table. The harbor was immaculate. Boston had spent a lot of money over the last couple of decades in clean-up efforts. Prior to, the shore was ringed with the sludge and oil from decades of motorboats. The air had been filled with the stench of dead fish and rotting vegetation. All this had combined to make the waterfront an area to avoid. The clean-up work had paid off. The water was clean again and numerous shore birds had returned. The waterfront was now a popular place for restaurants and small shops.

"Those rods you found ..." – Shelly took a sip of her coffee – "... have you gotten anywhere with 'em?"

Ian almost swallowed the wrong way but managed to recover. "I have four rods more or less finished. The skald in question was describing day-to-day activities. Nothing spectacular. I'm working on a fifth now. I'm having to balance school with research. Heavy schedule ... heavier than expected. Something's up, but that's above me."

She lifted her cup and paused before placing it on the table. Her eyes softened as she smiled.

Ian stood and extended his hand. They walked toward a small extension of the boardwalk where several trees provided a little privacy. A momentary awkward silence, then they reached for each other. A light kiss turned into another, then a much deeper and more passionate one.

They stepped apart. "Ian, I ... um ... that was nice."

Pulling himself together, he whispered, "Yes, it was." *Wait, she reached for me too?!* "You've been thinking about this?"

She smiled. "Uh, huh. Since Scotland."

Her gaze didn't seem as flirtatious anymore. There was no mistaking her thoughts. Words weren't required.

They walked back to his car and drove to his place.

The Rift - *Beginnings*

(HAPTER 16

After an incredible week with Shelly, Ian felt ecstatic. Not that he had been celibate his entire life – he just couldn't recall feeling this happy.

Maybe being single is over?

They would have to manage a long-distance relationship. But if it worked out, perhaps he could join the staff at Georgetown, or maybe Shelly could move up to Boston to work at the newly relocated Museum of Science. The latter was preferable to Ian.

Only a couple more weeks until classes would start, but Ian planned to spend every spare moment working on the mysterious rods. So far, he had deciphered eight spells though was only able to cast five. The more he deciphered, the more he realized the spells were useful for combat – *sleep, push, slip, web* – mostly for offense. Even a minor spell such as *finger spark* could be used for attacks.

The other three spells ... *well I know what they do, but I can't get the whole spell down yet. I wonder ... it took me a while to get past the first two. Maybe ... I don't have enough power? Yeah, right ... who're you gonna ask?*

Vaughn Collar

He felt his phone buzz. He smiled at seeing it was Shelly. "Hey, good looking! What's up?" Ian asked.

Shelly looked serious. "Ian ... turn on the national news. There's something happening in Brazil."

Ian switched channels.

> "... are dead in a remote village in Brazil after a howler monkey attack. The village is just outside the borders of Amazonia National Park. And now ..."

The screen displayed a map with the village just to the south.

> "... we have this small clip caught from the scene earlier today ..."

The clip was obviously from an amateur. The view was unfocused and blurred, bouncing up and down. As the screen cleared, a small group of monkeys charged into the village. Two wielded branches like clubs. The amateur screamed and ran as the scene blurred again before he charged through the trees. The sound of panting, and the scene focused before blurring again, as if held by shaking hands. The picture now centered on the main path. Two men lay dead, their faces in the dirt with blood pooling around their heads.

The two club-wielding monkeys turned, attacking a woman, driving her body into the ground. Other monkeys jumped onto the vehicle where the camera-person had hid. The view blacked out for a moment before a monkey screeched. The vehicle sped off with the sound of gunfire, fading in the distance.

Ian was not an anthropologist but he knew no monkey or primate should react this way. There were a couple of troops in the Congo known to attack each other and occasionally feed on the young they could catch – but none ever attacked humans.

The Rift - *Beginnings*

The news cut to a science reporter who was offering his opinion.

"The authorities are ..."

"This is wild," Ian remarked. "Howler monkeys are all bluff, unless threatened. This looks ... and sounds ... like an unprovoked attack."

Shelly nodded. "I know a little more. One of our people was down there and called in additional information. Are you ready for this? There were two attacks, not just one. The other ... two human infants missing are missing." She looked down. "I'd like to send you a copy of the report. There's more data contained in it. Is your home computer secure?" Her eyes showed shock and her voice trembled.

What in the hell is she sending me? "Um, use my university email." He sent her his secured link. Ian felt confused. *Shelly works at the Smithsonian. How does she have access to secure links beyond what the news channels have?* He shook his head. The download complete, Ian split the screen so he could still see her.

A large portion of the troop had attacked several huts on one side of the village. People had fallen to the ground, either stumbled or dragged by howlers. A large male knelt on top of a woman. He ripped into her neck with his claws.

The camera switched scenes – *no* – this is another camera at the other end of the village.

Two howlers crept through an open window and exited with an infant roughly cradled in its arms. It stopped and raised up on its legs and issued a loud call. The troop stopped and left as one. For howler monkeys to actually target human babies was completely unheard of.

Bizarre is closer to the truth. "Shelly, I have to ask. Why are you sharing this with me?"

Vaughn Collar

"Your specialty is in early human civilization. You have a well-regarded publication about observations from a chimpanzee troop, noting behaviors that would seem to suggest early signs of progression from a wild animal ... to something more."

Ian thought about his old paper. *But ... how in the hell did she even know about it?*

"Could it be possible this is something similar?" she asked. "Evolution?"

Ian sat back. He clasped his hands together, resting his chin on them. *Well, yeah ... a distraction is definitely a form of tactics. So was the call the one monkey made. The rest of the troop obeyed him ... like they were puppets on a string.* "Hmm. If you ignore several dozen generations of behavioral changes, then yeah ... I could see interpreting it that way." A stray thought crossed Ian's mind. "Were any of the carcasses retrieved? It would be interesting to examine the changes. These animals look larger and more aggressive."

She nodded. "A couple were preserved and on their way here. Look ... I want you in on this. There's a team forming to investigate this incident and others. I've acquired the pull to clear you without anyone questioning me. You want in?"

"Yes, definitely! How soon?" Her statement slowly sank in, not to mention the pull she would need to make it happen without question. *What?*

"Should be around eight hours or so. I'd imagine the flight has left Manaus within the last ..." - she looked at something behind the camera - "... thirty minutes or so. They're on a military flight and cooling equipment is onboard to preserve the bodies." She looked down before glancing back up. "You can probably guess it already, but ... this is a top-secret transfer. The Brazilians are having fits about us retrieving a carcass and with the event itself. Their military held us virtually at gunpoint. The flight left maybe five minutes ahead of the cavalry."

The Rift - *Beginnings*

Ian nodded. "I can imagine. I've never had reason, or frankly a desire, to go to Brazil. I've talked to a few people and that government is scary down there. They've repeatedly said they were never so thrilled as to see the border to Argentina." He pulled down a tab for his calendar. "I can be there for the weekend and perhaps a couple more days. After that, I have to be on campus."

The first sign of any levity crossed Shelly's face. "Are you sure? Just the weekend?" She gave him an impish smile.

He grinned. "You keep that up and my reputation as a staid history professor is going to take a beating." He laughed.

"Good! Well ... maybe not. I don't want it to get out that you're –"

"Shelly! Let's have some privacy." He chuckled before turning serious. "Look, I'll get materials ready, some pre-human and early human studies. I'll leave here first thing in the morning. I should arrive not long after the flight from Manuas."

Shelly donned her professional face. "I'll see you then. Meet me at the entrance to the anthropology section. I'll book you a room to keep covers satisfied. Thank you, Ian. For now ..." She blew him a kiss and disconnected.

Ian watched the news stream. The story was on a loop with nothing new. Just to double check, he pulled up information about howler monkeys. Nothing to reflect this level of violent behavior. Overall, howlers appeared to act more like an average schoolyard bully – all bluster and no substance. Definitely not murderously aggressive. *Tactics?* Other than vague rumors about orcas and a couple of observations about chimps, *tactics* were a human-exclusive trait.

Still, he couldn't deny what was on that video link. A clear ruse. And why two infants? He could understand if it was a desperate guerilla band fighting a meaningless war. But not howler monkeys.

Vaughn Collar

What the hell has Shelly gotten me into?

Ian arrived in Washington just before eleven in the morning. He found the correct lot and was walking to the specified wing when a side door opened.

"Mr. McGregor? This way." A security guard motioned to him.

He walked into the building, down a corridor that seemed to be used only by staff, and found himself in a conference room. Shelly was talking with someone.

"Ian ..." – Shelly motioned him over – "... this is Dr. Wayne Langston, head of genetic research at Johns Hopkins."

Ian shook the man's hand. He had heard of but never met him. He was supposedly one of the world's absolute best at interpreting a genome.

"Glad to meet you," Ian said. "I've heard much about you."

Dr. Langston smiled. "Not all bad, I hope." The grin was infectious and all three laughed. "I've been listening to Ms. Lang. Your paper about potential signs of civilized behavior in a chimp troop in the Congo is impressive."

The same security guard guided the three through empty corridors to the lab. On entering, the aroma of formaldehyde and decomposing flesh competed with the sterile environment. Two people wearing surgical gowns were discussing X-rays hanging from a stand. The corpse of a monkey was on the table. Ian noted it was not an ordinary specimen. Though it was a sub-adult, it was much larger than any howler Ian had ever seen. The facial structure was also slightly different – more human-looking.

One of the two examining the X-rays turned around. When she did, Ian realized it was Dr. Rachel Lafleur from Paris. She had a reputation as being one of, if not the most, renowned primate researcher on the planet. She smiled.

The Rift - *Beginnings*

"Oh, Monsieur Langston and Monsieur McGregor. How nice to have a chance to meet you!" she exclaimed in a heavy French accent. "I suppose we are to determine what has happened with this singe ... excuse me, monkey, no?"

Ian smiled. "That's the impression I'm getting, Dr. Lafleur. You have to admit, an incident like this is rather out of the ordinary ... enough to bring *us* together."

Dr. Langston glanced at Shelly, who nodded. "Doctors ... this is not the first incident. It's actually the second. This specimen is from the first attack. Dr. Lafleur herself was in that party when that attack happened."

Squinting at the petite French scientist, Dr. Langston asked, "You arrived ... three days ago?"

"Oui. The guide killed this one. I'm afraid there may be some decomposition. We had no way to preserve it at that time."

Ian felt more than a little out of place, a historian and archeologist in a biology lab. He glared at Shelly with a look of, *"What am I doing here?"* She smiled and touched his arm. Her demeanor became serious, and she surreptitiously pointed at the ceiling. Ian nodded, knowing the gesture meant higher powers were involved.

Don't question anything, yet. Okay?

The Feds were definitely involved, likely pulling in people from all over. No tidbit of information, or source of data, would be overlooked. Likely, the executive branch had started this chase.

Top secret? Hah! That's open press compared to what this is!

Vaughn Collar

CHAPTER 17

Doctors Lafleur and Langston, along with Shelly, Ian, and a government official, were sequestered in a comfortable office lounge. A waiter arrived to take their drink orders. For Ian, it was a scotch, neat.

Too many years spent in Scotland, Ian. He chuckled as the rest of the group looked at him. "Private joke." He waved off the attention. The others chuckled nervously as the room washed with strong emotions.

The door opened and a suited, muscular man entered. "Ladies and gentlemen, the president." He shuffled to one side.

Everyone stood.

Another man followed behind at a respectful distance.

Ian glanced at Shelly, who's eyes widened slightly, as if trying to control her reaction. His stomach tightened – things were becoming serious.

"Please ..." The president waited for everyone to seat themselves. "This is informal ... at least behind closed doors. This is my director of national security, Steve Hammond."

The man nodded as he pulled a tablet from his briefcase.

Ian was used to being one of the tallest around. However, Steve Hammond would tower over him.

The Rift - *Beginnings*

The president took the empty seat at the head of the table. "The subject matter makes it necessary, even if science isn't his ... or my forte. That being said ... Dr. Lafleur, you have some findings we should know about?"

Dr. Lafleur glanced at her notes before sitting up a little straighter. "Oui, Monsieur President."

Ian felt she was likely to be the only person not intimidated by the company.

"The findings ... zay are most disturbing and unusual." Her accent was strong.

The president glanced over at Ian and raised a 'brow.

Shelly grinned and looked away.

Ian shrugged and concentrated on the woman's words.

"But ... s'il vous plaît ... could we allow Monsieur McGregor to relay our findings? My English ... not good."

Ian's nerves progressed from slightly nervous to a cold sweat. He felt the gaze of the president and the director boring in on him. Shelly brushed her hand against his, giving him a little reassurance.

"Ian, please." The president chuckled. "I don't bite."

Ian took a deep breath. "Mr. President, I must agree with Dr. Lafleur. This incident and the results are indeed disturbing. The biggest diff –"

The president cleared his throat. "I've learned there are missing children. Have they been found?" He glanced around the room.

The director sat up a little straighter. "No, sir, not yet ... at least not to my knowledge. I've been led to believe the jungle is almost impassable. Unless we are extremely lucky, we'll never recover them."

The president frowned and sighed before motioning for Ian to continue.

Vaughn Collar

Ian took a sip of his drink. "The biggest difference is in the cranial size. Both specimens are around thirty percent larger than the norm for their age. The brains show clear development in areas of ..." – he glanced at his notes – "... analytic reasoning. In the second attack, a large number of the troop made a loud commotion that ..." – Ian looked at the president directly – "... worked as a diversion. Two individuals used the diversion, for lack of a better word, as a ruse."

The key tapping of the director's fingers on his tablet stopped.

"In regard to the kidnapping of the two infants," Ian continued, "we reviewed the footage, including recently obtained interviews by the Brazilian government." Ian nodded at the director. "They confirmed the videos. The two monkeys with the babies made a distinctly different call, and the troop responded." Despite the coolness of the room, Ian felt sweat trickling down his back.

The president glared at Ian. "You're telling me that ... a group of monkeys showed tactics? Including giving direction and verbal cues?"

"Yes, sir."

The president glanced at the two scientists.

"I can speak for Dr. Lafleur on this." Dr. Langston nodded. "Yes, sir, tactics were clearly displayed."

"Damn," the president whispered. "This is bad. Ian, sorry. I may interrupt a few times. This is ... well ... unbelievable."

"Yes, sir, it is." Ian took a deeper breath. "Okay ... the two specimens are larger than normal for their age. About ten percent overall, which follows the increased cranial capacity. Also, the pelvis has a somewhat different alignment. They would still be able to brachiate in trees, but they would be more comfortable on the ground. Both have been eating meat. For howlers, this is rare. They may cram the occasional insect into their diet, but otherwise their

The Rift - *Beginnings*

diet is almost exclusively fruits and seeds. Not these two. Autopsies showed over half their diet consisted of animal meat proteins. Lastly, we've sent away for DNA comparisons. Those results should be in very soon."

The president and director shared a look, and the president asked, "They're eating meat? Is there something important about that?"

Dr. Lafleur nodded. "Oui, monsieur. For a species to start ingesting a higher protein, usually within a few generations, we start to see an increase in ... neuron? ... no, neuron production. It is sûr ... excuse me, certain ... that these individuals were more cognitively advanced."

"Sir ..." – the director looked at the president, then everyone else – "... this is why I asked to be involved. I do not read DNA analyses, but from their report ..." – he motioned at the doctors – "... we have to start treating other similar accounts seriously." He opened his briefcase and pulled out some papers.

The president kept his expression flat and nodded.

The director handed one packet to Ian and another to Dr. Langston and Dr. LaFleur.

Ian glanced through the papers. It was the DNA analysis they had requested. *Why should I be surprised that the NSA already had it?* He glanced at the two doctors.

Dr. Lafleur's eyes widened. "Mon dieu!"

The scientists leaned over, reviewing and talking about the analyses. Shelly lightly grabbed Ian's arm. She made a miniscule jerk and rolled her eyes toward the president. The president was staring at him with more than a little impatience.

"Um, sorry, yes," Ian stammered. "The overall results are shocking, but our specimens have genetic alterations. Specifically, in the areas of cognitive processing, and oddly, it fits a larger production of testosterone."

Vaughn Collar

"It fits?" the president asked.

"Yes," Ian replied. "The increased production of this hormone can be directly correlated to the increased aggression shown. I'm more concerned with the cognitive advances, sir. Dr. Langston?"

Dr. Langston looked a little surprised. "Dr. McGregor is correct. The cognitive increase is worrisome. I used older studies to compare DNA with other specimens, along with precise measurements of the cranial capacity. These two individuals and evidently most of the troop are now roughly comparable to a certain hominid ... Homo Erectus. The smaller monkeys are not as advanced, at least not yet. But the comparison isn't a big stretch."

The room quieted, deathly silent.

The president's voice grew louder. "Are you serious?" He leaned over, eyes wide. One hand rose to his chin as he momentarily stared off. "Doctors, you do realize this is a little hard to digest?" He sat back and sighed. "Are you saying a new species is developing?"

Ian shook his head. "I'm not sure about a new species, but it is a little difficult to believe. We find new species in the Amazon all the time, usually a plant or an insect. Not anything remotely the size of a monkey." Ian met everyone's gaze. "We may be looking at a dramatic leap in evolution ..."

"But an evolution to what?" the president added.

The Rift - *Beginnings*

CHAPTER 18

Lucian used the rest of the summer to study the tomes in his possession. Slowly, he pieced together over a dozen spells and could cast all but one. He was unable to acquire the required component – bat guano – as they had become one of the most protected species on Earth. Frequent practice made Lucian feel more confident about using magic. Irritating and troublesome people were his favorite targets – when he was given the chance.

His ability was something he knew he had to keep secret. Not that this was difficult for him. Lucian was a loner and not actively social. Most of his character, he reasoned, was because ... well, no one matched his intellect. Well, maybe one, the alluring Natalya Goldobin.

Even with her on his mind, he yearned to continue exploring the monastery. A nagging suspicion told him there were more to be discovered – a lot more. *Next time,* he told himself, *I will return with better equipment like ground radar.* He knew that most older monasteries had basement chambers and doubted that this dig would be an exception.

The lindens and elms already showed fall colors, giving the campus splashes of reds and golds. A crispness to the air promised

Vaughn Collar

an early fall. The cooler weather was a magnet for those looking to escape the stuffy rooms. Students filled the benches and gathered in small groups on the open lawns. Lucian enjoyed the fresh air, though he stayed to himself. He overheard one group debating about the causes of human mutation. He stopped to listen, pretending to be watching birds.

What an odd topic. Human genome mutation?

After a few minutes, he resumed walking before stopping at his favorite bench that was shaded by an ancient oak. Pulling out his laptop, he searched for news concerning the conversation. He found an article from Romania, discussing a recent trend. In two small regions, around five percent of newborns had purple eyes and thick, black hair. Black hair was not at all unknown in the Slavic areas.

But purple eyes? Interesting.

The tower bell rang. He had study notes to finalize before his next class. Though purple eyes were certainly unusual, they had no bearing on his life.

Classes started and Lucian noticed Natalya sitting in the second row. He smiled, she was continuing her master's in history.

"Okay, everyone. Let's review the syllabus." Lucian looked at the class and tried to not be obvious that he was enthralled with Natalya. "As this is a graduate-level course, there are some things to discuss concerning grades. You will find notes bookmarked for this semester to assist while you study."

There was a flurry of tapping on various screens until everyone had accessed the syllabus.

He explained the study notes briefly before starting a short lecture. It proved difficult to keep his attention away from Natalya, and his eyes drifted to her frequently. She was well dressed – maybe

The Rift - *Beginnings*

a little too well dressed. Lucian noted several young men paying him no attention, but her a lot. Oddly, this behavior grated on his nerves. When she returned a smile to one of the young men, Lucian faced the board to keep his grimace from being noticed.

The class ended and Lucian waved as she walked by. "Excuse me, Ms. Goldobin. I have material from a recent dig written in classic Russian. Would you be interested in assisting with translation?" He took a deep breath to keep his focus on the work and not her. "I would be willing to give extra credit, and of course, a good way to attach your name to the research. If you're interested." Her perfume, or whatever she was wearing, smelled intoxicating.

She glanced down before looking up and meeting his eyes. "Yes, sir, I would be interested." She added a warm smile.

"Good. Come by my office at, let's say around three? I will be finished with my afternoon class by then. Would this be convenient for you?"

She glanced at her schedule and nodded. "Perhaps I can move a study meet. The extra credit would be great, Professor Ciobanu. I will be there at three. *Spasiba.*"

Lucian nodded. Being bold was usually out of character for him. He hadn't spent much time with a woman in - no, *don't think of it that way, Luce. She is a student and very intelligent at that. This is merely helping someone. Someone gorgeous and ... stop that, Luce!*

The afternoon classes crawled by. He kept glancing at his watch or the antique clock hanging on the wall. Finally, the last class ended and only a half hour remained before she would arrive. Her image filled his mind, so beautiful.

Luce!

He looked around and noticed one of the tomes on the table. He picked it up. After placing it in the cabinet, he pulled out a few sheets of the material to be translated.

Vaughn Collar

This should be enough for a good hour or two.

Exactly on time, she knocked on the door. He knew it was her by the perfume. He stood. "Good afternoon." He motioned to a stack of papers. "This is the material I was speaking of. Feel free to use the terminal. I will be working on a different project."

"Thank you, sir. I will get started."

"Oh, one suggestion. Open the documents on early Celtic and Futhark."

"Futhark? I haven't heard of that ... or is it them?"

He smiled. "Futhark is a script. I have a folder for you on the desktop. Futhark predates much of the writing in Europe. This paper, for instance, is written mostly in Celtic, but some of the runes have stylistic differences."

She pulled up the reference material. "This is what you were referring to?"

Lucian glanced over, averting his gaze from her eyes. "Yes. That shows the runes and the associated sounds. Most of this comes from early European alphabet, rather than a distinct population."

She nodded, running her fingers over the symbols, smiling.

"The thing with Futhark is that many of the alphabets of Europe stem from the script style." He paused. "If you need more information just use the databases. There are numerous articles about it. Could help to streamline the process."

"Do you have any advice about where to start? Maybe a certain page?" Natalya looked at him.

Her smile melted his reservation. "I would start with ..." – he scrolled through a couple of pages – "... here. The author used more recent styles. Should make it a little easier to decipher."

"Thank you, tovarisch. I'll get started."

Natalya clicked on the keypad.

Lucian watched from the corner of his eye. He was able to look away before she noticed his intense gaze. He shook his head.

The Rift - *Beginnings*

Luce, be careful ... He gathered his wits and returned to his notes. *Now, this wording ... I can change the intensity? Hmm, maybe even blind someone ...*

An hour had passed. Lucian jumped when Natalya cleared her throat.

"Sir, I have a study group soon, and I must eat first." She flashed a megawatt smile. "Where do you want me to save this?"

Lucian frowned. "I'm so sorry to take up your afternoon. In the same folder with your name on it. I can put everything else away. Just place the sheets in there." He pointed at a manila folder at the end of the desk.

She placed the papers in the folder and reached for her purse. "Professor, thank you for the opportunity. Um, same time, day after tomorrow?"

"Yes. Have a good evening." Though he tried to not watch her leave, his gaze lingered. Her smile was now an afterimage forever engraved in his mind.

"Luce, quit it! She's half your age ...!"

A snort of laughter, and he turned back to the spell, wanting to root this one to memory.

Vaughn Collar

CHAPTER 19

As the U.S. government was meeting with Ian and the doctors, the Brazilian government was conducting their own investigation. Brazilian intelligence had sent out a paramilitary team with orders to capture at least one or two of the monkeys. Finding the infants was their primary objective, but none expected this directive to be successful.

When they arrived, they were shocked to find the village largely destroyed. Huts were torn apart and belongings strewn everywhere. A few howler carcasses were scattered about. Behind the remains of a hut, three dead howlers surrounded the carcass of a jaguar. One howler had its arm torn off. Laying nearby was the arm with the stiff fingers still clutching a tree limb. The jaguar's skull was caved in.

An operator picked up the branch and studied it before placing it near the crushed skull – a perfect fit.

The men were surveying the damage as several howlers charged in from the jungle. The main body of the troop dropped from the trees and a few awkwardly ran.

The attack didn't stand much of a chance against the heavily armed group, though two men were hurt, one severely. The howler

The Rift - *Beginnings*

troop was decimated. Twenty-three members were killed before the rest scattered.

"Excuse me, Primero Sargento. Have you taken a good look at the macacos?" Terciero Bruno knelt, poking at one of the monkeys.

Primerio Sargento Aldo glanced over Bruno's shoulder. "Bruno, I'm a city boy. You're the jungle expert."

"Si, sir. Look!" He pointed to the backend of the nearest one. "The tail is too short. No way this one could have lived in the trees."

Sargento Aldo studied the four corpses. Even his untrained eyes could focus on what Bruno was pointing at. Still ... "Terciero, we are not paid to be curious. Bag them and let us leave this place. Do not say anything about this to anyone. Soldiers that are curious don't last long ... remember that."

The crew bagged the four carcasses along with the crushed jaguar skull, almost as an afterthought. Of the infants, only the head and upper torso of a doll and a diaper, stiff with blood, were found. Before leaving, the team placed several cameras around the village, all inside protective cages. The men were glad to board the helicopters and return to Brasilia.

When they arrived, the team was quarantined and warned that the mission was well beyond top secret. The carcasses were discretely sent to the University of Sao Paolo, where Dr. Leo Torres led a small group of primate anthropologists.

About a week later, Dr. Torres flew to Brasilia to present their findings to the premier and a senior cabinet member. The university's conclusions matched the American findings exactly. Dr. Torres returned to Sao Paolo to head the research. The Brasilia government's reaction was immediate. The park and the village were quarantined. Only a few scientists, such as Dr. Torres, were allowed in and only if under military escort.

Vaughn Collar

With the absence of humans, the troop quickly took over the area. The cameras were an object of curiosity for a short time before fading into the background. The research team observed that the troop leaders looked different from the average howler. One was approaching four feet, well beyond the norm. The altered members seemed more comfortable on the ground than in the trees. The largest walked on two legs. Closer observation revealed that their hip structure had somewhat changed. The leaders were now wielding clubs, and the top males led a band of over twenty individuals. Several females showed some of the same changes.

Their current tactics appeared to be the ceiling of their cognitive abilities. However, continued observations demonstrated they were now experimenting with the tools left behind. The quarantine of the park gave the troop a most precarious advantage. No distractions.

Ian walked toward his office as a well-dressed man taped a piece of paper to his door.

"Excuse me," Ian said, loudly. "That door isn't for notes."

The man turned with a bitter expression.

"Oh, it's you." Ian's grin turned just a little sour.

It was the assistant to the chancellor. Usually the one who bore bad news. "Hello, Ian." The man's expression changed from tart to disdain as he pulled down the note. "I can just tell you instead. Madam Chancellor would like to see you ... yesterday."

"Any particular reason?" Ian glared at the man.

The assistant took a step back. "That's between you and her." He laughed.

Ian's expression changed to anger.

"You won't like it ... that's all I'm going to say." He backed up, turned, and walked away.

The Rift - *Beginnings*

Ian heard a faint chuckle as the man disappeared around the corner.

You little shit.

Ian sighed and made his way to the chancellor's office. He nodded to the secretary. She gave him a wane smile, pointing to the anteroom. A tea service was out, along with a pitcher of ice water. Ian poured himself a small glass, then turned to sit. The door opened behind him.

"Ah, Ian." She held the door open. "Please come in."

Ian's guard raised. The chancellor was never as intimidating as when she was polite. She motioned to the nearby couch. Ian took a seat. The chancellor sat in the chair facing him.

"Ian ... well, as you know the campus is threatened by rising sea levels."

He nodded.

"I suppose the best way to say this is that our new campus plans were approved."

Ian was aware of the rumors. "The funding came through?"

"Yes. Each department has a scheduled date to close and reopen. Though, things are never quite sure until the construction is complete. The history department will be the first to close. In fact, this semester will be your last."

Ian arched a 'brow. "This is based on ...?"

"Enrollment numbers, primarily. The *soft* sciences, like history and psychology, are just not attracting students. The environmental problems draw the most attention these days, so ... the science department is drawing the most attendance."

He leaned back. *This is exactly what I need right now.* He softly huffed.

The chancellor's eyes widened. "There is a silver lining. Seems someone in Washington likes you. Your name has received recognition for the work you performed this past summer ...

Vaughn Collar

whatever *that* was." She looked at him, a question clearly written on her face.

No, that's beyond top secret. "I'm sorry, but I had to sign a lot of documents about ... well, about what happened. It doesn't affect the university. Far from it."

She looked a little disappointed. "You will be transferring to Washington and Lee in upstate Virginia. A visiting professor. We don't want to lose you, but we had to place you somewhere. Look at it as a great opportunity."

Ian blinked. He knew of Washington and Lee or at least of their reputation. Their history department was considered on par with Yale, Harvard, and Cambridge. *She's right, this is a great opportunity ... and closer to Shelly to boot!* "I, uh ... well, *thank you* doesn't seem enough."

"Ian, you deserve the best. It was my pleasure to approve the temporary transfer."

"I'll be able to bring my current research with me? I'm nowhere near finished with the material from Scotland."

"Yes, of course. I've already talked with the chancellor, Stanley Christiansen, about your long-term project. Your grant is secure." She glanced at the clock.

She must have several appointments like this today. "Thank you. The research is expanding into avenues I didn't expect. I would hate to put it aside."

She smiled with her eyes reflecting her happiness. "I wanted to tell you under better circumstances, but ... your grant *was* extended for another two years. This might be the perfect opportunity for a longer trip to Scotland. Washington and Lee won't be ready for you until the next academic year."

He sunk deeper into the couch. Two more years echoed through his mind, momentarily drowning out any negative

The Rift - *Beginnings*

thoughts. "Two years? This is totally unexpected! So, who's Santa Claus around here?"

The chancellor set down her cup and laughed. "I don't know. Maybe you have a fairy godmother in Washington." She gave him an exaggerated leer, then laughed again.

I can truly explore the site now. This is gonna be glor ... wait until I tell Shelly! "The students are being taken care of?"

She nodded. "Notices were sent out earlier today, letting them know about the closure after Christmas."

Ian stood and shook her hand. "Thank you for the good word. I've enjoyed my time here, a lot."

"Of course. You will be missed. I can't wait until you return."

He left the office, walking slowly. He glanced at the various notices on corkboards and reminisced about events that had happened in classrooms along the way. *The years have been good to me here.* He walked into his office. After locking the door, he called Shelly.

"Hello, Ian! This is a nice surprise. I wasn't expecting you until tonight. Is anything wrong?"

His face creased with a smile. "No, not wrong. I'm moving." He explained the news, stressing how he would be so much closer.

"That's great!" Shelly paused. "Wait a minute. What are you going to be doing until the next school term?"

"I'm headed back to Scotland. There's so much left undone. I figure I have through this coming summer, but now ..."

Shelly's expression changed. "I wish I could go with you. It'd be such a nice break from this madhouse here in Washington."

"I'd like that, if you could. I imagine work is complicated?"

"Uh ... yeah. Just a little." Ian could hear the sarcasm in her voice.

He chuckled. "You'll do great, don't worry."

Vaughn Collar

Shelly's smile lit her face. "Thank you. I really hope you're right. This is a lot more than I thought it would be."

"Don't let 'em worry you. Take care, Shel."

Hanging up, Ian stared at the phone, reflecting. *You're falling, buddy ... hard.* He shook his head, a faint smile on his face. Checking the time, Ian figured he had a couple of hours to devote to studying, and his lab was just a short walk down the hall.

He ran a spell through his mind, placing the words in the correct cadence. No headache accompanied the words, which was now fixed in his mind. The only thing missing was the component. As he reached for the door, he glanced at a corkboard on the wall where several advertisements attracted his attention. One boldly proclaimed they could help anyone write a paper, on any subject, and guarantee at least a 'B'. Out of curiosity, Ian took a closer look. He knew the student. *Good luck with that!*

Movement attracted his attention. A spider was hanging from a web, the ventilation providing just enough wind. Frowning, Ian pulled one of the ads off the corkboard and brushed the web aside.

Wait a minute ... a web. That's the component I need. It's your lucky day, Mr. Spider. I'll just take some of this.

A careful placement of his fingers and a quick flick, and Ian had his web. The spider scurried up, disappearing into a small hole.

He glanced both ways and listened. No one was around. *Time to try the spell.* An exit was at the end of the hallway, and Ian stepped outside and listened. Nothing ... no voices, no people.

"Here goes nothing," Ian whispered.

Focusing on a pair of pine trees at the entrance to the alley, he held the web in his hands, spreading out his fingers, he pointed at the trees.

"TELERANATE!"

The Rift - *Beginnings*

Web strands shot out from each trunk, meeting in the middle. A huge spiderweb now covered the ten-foot span between the trees. It was at least his height if not taller.

Oh my god ...

Ian pumped his fist several times, suppressing a scream of delight.

"Yes!!" he whispered. *Wait a minute ... how in the hell do I get this down?*

He darted back inside before anyone could see him. As the door closed, voices echoed off the walls. He turned and looked through the window panes. Two young men had just run into the web.

"Shit!" one yelled out.

The other froze, his hair stuck in the strands, splaying out. The web swayed with the impact.

Ian stared. *Should I help them, or ...*

He hadn't completed the thought before the web vanished, little tendrils of smoke drifting up. The two fell to the damp ground. Both slipped several times in the grass. They fled, panic and terror in their eyes as they disappeared into the darkness.

Ian doubled over and howled with laughter. His eyes filled with tears, and a painful stitch in his stomach helped him to regain control and catch his breath. As funny as it was, it was good that neither had been hurt.

Bet they don't try to cut through this alley again!

He turned for his office, and a wave of fatigue hit as if he had just finished running several miles. Casting spells seemed to cause fatigue, except for the really small ones - such as the one he used to light a candle.

Maybe I just need more practice ... or power? Something to think about.

Vaughn Collar

He looked around the lab to decide what to ship to Virginia and what to take to Scotland. The rest would go to storage until the new campus opened. Besides, Christmas wasn't far away and Shelly would be staying with him for the holidays.

What to get Shelly? Hmm ...

The Rift - *Beginnings*

CHAPTER 20

Ian and Shelly grew much closer over the two weeks leading up to Christmas. Although saying goodbye was painful, Ian's research was beckoning him back to the field.

The Scottish Highlands were not exactly a tropical paradise even in summer. Blowing snowstorms and icy winds were common. Though he'd spent much of his time at research digs in all types of climates, he still preferred to remain warm – at least every other day.

A call to a friend informed him that the village of Struy was almost rebuilt. There would be no need to travel all the way to Inverness for supplies. It took him most of a day to set up the camper trailer he'd rented from Glasgow International Airport, but making the trip into Struy and back was definitely easier.

Scotland welcomed him with a rare, calm day under an azure sky. Only a few wispy clouds drifted slowly to the east, and the trail to the dig site was still visible once he located the markers that were covered in snow. More importantly, it was void of any signs that someone had been there. The ruin's entrance had only a thin layer of snow and ice covering the ground.

Vaughn Collar

He sat on a partial step to catch his breath. Pouring a cup of tea from his thermos, he stared out over the landscape. The lake to the north, An Gorm-Loch, was still partially frozen except for a dark spot in the middle. Deer dotted the landscape near the tree line and the valley below. There were no signs of people.

Ian, ol' buddy, you're home. Well ... Shelly?

Ian felt bemused with conflicting thoughts of work and Shelly, but it would make the days pass quickly. The hike up the mountain was difficult. He needed to work himself back into shape.

The next day, his priority was the lower room where he had first found the rods. He started down the steep steps, holding out his hand. Standing quietly in the darkness, he took a deep breath.

"Luxor!"

A glowing ball appeared, and Ian concentrated on his hand holding the light. A sensation of heat radiated into his fingertips. As his arm moved, a disembodied hand moved with it. With another simple thought, the hand and light floated to the center of the room.

"Woah ... cool!"

The light was a different quality than a lantern, casting deeper shadows. But it still allowed him the ability to notice the subtle patterns on a far wall. He studied the designs, allowing his mind to wander as his eyes slowly adjusted.

"Another door?"

He ran his fingers over the contours, sensing a slight gap. Near the floor was a hint of a draft. Reaching into his pack, he pulled out two small pry bars and a hammer. Slowly, he worked the bars into the slender opening. Deep shadows hid almost everything and he missed his mark, hitting his hand.

"Shit!" *Damn, the spell's over.*

He searched for his lantern, turned it on, and stared at his now-bruising hand. Ian cursed again before turning his thoughts back

The Rift - *Beginnings*

to the ancient wall. He struggled with the bars and hammer, managing only a few inches. One last tap and the wall moved.

"Wait, this *is* a door!" *Hmmph!*

Despite the chill inside the room, a bead of sweat rolled into his eyes. Blinking, he reached into a back pocket and pulled out a bandana. He wiped his forehead. The growing dust made breathing somewhat difficult. The clearer air outside felt inviting but he yearned to enter and explore this new room. An opening just wide enough for his hands seemed promising. He pulled and the door dragged across the floor, small pebbles crunching into the ground. Dust motes swirled with the incoming air and a flinty odor hinted at something old. He peered inside.

Ian sat the lantern down and used his hands to pry the door fully open, revealing a dirt floor and a room with one wall caved in.

The blast wave could have done this. Hope nothing is too damaged.

A few pebbles rained down as he stepped inside. What looked like a rock shelf jutted out from the rubble. He sat on the dirty floor to think. The cold radiated up his back and made him shudder.

Okay, I need to brace these walls, so ... timbers ... hmm, lights ... would be kinda nice to see what I'm doing.

Ian stood and dusted himself off. He stepped out and glanced around. A large plastic case was just outside the entrance. He dragged it inside and pulled out the lights and their mounts.

A moment's thought, and he remembered that the solar panels were still near his camp. It took him only a short time to retrieve them and hook everything up. A little prayer for continued sunlight, and he flipped on the lights. The room lit.

Yes!

Ian selected several timbers stacked near a tree and dragged them inside. It was hard work placing them just so to reinforce the

Vaughn Collar

room. Dust hung in the still air and with every swing of the hammer, a cascade of grit and small pebbles fell into his shirt, collecting at his waist. Several times, he stopped to brush dust out of his eyes or to empty his shirt. With every hammer strike, his hands throbbed. He didn't want the grit to fall into more sensitive areas. Bracing the walls was only the first step. The cave-in had left a large pile of rocks on the floor that would need to be cleared.

Okay, I need ... what? Wheelbarrow, winch, a big pry bar ... water!

Just the thought of returning to his trailer and the steep hike made his muscles ache. Instead, he would bring everything down in the morning. With the few hours left of daylight, he cleared the rubble closest to the door. One misstep landed him on his rear, scraping his hand on the wall when he tried to catch himself. The dirt prevented the blood from dripping, but the sting convinced him to call it a day.

Oh great ... both hands. Tomorrow's gonna be fun.

A glance outside reinforced his concerns. Typical of Scotland, the weather was rapidly changing, and a storm was brewing over the far ridge. He had barely dragged in the solar panels when the first flakes fell and a brisk wind howled. He spread a canvas over the entrance, using rocks to keep it in place.

The walk down the mountain took longer than expected. The storm was now howling with snow thick enough to limit his visibility to just a few paces. Teeth chattering, Ian arrived at his trailer. It took a few attempts to open the camper since his hands were stiff from the cold.

He headed straight for the heater and stood close. It didn't take long for the feeling in his fingers to return. He rubbed his hands to ease the pins-and-needles of the returning sensation. He dug out a dinner to warm along with the tea and sat back to relax. His thoughts fell to Shelly.

The Rift - *Beginnings*

He never experienced a long, steady relationship before, not really. His emotions felt ... strange, and he missed her, *sure ... who wouldn't?* But she was much more than just a girlfriend. Thinking about their past conversations, a gentle smile creased his face. And her smile ... and her ...

Dude, you're in love. Wow.

He shook his head with a quiet laugh, and his smile widened just a bit more.

Okay, so now what?

He didn't know. All of this was new to him. Once, years ago, he had thought of asking someone to marry him. But the way he felt now made what he felt then seem like an infatuation. This was deeper – hotter.

He thought long into the night, playing out different ways to tell her his feelings. Time slipped by unnoticed until he glanced at his watch. It was past midnight. No wonder he was so tired. Still, he wanted to place a couple of spells in his mind for the next day.

A few hours later, he crawled into bed. The wind rocked the trailer as he snuggled deeper under the covers. Sleep came quickly.

Sunlight streaking across his eyes woke him. A long stretch eased his tightened muscles from the prior day's work. He sat up, trying to decide if another hour of rest was warranted.

Get up, lazy bones.

Large patches of snow, windblown into drifts, scattered across the landscape, adding to the glare. Some areas were bare, giving hope that he wouldn't have to hike through knee-deep snow to the dig site. A hot breakfast of bacon and eggs, along with a couple cups of tea, warmed him from the inside. He grabbed more tools and lumber and loaded them into the wheelbarrow. He filled a thermos with scalding-hot tea.

Time to head back up the mountain.

Vaughn Collar

The trail was exactly what he had hoped, mostly clear. So was the site. The wind was still strong, but at least the storm had passed. Only a few clouds were rapidly crossing the sky, almost as if they were chasing the storm.

Ian used the lumber to make a ramp. The solar panels and a toolbox were lugged outside. The rest of the morning was spent bringing out several loads of rocks and debris.

Time for a break.

He plugged in a portable heater and sat in front of it, his back to the warmth. Between the heat and the hot tea, his muscles loosened and the aches eased.

"You're not twenty-five anymore, bud ... or thirty." He snorted, laughing at himself.

With most of the room cleared, Ian needed more light ...

Ah ... "Luxor!" he said in a low voice.

The room lit with the warm light. Ian glanced around, and his excitement grew. Shelves lined the undamaged walls. Pottery, both pristine and broken, were scattered throughout. Picking out several more rods, he paused as his eyes landed on a sword still in its sheath. It was leaning against a broken shelf. Several carved walrus tusks looked promising. Examining the tusks revealed that one had the special script for magic.

"Yes!"

His hands shook as he tried to read the runes. He braced for one of those blinding headaches ... *and nothing.* No pain but he could feel the spell click in his mind. He picked up a few pebbles, the component, and mumbled the words.

"Cull hox carminate, ego vo tabernate."

He pointed at a rock slightly larger than a bowling ball. It vibrated momentarily before lifting off the floor, hovering a few feet in the air.

"I wonder ..."

The Rift - *Beginnings*

Centering his concentration, he moved the rock out of the room. He closed his eyes and could sense the force emanating from him to his hands. Opening his eyes, he walked outside to the rubble pile, allowing his concentration to lapse. The rock dropped.

Ian yelped and pumped his arms in the air. *Not even tired. Maybe another?* The spell ceased after a few steps and the rock fell. A wave of fatigue hit, and he reached for a tree.

He leaned back and watched as the clouds drift across the sky. His mind seemed clear. It was definitely his body screaming for rest. He ate a few bites from his food stores, feeling more alive than ever. His senses seemed sharpened. Sight, sound, smell ... everything felt augmented, hearing distant birds soaring on the wind that rustled through the trees.

Okay, levitation. This one may come in handy ... in a lot of situations. Back to work, Ian.

He slowly uncovered more artifacts, mostly pottery. A couple of small axes were under a large slab. Soon, the room was empty. He searched the walls for more gaps but failed to find any. Satisfied that this room was clear, he loaded the wheelbarrow with his tools and left. It was time to sort through what he had found.

By midafternoon, the gusting wind had calmed. Most of the chill was gone, but a fire would still feel good. The morning blaze had already died. After tossing new wood onto the embers, smoke rose but no flames. He laughed.

"Ian, you can use magic, remember?"

A minor spell that didn't seem to tax him came to mind.

"Digitate scintos!"

A flame appeared on the end of his index finger. The wind had no effect and soon the wood caught with the fire crackling to life. After warming his hands, he sorted through his day's work. Pottery went straight into a case filled with packing gel. He could study these at length in a more controlled environment. There were several small weapons – daggers, hand axes, spear tips, numerous arrow heads. These all went into a second case. One of the axes had a runic carving. Looking a bit more carefully, Ian found this to be a name ... Beorn.

Okay, Beorn. What else have you left me? And ... who were you?

The one walrus tusk was the only thing with the special carvings. Ian placed the other tusks into a case along with a section of a deer antler. By now, the sun was setting behind the mountains, and a chill had seeped into the air.

"Time to sleep."

In mid-February, Ian decided to head into Inverness. The weather forecast showed back-to-back fronts. There was bound to be several feet of snow dumped from these storms. Therefore, no point trying to clear a path to the dig site every day. Besides, he wanted a meal not cooked over an open fire or from a can. Mostly, he just wanted to call Shelly. He missed her greatly. Just hearing her voice would make the trip worthwhile.

The drive to Inverness showed that new construction was everywhere. Homes and businesses now filled the land cleared of destruction. People eagerly walked the sidewalks or along the river path. Life seemed to be getting back to normal.

Ian checked in at a local inn. After dropping off his bag, he entered the dining area where a waitress took his order. As he waited on the food, he sat back with a smile. It was comforting to watch others interact. He didn't have to talk to anyone. Just listening to the background of voices was enough.

After dinner, he crossed the streets, admiring the new construction. His stroll took him by Castle Inverness, then the museum. His heart tightened as he thought about Shelly. He wanted to call her, but she would still be at work. He returned to

The Rift - *Beginnings*

the inn for a long, hot shower before stretching out on the bed, just meaning to close his eyes for a bit.

The alarm startled him. It was midnight. Shelly should be home by now. Scrolling through the numbers, he selected hers. On the third ring, she answered. Her face lit the screen, matching the smile on Ian's face.

"Ian! How's Scotland? I miss you!"

"I miss you too. Scotland's great. Cold, but great. I feel at home here. How're doing? Work keeping you busy?"

They talked for a bit, sharing their thoughts and feelings.

"There's some really strange things happening," Shelly finally said, biting her lip. "The media is slowly making their way through the intelligence world."

"Oh?" Ian was wide awake now. "Like ...?"

Shelly looked as if she had lost her train of thought or perhaps didn't know how to say it.

"Shel?"

"I'm here." She shook her head. "A series of strange reports are showing up from the lower Appalachian area. In and around the Virginia-North Carolina border. You're familiar with amniocentesis?"

"Yeah. Samples taken of cells in the fluid around the fetus."

"But ... we have access to the lab's analysis. Odd DNA reports."

"Such as?"

"At first, just unusual eye and hair coloring."

"Why is someone's eye and hair coloring making its way onto the government's radar?"

"Let me finish. There wasn't much at first, just a few children here or there. But now there are enough to show a pattern. A closer look was deemed prudent."

"Did someone hack the amniocentesis labs?"

Vaughn Collar

"Uhm ... yes. The results were forwarded to the genome project jointly worked by Yale and Oxford. They were tasked with determining if the preliminary results were accurate."

"And?"

"And what we have is concerning. The majority of these children have purple eyes and extremely black hair. Others have white-blonde hair and *golden* eyes." She grew quiet.

"What else, Shelly? New hair and eye colors aren't that significant."

She shrugged. "It's beginning to feel like I'm following a little, white rabbit."

Ian laughed. "Understood. Tell me what you can. I hear the word *classified* coming on."

"It's a little more involved than analyzing a DNA sequence. Most of the talk is way above my grade level. But, I really listened when they mentioned the ... death gene."

"Death gene? You mean ..." – Ian took a deeper breath – "... we can determine longevity now?"

"Uh ... yeah. But back to the kids. They're estimating that these children could live a hundred and forty years. Maybe up to two hundred."

"Two hundred?" He refocused. "Damn."

"Ian, the classification is as high as anything I've ever seen. This is way above me."

Ian realized Shelly might not be free of Washington anytime soon, and he wanted to see her. "Any way you can break free for a couple of weeks? Say ... April, May?"

"I should be able to swing that." Shelly smiled. "I'll look at my calendar and get back with you."

They talked for a little while longer, promising to call again soon. They said their goodbyes, and the line disconnected. Ian looked at the screen and sighed. He missed her already.

The Rift - *Beginnings*

Bud, this is getting deep. He chuckled. Then he thought about what she had said about the genetics reports. People living for two hundred years? *Woah.* And what about his magic and some of the other things happening? *What the hell is going on? And what else that we haven't heard about?*

CHAPTER 21

Lucian glanced at the time and sighed. The clock seemed to be moving absurdly slow. Ms. Goldobin should arrive any minute. She was an incredible person – intelligent and exciting. Their talks were always stimulating. The time spent working on the Russian material had been productive. Final exams were already graded and recorded. Lucian always looked forward to the end of a term.

Instead of the constraints of a student-teacher relationship, he was thinking about moving forward. In class, he often felt her tender gaze. Every time he looked back, she always had a warm smile. Her questions seemed to contain more content than just an ordinary student looking for answers. Lucian felt the time was right to approach her personally.

Earlier, Lucian had asked about her assisting with a document from the early 1800s. He told her that it was in Russian, but the style was something more poetic, and he wasn't sure about the right nuances. She said she would be delighted to help. He made sure to arrange everything, including a bottle of a highly regarded white wine from Crimea, ready to pour.

A light knock on the door startled him. *Already?* He glanced at the antique clock. *Right on time.* "Come in, Ms. Goldobin."

The Rift - *Beginnings*

She smiled as she entered. "Sir, this is not school. Please, it's Natalya ... or even Nat'ya."

He returned the smile. "Certainly ... and please, call me Lucian."

His heart raced. He was glad she didn't see that his hands were shaking. A deep breath, and he felt a little more under control. He walked over to the material, waving his arm.

"These are the documents. I felt it would be ... better to have someone whose native language is Russian. I doubt mine is good enough for this. Too much is archaic. Having you here, Nat'ya ... makes the task more enjoyable."

He wanted to touch her hand as she sat down but resisted. Although classes had officially ended, a part of him remained fearful of contact with someone who had been a student. His hands were clammy from being so nervous. He turned away momentarily, surreptitiously wiping the small beads of sweat from his upper lip. He drew in a slow breath, trying to calm his racing heart. Feeling a bit steadier, he acted as if he had something important to work on.

"I have a project to finish. But please don't hesitate to ask questions."

She looked at him, warmth behind her smile. "Spaceba, Prof ... Lucian."

He stood at another table and moved the stack of paperwork hiding the tome he was currently working on. It was the tome from Petroşani, but not the one that contained magical writings – or so he thought. He opened it and found a full page of script. Two words in and the blinding headache hit. He wasn't fully aware he had made a grunt. As he grabbed his head, a warm hand touched his shoulder.

"Professor, are you all right?"

Vaughn Collar

He managed to close the book before she saw anything. "I am fine. Sometimes I get these headaches that come on rather quickly. It's nothing ... something left over from my youth." He looked at her.

Her piercing, blue eyes stared back with concern – or something else. "Perhaps you should take a break. I have something to show you. Let me bring it over."

She handed him pages of scribbled handwriting. One was a full translation. He glanced at the clock.

Had it been an hour already?

She pointed out a particular section. "I can see why this was troubling. It's a local dialect translated into Russian of that time. I have a great uncle from that area. I used to listen to his stories and picked up a few words. Like this one." She pointed to the middle of the page. "It means *expedition*."

"This is great! Have you determined what this represents?"

"Yes, I believe so. I think this is a journal or diary. The author must have been a scribe. There is a section, um ... here ..." – she flipped a couple of pages back – "... describes the travel to the site of an ancient settlement."

"How ancient?"

"As best I can figure, this group believed it to be from around the second millennia B.C."

"The Sintashta? Of course. They would have inhabited the area at that time. Interesting, but not what I was hoping for."

"Hoping for?"

"I have devoted many years to finding the earliest origins of the Celtic peoples. Still, this may prove useful."

"How so?" she asked.

"Well ... it may eliminate areas, help refine where my search needs to focus. Anything else? I can see you've gone through a lot of this already."

The Rift - *Beginnings*

"Most is the mundane day-to-day observations of men stumbling through the unknown area. To this point ..." – she carefully turned the page to where she had placed a small marker – "... the one village was all they found."

He looked at her, even more intrigued than before. All this intelligence and drive – and looks? *She'll go far. Even farther if I can be there.* "Would you like a glass of wine ... to celebrate a good semester?"

Natalya's eyes widened and a slight frown formed. "Perhaps another time. I've already made plans with friends." She glanced at the time. "Well ... maybe a small glass."

Lucian made a bit of a show opening the wine, making sure she could see where it was from. He handed her a glass.

She took a sip, then stared at it for a moment. She slowly set it in front of her. "I am not sure how acceptable this is."

"What do you ... why not?"

She looked away. Sighing, she haltingly stated, "A few of my friends told me not to come here. Not to spend ... social time with a professor."

"I see." He nodded. *She didn't say no.* "Then, to a good evening?" He raised his glass. "Maybe we can arrange another time when you don't have plans."

She gave him a flat look, no emotion visible. "No ... I don't believe we should ... be helping each other like this."

"Like ... what?" he asked. *No, she just means tonight!*

"You know. After hours."

Lucian set his glass down, displaying his best smile. "With classes over, it would not be a conflict. It would be fine for you and I to be friends. Maybe more."

She closed her eyes, taking in a deeper breath. She held her hand to her mouth momentarily before reaching for her purse. "Mr. Ciobanu ... Professor ... I must leave. This was not a good

Vaughn Collar

idea ... me coming here. I am so sorry. I did not mean to give you a false impression."

Lucian felt his heart tighten. He nodded. "I see. I shall not take any more of your time. I will make sure this research goes into your file. Thank you for your assistance with the document."

He walked to the door and held it open. She stepped into the hall, then turned. The look on her face appeared cold and expressionless. He felt her gaze hit his heart like piercing daggers. She turned away with the sound of her heels receding into the background – then she was gone.

He looked back at the room. Papers were scattered across different piles. A bottle of wine, opened, the condensing moisture on the glass forming a ring at its base. He could still smell her perfume, subtle but enticing. A fly buzzed against a window. The sound of it irritated him. Grabbing a magazine, he rolled it up and savagely swatted the insect, obliterating it. He swatted it again and again, then stopped. There was nothing left except a smudge on the window. The rolled up magazine was in tatters.

What have I done? Why are you trying to fool yourself?

He shook his head, the anger dissipating. Replacing it was – nothing. He could feel his emotions drain. The thought of continuing to teach felt repulsive. He glanced around the office again, his sight stopping at the tome he was working on.

That's what I can do. I can go back to Petroşani, see if there is anything left in those ruins.

He walked over to the wine bottle, took it over to the sink and poured it out. He wanted his mind clear. It was time to leave. The department head position he had so yearned for now seemed like a waste of time. What did he care about politics, anyway? In fact, what did he care about people? It was then that he caught a look at himself in the window, the darkening sky reflecting the light of the office. A small, unattractive man stared back, a little underweight,

The Rift - *Beginnings*

graying at the temples. The unsightly scar he still bore from his youth.

"Lucian, you're fooling yourself to think she would be interested in you. You're old enough to be her father. Yes ... it is time to leave."

He didn't doubt that she would tell her friends about this, and of course at least one would blurt it out to the wrong person. With the decision to resign, he sat and accessed his investment accounts. At least, he had chosen the right person for that. His current worth was well in excess of three million dollars. He snorted a bitter laugh at himself.

He stood, took a step, and tripped. The cork from the wine bottle was half-flattened. He must have knocked it off the table. He looked at the bottle standing next to the sink. His anger flared. He grabbed the bottle and threw it at a far wall. It shattered into thousands of sparkling shards, the remaining liquid staining the bricks, the sound echoing through the room.

"Never again. Never!" he cried out.

Looking at the glass on the floor, he felt his heart close. Hopefully for the last time. He thought about what he needed to do before he left for Petroșani. He could easily live off his investments, thus giving him all the time he wanted to focus on the dig site.

Yes, time to leave.

He felt there were so much more to discover. Now that he had the time.

Natalya walked into the bracing cold of that December afternoon.

What a fool to think I would be the slightest bit interested in him!

Vaughn Collar

She knew she had led him on and more than once with her coy smiles. Sitting in the front row, making sure she showed off her legs.

And who's the fool now, eh, Nat'ya?

The echo of shattering glass, mixed with an incoherent yell, spread out from the building she had just left. For a moment, she thought she would run back.

No, not a good idea.

She hadn't actually lied to him. She did have plans that night with friends. And – she had been looking forward to working with him. But – there was a new guy in the group she found intriguing. She had never met a Native American before, not in person. And this one was rather nice to look at.

With that thought, she quickened her steps, not looking back.

The Rift - *Beginnings*

CHAPTER 22

By early summer of 2078, the small town of Boone was the target of increasing media scrutiny. News had spread about the birth of a child with purple eyes and jet-black hair. Over the next several weeks, four more were born with similar characteristics. Then, a child with golden eyes and silky, white-blonde hair was born and reporters were drawn to the area like mosquitoes to blood. Outpourings of news were becoming much more frequent. The parents, uniformly, tried to keep a low profile. They didn't want their children to be a world story. All they wanted was to be left alone. Many a night passed with one, or several, of the mothers crying herself to sleep, cursing the curiosity of reporters. They wondered, *Why me?* Emotions grew so tense that a local psychiatrist offered her services for free.

By the end of the summer, the unusual births were up to ten, just within the boundaries of Boone, North Carolina alone. News of other births were circulating. All located in a small area spanning the mountains of North Carolina and Virginia.

Shelly sat at her window seat and thought about Ian. D.C. was a sea of lights spreading out to the horizon. Her phone dinged,

Vaughn Collar

startling her. Seeing the familiar area code of 202 gave her an unsettled feeling.

"Ms. Lang?"

"Yes."

"This is Angela Rhodes, secretary for the director of national security. A driver is on her way to escort you to a private meeting. I will remain on the line until she arrives. Are you dressed?"

"Not exactly. How long until she gets here?"

"I will ask the driver. Please do not hang up."

Shelly cursed quietly, walking to her closet. She pulled on some clothes and ran a brush through her hair. *I look like a mess, but yah know what, they didn't warn me.*

The doorbell rang.

"Ms. Rhodes," Shelly said to the phone, "is the driver here?"

"Yes, she is. Please do not hang up."

Shelly grabbed her purse and opened the door.

A woman stood quietly, wearing a dark business suit. "You can hang up now," she said. "I apologize about the late hour."

Shelly smiled and nodded. They did not talk on the elevator, and when they reached the street, a man held the SUV's door open.

The tinted windows made the outside world seem vague and bland. After a quiet thirty-minute drive, the door opened. Shelly looked around. They were in an underground parking garage. Their footsteps echoed, blending with the faint sounds of outside traffic. D.C. never truly slept.

She followed her silent escorts to a single elevator. Oddly, there were no floor markings. When the door opened, two men greeted her. As they walked the corridors, Shelly realized she was in the White House. She was led to the Situation Room, her nerves already on edge from the suddenness of the meeting. Now, her stomach started to flip.

The Rift - *Beginnings*

The president and the director turned and nodded. She was the only one wearing a suit, except for the Secret Service. The director was in jeans and a sweatshirt, the president in khakis with his sleeves rolled up and his tie just visible in one pocket. A few others were present, all in casual clothing. A loud laugh brought her gaze back to the president. A bottle of bourbon was on a long table with several seats on either side – a podium at one end. Almost everyone had a drink in their hand.

The conversation was rather quiet, their stance stiff despite the laughter. She took in a deep breath, making her way over. The president smiled. The director and vice president stopped talking. Another man stood. Shelly recognized him – a Dr. Scott Holland from Johns Hopkins.

"Good evening, Ms. Lang," the president said, reaching out.

Shelly took his hand and smiled. "Evening, sir." She glanced at the men and suddenly felt small. They were so tall.

"I apologize for the abrupt interruption of your evening," the president said. "We have a unique situation requiring special attention." The lights dimmed and he made a hand motion for everyone to sit. "Mr. Hill, the floor is yours."

Shelly looked over at the podium. She had not seen the man standing there when she entered. If anything, he looked more nervous than her. His appearance was at odds with everyone else. He looked as if he hadn't slept in days. The shadow of a dark stubble blurred his chin. His tie was crooked, and a couple of buttons missing. His darker skin did him well as it helped to somewhat hide the circles under his eyes.

And I thought I was nervous!

He stepped up to the podium, gripping it tightly to steady the tremor in his hands. "Thank you, Mr. President." His voice was soft and low.

Shelly turned in her chair and leaned forward.

Vaughn Collar

He cleared his throat and took a sip of water. "Ms. Lang, I'm Damon Hill in intelligence."

She smiled and nodded, hopefully reassuring him.

"I'm tasked with following the research of other institutions. Usually medicinal advances."

She glanced over at the president.

"Carry on," the president said. "Mr. Hill. Please connect the dots for us."

Mr. Hill nodded. "Two countries with no real connection, Brazil and Tanzania, are researching the same issues. Wild animals showing signs of rapid ..." – Mr. Hill cleared his throat – "... evolution."

"Evolution?" Shelly repeated. *Wait ... Brazil? The howler monkeys?* She placed a finger to her lips.

"Ms. Lang, you have a thought about this?" the president asked.

"Brazil. The howler monkeys," she replied. "Remember the last meeting, sir? We discussed potential evolutionary changes."

"Yes, ma'am." Mr. Hill nodded. "I was made aware of your research. And yes, what we are seeing is apparently a continuation of that event. I have additional information." He tapped on his computer as he talked. "The village in Brazil was abandoned. But ..."

A photograph of small homes appeared on the screen.

"The military left a few cameras in place," he said. "I've been able to pirate the download."

"Pirate? You've hacked into their live feed?"

"Yes. The Brazilian government hasn't caught on yet." Mr. Hill tapped on his computer again, and a video started.

Several howlers walked across a dirt road. Two large males were being groomed by several smaller monkeys. A few younger ones

The Rift - *Beginnings*

were playing nearby with an adult watching. The scene appeared totally normal. Just an average troop.

"Okay," she whispered. "What am I looking for?"

"Keep watching," he whispered.

Three large males walked into view – on two feet – looking totally at ease upright.

"Those three," he said. "Keep watching."

Shelly was struck at how large they were. One was carrying a tree limb as a club. The younger monkeys screeched and ran into the nearby brush.

"He's carrying a weapon?" Shelly felt perplexed.

"Just watch, please," Mr. Hill repeated.

The large males spotted the two being groomed. The smaller members screeched and fled. The three newcomers ran after the smaller males. The one carrying the tree branch caught the nearest one and clubbed it on the head. The other smaller male escaped. The fight lasted only a few moments before the targeted animal was in the road, dead. A cacophony of hoots, screeches, and howls was almost deafening.

"My god!" Shelly was shocked.

"This next part is important." Mr. Hill zoomed in, bringing the trio into a closer view.

Two males tore apart the body, twisting and pulling, dismembering the carcass. The blood pooled and the three devoured the raw flesh.

Shelly cupped her hands over her mouth, feeling nauseated, her eyes widened. "Wha ... what?" Shelly muttered, looking around.

The president closed his eyes. Several others stared at the screen, eyes wide and mouths open.

Mr. Hill shook his head and pointed. "Watch what happens next."

Vaughn Collar

The three, now covered in blood, walked away from the corpse. With a screech from the largest, one stopped and walked back to the dead body. He picked up the head and stared at it for a moment before closing the eyes. It made a soft noise, then placed the head back on the corpse.

"We think the dead was the former alpha male." Mr. Hill stated.

Shelly sat speechless, horrified. The behavior was nothing she'd ever seen. Other species may have eaten parts of the carcass, but none would have handled the skull like she'd just witnessed.

"Ms. Lang," the president said, "your expertise in early civilizations and culture is why you're here. What do you take from this video?"

Trying to organize her thoughts, Shelly tapped a pen on the pad in front of her. "Mr. President, as ugly as that was, it clearly shows a level of intelligence not seen by any species ... except humans. The attack on the leader, yes, that happens. But the cannibalization of the remains? Closing the eyes?" She replayed the image in her mind. "Mr. Hill, can you play back to the image right before the attack?"

He nodded and brought up the video. He hit play, only to have Shelly and the vice president yell at the same time.

"Freeze it!" Shelly ordered.

"Right there!" the vice president hollered.

The simultaneous yelling rattled Mr. Hill and caused him to hit the wrong button, jumping the video ahead by twenty seconds. "Uh, sorry. Hold on ... okay, here it is."

The requested frame appeared, and Shelly asked him to enlarge it. "Stop!" Shelly pointed at the screen. "Can you zoom in on the far-right monkey?"

The frame enlarged a little more.

"Look at the scar on the right shoulder."

The Rift - *Beginnings*

"All wild animals get injured," Mr. Hill said.

"Yes, but remember, the initial patrol fired at several of the monkeys when they scattered the troop. That ..." – she pointed at the circular scar – "... is a bullet wound that has healed."

The vice president added, "I agree. I've seen enough from the war."

The president looked between the two and frowned. He picked up the bottle of bourbon and poured a little into his glass. "Mr. Hill, you have another?"

"Yes, sir."

He brought up a video of a man holding a dead lizard. As he laid the carcass on the ground, the president and Dr. Holland raised their voices. "Freeze that image!"

Shelly laughed to herself. "Can you expand on the series of small spikes just behind the lizard's shoulders?"

Mr. Hill adjusted the picture. Starting between each shoulder blade and the backbone, a series of small spikes ran down the lizard's back. The ones in front were definitely larger. More detail wasn't obvious as the picture was a little grainy due to the close up.

"By the time the lizard was examined at a lab, some deterioration had taken place," Mr. Hill stated. "But they took a full series of X-rays. Um ... here they are."

A full skeletal structure was now in view, matching the series of points on the lizard's back as shadowy spots.

"Those dark spots. Were they identified?" Shelly asked.

"X-rays don't usually show cartilage ... which is what those bumps are. At least, the front two."

Shelly stood and walked over to the screen.

"This particular specimen was just under five feet in length," Mr. Hill added, "and around two years old, judging by the growth rings on the scales. We have been receiving sporadic reports about

Vaughn Collar

monitors becoming scarce. This includes the black market. Sadly, that's one of our best ways to determine species scarcity."

"How so?" Shelly asked.

"Tanzania and Kenya are high on the list of countries with quarantined exports. Seeing animals like this with greatly diminished numbers being sold is a good indication of species rarity."

Shelly looked at the screen one last time before returning to her seat. Her thoughts went out to her sister in Abingdon, Virginia who had heard rumors of children being born different. Both knew the Appalachian area was ripe with gossip of strange people and patently false tales. Truth was about as hard to find as the proverbial needle. Yet, the newest tales about the children were just a little too coincidental. She remembered talking with Ian and was able to keep her face straight when she realized what else was coincidental to this timeline.

How can I ask Ian about this?

The president looked around the room. "Okay, people. That's two species with strange changes. I don't believe in coincidences. Any ideas?"

"Mr. President," Shelly said, "the only correlation I can surmise is the similarity in timelines. Are we looking at random evolutionary changes?" She looked over at the director. "Sir, have you spoken with anyone in the astronomical fields?"

He looked at her, a sincere expression of puzzlement on his face. "Um, no. What are you thinking?"

"Something occurred to me that could cause global changes. Could there have been an extremely powerful solar flare? Or maybe a gamma burst? One of those could possibly cause DNA changes from the radiation." She bit her lower lip. "Maybe mid-to-late summer a couple of years ago?" She had thought of the reactor

The Rift - *Beginnings*

incident, and how it could potentially lead back to Ian, and therefore, didn't want to include it.

The director's 'brows raised, then he chuckled. "That is exactly why I requested this meeting. I tend to focus on politics and hidden agendas."

Environmental problems would not have occurred to him or the president. The two had started their careers during the worst of the political upheaval, some twenty-plus years earlier. Both were lawyers in the late 2050s and 60s when civil unrest was at its peak.

"I will have that question forwarded," the director said. He looked at the president. The two showed their long friendship in the way they communicated by just a look. Obviously, the president had *said* something. "As soon as we leave."

"If anyone discovers any other reason for any of this ... any reason at all," the President added, "I need to know. And don't worry about the time ... just contact my staff. This may not be our most pressing issue, but I don't want it ignored. Thank you for your time."

Everyone gathered their materials and the president was almost through the door when he stopped and turned. "Director, Ms. Lang ... I understand the press is making a nuisance of themselves in the Appalachian area around southern Virginia and North Carolina. They're asking questions about changes in newborns. Shut it down. Now! We don't need the press, and frankly, those folks don't either."

The director's face assumed a blank stare, before glancing at Shelly. The look was obvious – he might as well have said, *You're not going to like this.* He nodded at the president. "Understood, sir."

"If it is truly serious ..." – the president sighed – "... then do what you have to do. Just don't tell me what you have in mind. I don't want to know. Just make it happen." The door shut behind him.

Vaughn Collar

Shelly tried to keep the fear off her face. She was now a part of the president's inner circle. The thought of what could happen frightened her – should she step out of line. She was glad she wasn't driving as distracted as she felt. Then, she remembered something Ian had said soon after he found her at the museum.

Oh shit! Ian, I've got to talk to you!

Arriving home, she grabbed her phone. *He's in Scotland ... not Boston.*

Doing the math, she figured he would be asleep. She decided that he needed to be fully awake for this. Not awakened by a call in the middle of the night. She set an alarm for midnight.

In her kitchen, she looked at her tea.

No, this requires a little more caffeine.

She opened a cabinet, moving aside cans to grab a small container. The aroma of Columbian coffee filled her senses. This was definitely a night to indulge.

Now, how do I do my job and protect Ian?

The Rift - *Beginnings*

CHAPTER 23

Ian sat with his first cup of tea for the morning when his phone pinged. He smiled when he saw it was Shelly.

"Hey there ... what's up?" Ian asked. *It was midnight there!*

"Did I wake you?"

"No. Is something wrong?" He sat up straighter, almost knocking over his tea.

"You said something back at the museum. I didn't pay much attention then, but ... there are some things happening and ... well, what you said could be important."

"Okay?" Now, he was even more puzzled. "Uh, mind giving me a clue?"

"You said something like ... you were seeing things a little more clearly, and you felt, well, different."

"Okay. Doesn't ring a bell ... wait. Yes, it does." He rubbed his eyes, trying to clear them from a sound night of sleep.

"Have you mentioned this to anyone else?" Her tone was soft.

Ian shook his head. "No, I haven't. Why?" She looked worried. *What the hell has rattled her?* "Shel, what's wrong?"

She paused. "Ian ... not over the phone. I'm flying over."

"Where?" *What ...* "Here?!"

173

Vaughn Collar

"Yes, I'll catch the first available flight. We have to talk ... privately."

He chuckled. "I'm in a trailer in Struy, about a mile from the nearest ... anything. Can't get much more private than this." *This isn't a relationship visit, that's for damn sure.* "What about your job? Won't they question why you're catching first-thing flights to Scotland?"

"I doubt it. I can call it an unofficial visit quite easily. No one will question the trip. Besides, I have several weeks of vacation saved. Time to use some."

"Sounds great to me. Although, well, I guess I'll learn more when you get here."

"Yes, and it's getting more complicated every minute. Can you pick me up at Glasgow International? I'll let you know what flight as soon as I can."

"Sounds good, Shel. Are you trying for the first flight or the fastest?"

"Whichever gets me there the quickest. I'll meet you at the little pub next to the first concourse."

"I'll be there. Can't wait to see you."

The line disconnected. He sat back, thinking about their conversation, glad that he had installed that small satellite for calls just like this one. The little amount of time he spent at his trailer didn't include watching the news. The trailer was for showers, a warm meal, and a clean bed.

Maybe I need to catch up a little.

He turned on his tablet and pulled up Sky News for an up-to-date report. Within a few minutes, a story came across about a potential government cover-up in Brazil. Supposedly, a small village was to be relocated due to the amount of high tide salinity flowing up the Amazon.

Yeah, right.

The Rift - *Beginnings*

There was no way ocean salinity could flow up the Amazon that far. Especially to flood-cultivated land with enough salt to stop growth.

Chuckling, Ian smiled. This was definitely a cover story, most likely to quell rumors of strange events like the howler monkey attacks. The remainder of the news didn't cover anything he found interesting or even remotely connected to changes around the globe.

He glanced around and sighed. The interior looked like a tornado had visited. Dirty clothes were piled haphazardly across the sofa. The sink was hidden under a ton of dirty dishes.

Nope, not going to the dig today ... start with the sink.

The stack had shrunk considerably when a news report attracted his attention.

> *"... small towns in the Appalachians of North Carolina ..." an announcer stated, "... and Virginia are reporting an epidemic. The authorities are urging people to find detours and avoid the area. For now, the Blue Ridge Parkway has been closed ..."*

Ian turned the volume up, accidentally knocking a few plates off a stack of clean dishes with the towel he had forgotten was on his arm. "Damn it!" Nothing broke, but he missed some of the story.

> *"... social media is coming out of the area. Another government cover-up? One of our reporters was turned away from ..."*

Ian quit watching. *The government is always trying to control the news, even when ... wait! Didn't Shelly say something about kids in that area with DNA changes? Oh my god. No wonder she's flying over.*

Vaughn Collar

With his mind distracted, he glanced around, a little shocked to see the dirty clothes were out of the way, the dishes done. Even a scented candle was burning to mask some of the stale odors.

Hmmph! Maybe I should be this distracted every time I need to clean!

The prior week had produced several new rods with the Futhark script. Two had the hidden magic. Ian tried to work out the writings, but the familiar blinding headaches erupted. By now, he understood he lacked either the expertise or power. He closed his eyes and leaned back. A couple of the words he couldn't decipher.

Try again, Laddy.

He read the spell. Only a slight headache this time. His vision blurred then focused.

"Cum hox tibe tu noctemate vısıus."

What he couldn't make out was the spell's component. No headache, but it was as if he were looking at something underwater through a clear, swift-moving stream. He knew he was close. Another day, perhaps.

The second staff proved much more promising. He was able to easily read four new spells. One, in particular, looked useful in a number of situations. It would allow him to understand any language written or spoken, except magic. He re-read the spell and felt it *click* in his memory.

Time to test it. Let's see ...

He searched for a streaming video in a language he knew nothing about. A Japanese news program came up. He cast the spell, and within just a few words, he found he could understand everything.

Alright so far ...

The Rift - *Beginnings*

He found a Japanese website. It took him a few seconds to realize the Japanese language was written right-to-left. He spared a quick laugh at himself before easily reading the page on his computer screen.

The other spells did not look as practical. Falling slowly or jumping a great distance might be fun, but when would he actually use them? The last spell almost seemed like a waste of time until he thought about it a little more.

Hmm ... open an area, cast the spell, and see if any magic is present? Yeah, I can see that being useful.

While contemplating what he could use the spells on, his phone chimed. It was Shelly.

"Hello there! Waiting for your flight?" Ian asked.

"Yep. I've got a little spare time. I'm on one of the Concordes."

"Concor ... okay. Sounds like I better get going. How long is that flight, hour and a half?"

"About that." Shelly's expression changed. "Ah, yeah ... I'd better let you go. I'll see you soon." She blew him a kiss, then signed off.

Ian sighed, missing her already. He needed to pick up a little more before he left. Especially, the magic materials. He didn't know if he was ready to reveal himself yet. He carefully placed the rods into boxes, swallowed his tea, and ran out the door. He hadn't been able to get an aircar, not on such short notice. But there shouldn't be too many police out, not this early and not on the back roads.

Okay, I can push it.

He made the drive in only a few hours, cutting an hour off what it should've taken. Ian ran into the lobby, looking for the arrival boards. He found her flight just as the sign changed from *On Time* to *Arrived*. It was a short jaunt to her gate. Only a few moments passed before Shelly walked into view.

Vaughn Collar

Her eyes widened and a warm smile crossed her face when she spotted him. "Ian!"

He held out his arms, and she quickened her pace. They embraced in a long hug.

"I needed this," she murmured into his chest.

"Me too," he replied. "So, how was the flight?"

"Not bad. Fast."

They walked hand in hand to retrieve her bags and then to the car. With the doors closed, they leaned over for a long kiss.

He smiled. "So ..." he said, starting the car, "... what's the emergency? Looks like you just dropped everything to get here."

"Pretty much," she said, yawning. "There are events happening around the world. On their own, just a little concerning. Put them together ... I don't know, Ian. I don't know how much longer it'll be until someone in the press adds things up."

Ian grinned. "You're rubbing off on me, honey. I can also see the strings tying together. You're talking about Brazil?"

"Yes ... and more. I think I've figured out when everything started."

"And ...?" Ian gestured, a rolling motion with one hand.

A long sigh. "The reactor."

Ian's 'brows rose. "What would *that* have to do with anything?"

"I don't know exactly *what* happened, but the timeline is too coincidental. The howler monkeys ... the changed ones are about that age. There are a couple of other things." Shelly yawned again.

"You must be tired."

"What gave you the first clue?" She chuckled. "It's only about three in the morning for me."

Ian reached into the backseat and grabbed a pillow. "I figured you'd want a little more shut-eye."

Shelly gave him a warm smile and a quick hug. "You're so thoughtful. Thank you and yes, a little sleep does sound good."

The Rift - *Beginnings*

She propped her head against the pillow and was out before they cleared the airport. A steady mist limited visibility on the way back. With the silence, Ian had time to think.

Do I tell her about me?

His thoughts raced, never slowing to complete an idea. When they approached the turnoff to his trailer, he had finally come to a decision.

Tell her. You can't start this relationship hiding truths.

He parked and reached over, gently nudging her awake. She opened her eyes, looking confused.

"We're here," Ian said. "I'll get your things from the trunk ... pardon me, the boot."

Shelly shook her head with amusement at his muse. He unlocked the trailer and opened the door. It was definitely an *Ian* place. Anything that didn't pertain to the dig was placed in an open spot. Anything to do with the dig was carefully piled in neatly organized, discrete stacks or pottery bins. His laptop was set to one side, dangerously close to a pot of now-cold tea.

The misty rain seemed to be lifting. The sun was visible through the clouds as the weather had cleared just in time to welcome her to his home.

"Care for some tea? Um, fresh, not that." He waved at the pot on the table.

"Please."

"Anything to eat? You've got to be hungry."

Her stomach growled.

Ian laughed. "I'll take that as a *yes*."

Shelly giggled.

Ian started a pot of water, raided the fridge for milk and cheese, and found a box of crackers in the pantry. He joined Shelly at the table just as a ray of sunshine poked through the window. Dust particles swirled, following Ian's movements in the kitchen.

Vaughn Collar

"This is so ... *you*." Shelly motioned around. "I almost feel like I'm back in your apartment." She poured her tea and sat back. "Ian, what I told you over the phone. That was the part that the public knows or at least can easily find if they look. But there's more."

"Like what?"

"Those aren't the only animals that seem to be affected. Rhesus in Japan. Horses in Montana. Children, Ian. Children in the U.S., Europe, Japan. And all seem to have the same timeline."

"The reactor explosion. Yeah, I see where you're going." Ian looked out the window and caught his reflection. He stood and turned to the fridge, trying to hide his shaking hands.

Her eyes were on him as he turned back. "There's one more thing. Remember what you told me just after the incident? About seeing things more clearly? What did you mean by that?"

His heart raced, his hands felt clammy. He was about to open himself more deeply to her than ever before. This was a huge secret to trust with someone. For just a second, he thought about avoiding it, but – *It's now or never, Laddy.* "Let me start from the beginning ..." Ian told her about the strange wave and finding the root cellar and staves and the script writing.

"I remember. Did you ever contact Professor Arbanas?" she asked.

"Yes, and he definitely helped. I traced the writings back to the origins of Norse runes. Most of their base script originates from Futhark that traces back to the second or third century B.C., which corresponds with the oldest rods. The wood came from trees indigenous to an area of Europe that's now Albania."

"Wha ... Albania? How would a staff from Albania end up in the Norse regions?"

Ian stood and leaned against the wall. "I wondered about that until I remembered something. Not all of the original Norse came

The Rift - *Beginnings*

from Germanic heritage. Some of the older tribes seem to be from the Mediterranean." He sat down. "I'm getting sidetracked. It's the script on the material making things interesting." He picked up a rod from inside a box sitting beside him and ran his finger just above the script. "See this? The same Norse script."

Shelly shook her head. "Ian, there's nothing here."

"You can't see ... anything?"

"No. I see the script here." She pointed to the top few lines. "And here." She pointed to the last line.

"Hmm." He frowned, put the staff down, and picked up another. "See anything now?"

"Again, nothing. Ian, are you okay?"

"I'm fine." He glanced out the window and smiled a mischievous grin. "You trust me?"

She gave him a suspicious look. "Yes. What else do you have that isn't here?"

He laughed. "You'll see. This, you will see."

He pushed the door open and stepped out. The sun beamed down, reflecting sparkling lights off raindrops in the surrounding trees. Ian pointed at a pile of large rocks a few yards away. He drew in a deep breath and slowly exhaled as he briefly closed his eyes. Opening them, he said a few words that sounded like a mixture of Latin and Greek. A ball of light formed in his hands that emitted crackling sparks. Ian aimed at the pile, and the light split into four smaller balls, shattering the rocks into smaller pieces. The sound echoed around them. Ian turned and smiled.

Shelly's eyes widened. She looked at Ian, at the rocks, and then back at Ian. Cautiously, she walked over and picked up one of the pieces. She touched a darkened spot and her finger swiped away soot. The rock's surface was cratered at the impact point.

"It looks like it was hit by lightning!" She turned the rock over in her hands. "How ... what ... how did you do this?"

Vaughn Collar

Ian's eyes sparkled and his grin matched. "Magic."

The Rift - *Beginnings*

CHAPTER 24

"Magic? Ian, seriously? If you're trying to be funny, you're not." Shelly glared at him, still holding the fragment of rock.

Ian met her gaze. "No, this is serious. I don't know how this happened, but I know when. Since the reactor incident, I've gained abilities. Like this one." He walked over and gently held her shoulders. "I'm being serious. That broken rock is real, right?"

Shelly looked at the rock, then slowly back up at him. "Yes. But –"

"I can't explain it. Ever since the explosion, I've been able to do things. I call it magic. I don't know what else to call it." He waved his hands in the air, searching for the right words. "Those rods you were looking at. The area you thought was blank. It's not. There is writing that explains what actions to take. What materials to use and the associated words. Like this ..." He looked around and spotted two trees separated by about ten feet. He closed his eyes, allowing the spell to flow through his conscious thought. Reaching into a pouch on his belt, he removed a small, white ball. He spread out his hands, palms facing the trees, thumbs touching.

"TELERANATE!"

183

Vaughn Collar

Strands of material shot out of the trunks, colliding in the air. A small mass formed in the center, happening almost faster than their eyes could follow. A large web now occupied the gap, rippling in the slight breeze.

Shelly's eyes widened. "Is that a ..."

Ian nodded as a smile spread across his face. The web was the same as the one he had cast in Boston, but larger. Shelly walked over, still entranced by what she had just watched. She bent down and picked up a small branch, tossing it at the web. The branch stuck. She reached out to touch it.

"I wouldn't do that. It can hold two large men in place."

Shelly withdrew her hand. She turned with an expression of puzzlement. Her mouth opened and closed a couple of times but made no sound.

"Why don't we go inside," he said, reaching for her. "It looks like it could start pouring any minute." Ian gestured at the low clouds filling the sky. A light mist started before they made it to his trailer. Ian draped his coat over Shelly and led her inside. Shelly sat at the table, still clearly puzzled. Ian turned on the stove to warm up some water for tea.

"Ian ... I don't know what to say." She grinned. "Is this what you meant by saying you felt you were thinking clearer?"

Ian smiled, bringing over the now-steaming water. "When I came down from the dig? Yeah, that's about right. I remember looking at one of the rods. I had hoped it wasn't damaged by the ground shaking."

"You felt that up there?" Shelly motioned toward the window where she could see the base of the mountain, its peaks hidden in the clouds.

"Oh yeah, I definitely felt it. It knocked me off my feet. Didn't hurt the tents, which was my main concern. All the material from the dig was inside."

The Rift - *Beginnings*

Shelly reached over, taking his hand in hers. "I'm glad you were safe. But what happened up there?"

Ian sat back and looked at the ceiling. He paused to collect his thoughts. "There was the initial jolt. Then, a wave of energy came through. I remember it becoming really bright. There was a sensation of ... I can't actually describe it. Like an electrical shock, but not exactly."

"And that was when you noticed a change?"

"Soon after. I walked up to the top of the mountain and saw the devastation. I went back to the camp, looked inside the tent, and found the rods on the ground. But not damaged."

"And ...?"

Ian chewed his lip, trying to recall. "I noticed one of the rods had writing on it. Writing I hadn't noticed before. When I looked closer, a blinding headache hit." He picked up one of the rods. "This is the script."

Shelly looked at the staff and then back at Ian. "I don't see anything."

"Really? Not even here?" He pointed with his finger.

"No. Nothing."

"Can you see this?" He pointed at the bottom of the rod where carved runes were very present.

"I can see those, yes. Do they ..." – she placed a finger lightly on the runes – "... describe anything special?"

"No. That's the start of a tale. Hmm ... let's try another." He walked over to a closet and pulled out a longer rod. "Here. The script wraps around it. It describes a ... spell. I guess the best words would be ... to allow a person to see in the dark."

"But I can't see anything on here."

"Maybe you have to have the ability to use magic to read magic. Certainly fits in with the royalty having abilities the commoners didn't, and the tribal leaders would have kept this to themselves."

Vaughn Collar

She put her cup down, still searching his face for answers. "And this all started with the incident?"

"Yes. I've re-examined everything, and looked a little more carefully at everything I've brought out since. So far, I've identified about a dozen spells. But there are so many more. Some, I have a good idea what they do. Others, I can't even read the first letter before the headache kicks in."

"You mentioned a headache back then too. Do you think there's a connection?"

"Yes, I do. When I'm trying to read a spell more advanced than my abilities, the headaches hit. Come to think of it, it happens when I try to memorize more than just a few spells. And my power ..." – Ian ran his hand across his beard – "... and numbers of spells I can memorize have increased. Hadn't really thought it through before."

"Power?"

"When I first started, I could read and use just a few spells. They were simple ones, like producing a light or a little flame. Now those are easy. But there were spells where I could read only a few words or none at all. Just a couple of days ago, I was able to figure out a spell that can move dirt the same as using a shovel."

"That would come in handy. Hold on ... you said *number of spells?*"

"Don't you know it! And yeah, I've progressed from one to five daily."

Shelly stood, taking her cup to the sink. She stared out the window, then closed her eyes, pressing her fingers to her forehead.

"What are you thinking?" Ian asked.

"I'm not sure, honestly. It all sounds crazy, but ..." – she motioned at the rock pile outside – "... I didn't hallucinate those rocks breaking."

The Rift - *Beginnings*

"Shel, you oughta see it from my side. All of a sudden, I can do things only sci-fi fans can dream about. I mean ... magic?"

Shelly looked at Ian. Her eyes were full of love, not the least bit cautious. "It's funny. I came here to talk about *things* happening around the world. Now, I discover that my boyfriend is one of those *things* happening."

They laughed.

Ian stood, taking one of Shelly's hands in his, leading her to the couch.

"Might as well be comfortable." Ian leaned back, facing her. "This feels like a long talk."

"Probably. And your magic actually fits in with these events." Shelly went on to list the strange occurrences happening around the globe - the relocation of the Amazon village, the monitor lizards in Africa, the DNA anomalies in the Appalachians. "There's another that's more than just a little alarming."

"Really?"

"In British Columbia, the mosquitoes are growing larger. Much larger. As in four or five inches. Thankfully, it's in an isolated area. It came to our attention when a small child almost died from blood loss."

"Five *inches*? That's not a mosquito ... that's a little vampire!"

They giggled.

"Uh-huh. The child's father brought in a few specimens. Scientists at the University of British Columbia tracked the lineage. They estimate these bugs are around two years old."

"Two years? Damn." Ian realized where Shelly was heading.

She sighed. "Something came out of that reactor explosion. It's changing the DNA in multiple species, including humans and not in just one area, it's across the world. And now ... you ... and ..."

"And magic."

"Yes," Shelly replied.

Vaughn Collar

"And this is why you were drafted by the president?"

"Yes. I'm the head of a new department. The funding, even the existence of the department, is beyond black. But so many things are happening, I don't think it will be too much longer until someone turns on the lights."

"And then the whole world will know?"

"Probably. I came here to get an outside opinion. Now ... well ... consider this a warning. You must keep your new abilities hidden. The committee would just love to get their hands on you."

Ian reached for her, holding her in his arms. "I will. Believe me, I will."

They sat in silence, enjoying the warmth of each other's embrace.

A disturbing thought crossed Ian's mind. "Have you heard of anything else? I mean, to do with other people?"

"Other than the kids in Virginia, no. Why?"

"Just because *you* can't read the hidden writings doesn't mean nobody else can."

Shelly sat up. "Yeah, and ... oooh. Someone else able to use magic ... someone not as nice as you."

"Exactly."

Shelly closed her eyes in thought. She took in a deep breath and slowly exhaled. "Okay, I see where you're going. Hmm ... I can't use my system in D.C. to search for people like you. But I still have my security clearance at the museum in Inverness. Maybe I can use their system." Shelly moved to stand.

Ian gently grabbed her arm. "I've got a better idea, at least for today." Ian raised a 'brow, a lopsided grin on his face.

Shelly sat back and wrapped her arms around him. One long kiss led to another, which led them to the bedroom.

The Rift - *Beginnings*

The next day, they drove to Inverness, separating after renting a vehicle for Shelly. She headed for the museum and Ian for a store. He returned to his trailer, a car full of groceries, and his mind on the newest material from the site. Maybe there was something he had missed.

Ian fixed a pot of tea and thought about their conversation. What if there was someone else out there? If so, would he or she be dangerous? How could they find him or her? Would another government agency interfere? Surely, he wasn't the only person on Earth affected.

CHAPTER 25

Lucian settled into a small house in Petroșani. He had spent a few days shopping for furniture and such. Once done, he hiked back to the monastery. After a full day setting up his campsite, he spent almost every waking hour exploring the ruins. His time was not wasted. A few days of clearing rubble led Lucian to the column with the protection glyph.

"I wonder ..." It was not difficult to tell what stones came from the accompanying column. *There has to be more than just those two tomes. Protection glyphs aren't easy. What else are you hiding?*

Lucian kept removing rubble, but at a slower pace. Every time he cleared a meter or so, he would stop to inspect the area. His efforts were rewarded early one afternoon. Not far from the column with the protection glyph, he found a hidden entrance. Another hour of hard work, and the rubble blocking the doorway was cleared.

Winded and with his back aching, he rested for a bit. The faint outline of a door was now visible. The stones from the crumbling walls had moved the door just enough to reveal its presence. He admired the efforts of the long-ago builders. Without the damage, this door would not have been visible.

The Rift - *Beginnings*

Selecting his tools carefully, he opened the passageway and reached for a flashlight.

Wait, you don't need that. A quick command ..."Luxor ..." and a ball of light appeared. Holding his hand high, he gasped. Lining the walls were shelves filled with books and scrolls. Cobwebs covered everything. There wasn't much debris on the floor, letting him know that this room had been relatively undisturbed.

How long, I wonder?

He barely worked through a quarter of the room and found four more tomes with magic writing. His backpack now held enough research to occupy him for weeks and weighing as much as he felt comfortable bringing back in one trip. He also needed to resupply.

It was an afternoon's hike down the mountain and to his new home. The next day, with his backpack full of food, water, and other needed items, he hiked back to his camp. He repeated this pattern, and it was difficult to not stop and read every tome. But he knew if he did, it would be winter before he was even halfway done.

Where do I start?

His main table was covered, as was his couch. His hands trembled with excitement.

Get a grip, Luce.

He started with the pile closest to his desk. Over the next few weeks, he worked on preservation in the mornings, then reading in the afternoon. Some nights, he was in bed late, having tried to cast the spells that he could. Most of the time, he was exhausted from the off-and-on headaches. Still, he made progress.

Most of what he could understand were spells designed to alter appearances. He could change his facial features entirely, add or subtract up to a foot to his height, vary his weight up to about fifty pounds, and switch out his clothing. A few times, he set aside the

Vaughn Collar

research and ventured out with his appearance altered. No one seemed to notice anything out of place, at least that he could tell. One time, the spell was expiring before he was ready. Luckily, he was able to duck into an alley before anyone would see him change.

There were spells for physical attacks too. Those, he largely ignored. One spell, however, particularly intrigued him. With it, he could read and understand different languages. He tried this by accessing news programs from other countries, along with written material. Without fail, he understood every word.

Hmm ... maybe now I can understand some of those ancient Irish and Russian works.

He returned to the monastery determined to empty it of all its secrets. An old cabin not far away could serve as a shelter if restored. The passage of time blurred until he noticed the days shortening.

If I was still teaching, I'd be getting ready for another semester ... so glad I'm not.

Lucian reached the farthest wall from the entrance later that summer. Seemingly, there was nothing left to discover. He lit a small clump of wet grass and tendrils of smoke rose curving toward the far wall, disappearing behind a couple of stones.

Wha ... another room?

He moved a large rock to find an entrance leading underground. Moving the rest of the rubble took a few days. But he could see a few steps curving down and into the darkness.

"That first rock was well placed. On purpose, maybe?" He stepped down only to find another wall. After examining the opening more cautiously, he was rewarded. "Ah hah! Another glyph." Markings glowed faintly in the darkness and shimmered as if reflected off water. The script was unknown. He had never seen this language before.

The Rift - *Beginnings*

He took out his pouch and spoke the language spell. "Legan quod non posseb."

The glyph flowed into words he could read.

"Citeste-ma Si Treci." Lucian chuckled. *Read me and pass? Really? Well ... give it a try.*

Saying the words aloud, the glyph faded. A scraping sound echoed from somewhere in the dark as if a large rock were being dragged across gravel. He shone his light and watched as the wall disappeared into an opening. More stairs were now visible.

Hmm ... nice glyph!

Casting his light spell, Lucian slowly descended the stairs that led down. Holding his hand up high, he looked around. Most of the room was visible with only a few areas still dark. His attention was drawn to a pedestal in the center about waist high. A pair of hands formed a bowl with the thumbs curving over the palms. The stone was worn in several places. He determined the hands were the support for a book, and the thumbs served to hold the book open. The supporting pillar was carved with an image of a boar's head superimposed on the body of a dragon.

This is familiar, but where ...?

The image seemed to have similarities to both Celtic and Slavic themes. Distantly troubled, but unsure why, Lucian studied the walls. The room appeared to be carved from the rock itself – no brickwork visible. A few roots had crept through and water dripped forming shallow puddles. The room smelled musty with a faint hint of – *rust?*

Lucian brought his light closer and found worn carvings in the palms. The stone was rough from years of exposure to damp air. Seams could be seen, showing that the pillar was built in pieces. Many of the finer features were eroded. As he felt along the dragon's spine, Lucian jerked his hand back. The carving was a representation of an old Slavic god, Veles.

Vaughn Collar

But what is it doing up here?

From what Lucian knew, Veles was almost exclusively a god of the lowlands. Mountain people feared him. Veles represented magic, and the mountain people were more practical, fearing magic.

Lucian sat down to rest his feet and to think.

"Veles ... wait a minute. Luce, think. Veles is also one of the old Slavic gods for the underworld. What *is* this place?"

Now, he was even more confused as to the purpose of this monastery. His discoveries answered one question but led to two or three others.

"Well ... you wanted more. Be careful what you wish for."

He shook his head, chuckling a little at himself before getting back on his feet. He continued exploring the pedestal. On either side, carvings of a zither, a stringed instrument, and a fujara, a type of flute, were visible.

"This pedestal had a purpose," he whispered. "People used to believe music would enhance magic, make it more powerful. So where are the instruments?" *And why so isolated? What am I missing?*

There was more of the room to be explored, which was maybe thirty feet across and formed a square. The ceiling was just above his outstretched hand, somewhat more than seven feet. His light pushed against the darkness to show a basin at the base of one wall. Above it were four odd openings about a square foot each.

The remainder of the room was plain, unadorned. He was about to leave when he noticed a seam close to the stairs where water had dripped, creating a long, white stain. Running his fingers along the seam, he gently pushed. The wall gave way, a little. A closer look revealed a small opening intricately carved to hide a small alcove.

A hidden shelf?

The Rift - *Beginnings*

He pulled out a pry bar and worked it into the almost invisible line. Inside was a leather bag. Within that was an ancient fujara. Lucian handled the instrument almost reverently. He had always loved the sound they made. Indeed, it was almost as if it spoke to him. The wood looked to be in good condition, enough that the instrument could be handled gently. Even so, he gingerly placed the fujara back into the bag. He had one last look around before leaving.

Lucian set out the fujara. Due to its age, he treated the instrument with care as he cleaned it. He blew a soft note. The sound sent his mind reeling back to watching travelling musicians during his youth. It was one of the few nice memories he owned. The warmth of the sound seemed to almost touch his soul. Something else happened, though. Something totally unexpected.

Normally, whenever he cast a spell, it was instantly gone from his mind. Before he could cast it again, he had to re-read it. But the sound of the fujara enabled him to recall every spell he had cast that day. He could feel the magic coursing through his body like blood through his veins.

This is what power feels like! Time to test this out.

Stepping outside, he looked around until he spotted a boulder. Letting the energy build within, he cast the spell. Five globes projected from his hands and crashed into the large rock, shattering it into pieces.

Wha ... oh wow! Five ... not one? He glanced at his hands and saw no difference, no damage. Nothing apparent, although he could feel a tingling sensation.

The magic of the fujara was still coursing through him. There was one spell he wanted to try and this seemed like the perfect opportunity. He opened his notes to find the spell he wanted. One that allowed him to detect magic. Holding the proper component, he played the same note as before and cast the spell.

Vaughn Collar

A *glow* appeared above a crate in the corner. Opening it, he found a small box, the source of the light. A ring made from silver with a black tourmaline inset was tucked inside.

"Not exactly a masterpiece, is it?"

The glow diminished as the spell expired. He placed the ring on his finger.

Too big.

A minute tremor and the ring shrank until it fit. He felt a faint surge course through him. He thought about taking the ring off, but it seemed to suit him. With no idea what magic it held, he could only guess at the powers of the ring. Though the power he felt had a distinct chill.

"Protection, maybe? But from what?"

The end of the summer also signaled the end of his time at the monastery. Lucian had a productive but tiring dig. The very thought of continuing when the weather was changing to cold and wet just made his bones ache. The first signs of snow in the mountains were the final straw. It was time to remain in Petroșani.

He considered his dig a spectacular success. His repertoire of spells had increased dramatically. Through constant trial and error, he figured out the best ones. He loved walking through town disguised as someone famous. Another favorite was to appear as local law enforcement. The experimenting wasn't limited to just changing his appearance.

One spell warned of side effects, though it seemed like it could be useful. What could go wrong with moving faster? Still, he figured it would be best to pay heed to the warning. It was a quiet, warm afternoon, and he decided it would be a good time to try it out. His target was a butterfly, slowly flitting from flower to flower. He pulled out his spell pouch and muttered the words.

The Rift - *Beginnings*

"ITE VELOCI MAXUM."

The butterfly now acted more like a hummingbird, jerking around. The effect lasted just a few seconds. Landing on a flower, the butterfly seemed weakened and fell to the ground, its wings only vaguely moving. A bird swooped down and snatched the insect in its beak.

Lucian shrugged. "Oh, okay. The spell takes a lot of energy. Have to remember that."

On his final trip down, Lucian used the forest cover to stay dry. He'd been looking for a willow tree to carve a new fujara. The instrument he had found was drying out and cracking now that it was exposed to the elements. The tree he found was perfect with several branches straight enough to use. Research determined that the willow was Veles' favorite.

He visited a local craftsman with a reputation for well-made instruments and preferred by players at cultural fairs. Lucian paid well for the new fujara and picked it up just after New Year in 2079.

He had remained busy through the fall, either reviewing material or learning new spells. Life in Petroșani was relaxing with little to no crime, people generally got along. What little crime existed was mostly theft from unwary tourists, with some conflicts around soccer matches.

Lucian now had a repertoire of a dozen spells. He would walk around town, watching for people being hassled. Commonly, this would be teen boys harassing either a less popular boy or an unfortunate young woman. Spells used for more direct purposes were *push*, *slick spot*, and *shrink* or *enlarge*. A bridge over a small river flowing through town provided a nice stage, watching people fall into the river as the railing shrank. He told himself his targets deserved to be punished.

Vaughn Collar

He only once used spells to directly help himself. He had visited one of the better diners in town for a treat as he had finally figured out a complicated spell to alert him of possible intruders. Upon arrival, the hostess led him to a small booth.

"Will this do, sir?" the hostess asked.

"Yes, thank you."

Lucian picked up a menu and selected his dinner. The wine list also looked good. *Maybe one glass tonight.* The waitress took her time before she arrived to take his order. Her expression was familiar, and Lucian knew this expression quite well – a scar on the left side of his face ran from just under his eye and down to his jawline. The scar was from a knife wound in school, courtesy of a bully. Not only was the service here bad, his meal was a little cool when he received it. Rather than complain to the manager, Lucian decided to directly intervene.

He came back the next night and asked to be seated in her area. A spell had changed his appearance to look younger and no scar. The waitress had a completely different approach, to the point of flirting with him. He ordered the most expensive meal on the menu along with a bottle of wine. He waited until he had almost finished and went to the restroom. Once there, he canceled the spell.

Instead of returning to his seat, he sat at the bar and pretended to watch a soccer match. The waitress walked by his table several times before talking to her manager. The manager was displeased and soon the girl left in tears. Lucian laughed to himself.

About what you deserve.

Some days later, Lucian was walking back to his home, full from an excellent lunch, when a commotion erupted on the other side of the street. A man was loudly berating a lady operating a pretzel stand. Lucian could easily make out the angry Russian

The Rift - *Beginnings*

accent. Other customers walked away rather than become involved. Lucian could see the woman was close to tears.

Nememic (asshole)! I'll show you!

Lucian glanced around and no one was paying any attention. He smiled as he cast his spell. The man stumbled into the street. A car was moving too fast to avoid hitting him. Tires squealed and a loud bang sounded as the Russian was catapulted into a nearby light pole. Lucian clearly heard the bones breaking on impact. There were several screams from people yelling for an ambulance.

Lucian looked at the man as he walked by. He was obviously dead, his head at a very odd angle to his chest. Blood oozed from several places, already collecting into a small pool, trickling down the sidewalk to the gutter. An expression of fear was frozen on the man's face. Lucian shook his head and kept walking.

Once home, he poured himself a small drink and sat back to think about the incident. He felt a little troubled that he didn't feel anything for the death. True, he had never been the warmest person. But to not care ... at all?

Wait ... Russian. And ... Natalya was Russian. Ahh ... yeah.

He nodded to himself. He may have cared, a little, if the man had been anything but Russian.

"Oh well, such is life. Now, where was I on that last tome?"

Vaughn Collar

CHAPTER 26

The summer of 2079 was mostly just another summer. However, some of the events were changing the world. In a small glade, somewhere in a southern state, insects much larger than usual were hatching.

A luna moth landed on a narrow twig that bent from its weight. The moth was much larger than usual with a wing span of close to ten inches. Nearby, a praying mantis was climbing up a thick stalk of grass. It too, was large, close to eight inches. The two insects spied each other and froze. The mantis extended a foreleg but not at the moth. The claw had an opposable digit almost a thumb. It pointed at a distant house. The sound of children playing echoed through the glade. The moth reached out and touched the mantis' claw and nodded its head. Both flew off.

The little glade was not far from another place experiencing enlarged insects. People spoke of strange rumors about bugs the size of small birds. Family pets went missing, turning up later unharmed, physically. However, the pets refused to venture outside alone and cowered when near an empty field. Because of the increase of unusual insects, patches of land zoned for construction remained wild.

The Rift - *Beginnings*

One such place was rezoned for residential. Initially, a few small incidents caused some delays. However, when workers were spooked, work ceased. Cables and wires were damaged with strange teeth marks. Hand tools inexplicably vanished. As time passed, more incidents happened. The crew walked out after a worker was bitten by an overly large grasshopper, actually severing a small tendon in the man's hand. The site was soon abandoned.

Randall McTavish spent his days ferrying scientists from Vancouver to an inlet across the Queen Charlotte Strait from Port McNeil. To him, they were seriously delusional.

Five-inch mosquitoes? Oh well ... as long as they keep paying, I'll keep bringing 'em. At least, I'm getting some of my tax money back!

Sue and Mark Hancock were the lead scientists. Though they had not actually seen the overly large mosquitos, they had seen pictures of the specimens brought back a year earlier. Since then, rumors spread through the university that the bugs were growing even larger. An emergency grant funded their trip with two graduate students, Steve Sinclair and Melody Stanton, who were working on furthering their education.

The boat arrived in the early afternoon, and they quickly set up the mosquito netting. Summers in British Columbia were a haven for flying pests. Anchoring around a hundred yards from land would keep the majority away. Sue and Mark drew watch the first night.

The sun had just set behind the mountains of Vancouver Island when the aurora borealis waved its ghostly tendrils, hiding the stars. A faint high-pitched hum was growing louder, and Mark turned, trying to figure out what it was.

He whispered, "Sue, hear that?"

"Yeah, I do. They must be close to be that loud."

Vaughn Collar

Something smacked against Sue's head and she ducked. They readied their cameras, and their hands shook as they waited. It didn't seem to take long before the swarm arrived, and the air thickened. Sue took a step back as the sky darkened. Together, they hid behind the net.

"Damn!" Mark stated. "Look at the size!"

Sue's voice quavered. "Those things are what? Four inches ... or bigger!"

A quiet ripping sounded, and Mark took several steps back. The darkness sent chills up his spine for the stars seemed to have disappeared. The mosquitoes were slowly forcing themselves through the net.

"Sue! The duct tape!"

"Where is it?" she yelled.

"In the duffel bag, under that ..." – he pointed – "... seat!"

She opened the bag and grabbed the tape, tossing it to Mark. He pulled off a strip and covered the opening. One mosquito had made it inside.

"Ow!" Mark swatted at the thing. "Dammit, it got me!" Mark held out his hand. He slapped again at the bug and it sounded like a balloon popping. Blood squirted across the floor.

"Oh shit!" Sue pointed to another rip. "Gimme the tape, another hole."

Several of the oversized mosquitoes made it through before she could repair it. Mark and Sue screamed as they were bitten several times. Sue pushed Mark into the main cabin.

"Get in!" she yelled.

Mark slammed the door as several mosquitoes slapped against the windows with audible thumps.

Randall stepped out of his sleeping quarters, bleary eyed and looking annoyed. "What the hell's going –"

The mosquitoes swarmed on the glass.

The Rift - *Beginnings*

"My god." Randall wrapped his arms around his chest. "It's true?!"

The two students stepped out next, looking equally stunned.

Mark glanced over at Randall. "Looks like we're staying inside. That netting won't hold." The pounding against the glass reminded Mark of being inside a drum.

"But ... they're just mosquitoes!" Randall stated. "They can't tear through a net, can they?"

Sue shook her head. "Ordinarily, you're correct. But look! Look at their forelegs."

They stared through the window. It was readily apparent the forelegs had been altered. The claws were no longer just a pair of claws. An opposable digit was now visible and being used to tear through the barrier.

Mark and Sue glanced at each other, a smile spreading across their faces.

"There's our grant extension." Sue chuckled, pointing.

"Yep and enough for us too," one of the grad students said.

The mosquitoes slowly dispersed.

Taking turns running outside to bring in the equipment, they didn't escape completely unscathed. All suffered at least four or five bites. Mark was the worst off and was feeling somewhat dizzy. Sue helped him to his cabin.

The two students set up the night cameras. This area of B.C. was about as wild and untouched by man as anywhere in Canada. The sky was clear, with a half-moon overhead seen through the green curtain of the aurora. They hoped to observe some of the nighttime animals and were not disappointed.

A grizzly ambled from the forest, walking along the shore, turning over rocks for grub. It stopped momentarily, then spun to bite at its hind quarters. Growling, it reared up on two legs before

Vaughn Collar

falling back onto all four. Its irritated growls grew louder before it bolted into the trees.

The two students looked at each other.

"Evidently bears aren't immune to these giants either," Melody said.

They chuckled.

By three in the morning, the two were feeling a little drowsy. Melody stood to stretch. A movement through the window caught her attention.

"Steve!" She hissed and pointed outside. "Look!"

Steve reached for the night scope. Something was walking along the beach on two feet. Dark fur covered its body. It was at least eight feet tall if not taller.

Melody had problems trying to focus the night camera. Her hands shook with excitement.

"So the rumors are true," Steve said. "They do exist." He kept watching as the creature flipped over a log. Kneeling down, it picked through the sand and gravel, looking for clams and crabs.

The creature slapped itself before performing a full-on dance as it swatted at the air. It roared, a sound none would ever forget, halfway between a human cussing and a lion's roar. The creature ran to the edge of the forest and pulled up a plant. It used it like a fan to ward off the mosquitoes. The plant disintegrated and the creature gave up, running into the forest.

Steve looked over at Melody. "Tell me you got that," he exclaimed.

"I did. Wow!" She looked at Steve, her eyes large. "This ..." – she patted the camera – "... is going to set the world on fire."

They gave each other a hug, then pulled back, embarrassment on their faces. Melody was just tall enough to see over Steve's shoulder. There was movement again on the shore.

"Steve," she whispered. "Another one!"

The Rift - *Beginnings*

He looked through the night scope. "Melody, get the camera going again. Either it's back or it's another one."

She was already pointing the camera at the shore.

The creature warily looked up and down the beach. It seemed smaller than the first. As it cleared the brush, they could see more definitively what they were looking at.

"Mel, that's a female!"

The creature had breasts. It stared into the forest as a small tree moved and a much taller creature walked out. The two exchanged a look before the taller one made a motion, indicating a log on the shore. They moved the fallen tree aside. Both knelt, picking at the ground.

A light shone from the cabin below, illuminating the shore. The creatures stood, and the female darted into the forest. The male turned and stared at the boat. It bared its teeth and growled. Melody managed to capture the creature staring at her, its eyes glowing in the night before it vanished into the forest.

"Dammit!" Melody stated. "Oh well, we've gotten enough to convince even the most skeptical."

They were all smiles when Sue and Mark entered the watch station.

"Tell me you got that on film?" Mark asked.

"Oh yeah ... all of it," Steve said. "Screw the mosquitoes. This made the trip completely worth it." Steve's smile was infectious.

A bleary eyed Randall watched the video. After marking the location on his GPS, he sat back, calculating how much money he would earn chartering trips to this inlet.

The research group spent the day on the beach, obtaining samples of hair and blood along with plaster foot casts. They attempted to move the fallen tree the two creatures had moved, but all four could barely budge it. The site was filmed, using Steve as a size comparison. He placed markers on the tree where the two creatures had stood. None were surprised that the male was somewhat over eight feet and the female was just under seven.

News from the Amazon slowed to a trickle. What little did escape the blanket of secrecy was devoted to the howler monkeys. A second group was found. Contact between the troops was unknown but not likely as the two were many miles apart. However, they weren't the only species affected. The initial wave traveled along the river, passing through a large pod of freshwater dolphins.

Several of the pod were female and pregnant. The newborns showed apparent differences. The pectoral fins were a little longer with enlarged bone growth, giving the fins a jagged appearance. The dorsal fins were not as high but ran farther down the spine. The snouts were shorter than normal, and behind and below the eyes were small bumps.

In the woods near Boone, North Carolina, several nests of small lizards were washed over by the wave. These reptiles were affected similar to the monitor lizards of Africa. One or two hatchlings were larger than the rest. They too had the slight ridge encircling just behind the head and two bumps over the front legs.

Two generations later, the changes were not as advanced. Most of the affected members had either mated unchanged or hadn't survived long enough to pass on the altered genes. However, one place where two nests were closer together experienced mating between changed individuals. The third generation was almost unrecognizable from the original. They were twice the size of the unaffected ones. The slight ridges on their backs had become a set of small spikes that elevated when threatened, revealing a thin membrane. Lastly, the larger members had added plants to their

The Rift - *Beginnings*

diets, along with fruits and berries. The Paw-Paw fruit was now a sought-after delicacy.

Though not observed by people, the forest held a few other surprises, particularly with insects. The largest were basically the same size, if not larger, than the lizards. The changed reptiles avoided the larger insects, refusing to prey on them, even if the opportunity presented itself.

Three small villages in northeastern Romania were experiencing a series of human births paralleling those in Virginia. Over one-hundred children were born within the last couple of years with the same silky, black hair and purple eyes. A few others showed the same white-blonde hair and golden eyes.

Dr. Shevchenko was sitting in her office, looking at data concerning this pattern. To her knowledge, no trends like this ever previously existed. She was waiting on a return call from a friend in the government, curious if she could gain access to classified records. Her phone rang. It was her friend.

"Maryia, thank you for calling back."

"I wondered if I would get the chance, Olga. There are villages in our home country asking this same question."

Maryia Melnyk and Dr. Shevchenko were both originally from the Ukraine but relocated to Romania with their parents twenty-odd years prior.

"Really? Then this is not a localized event?" Dr. Shevchenko asked.

"No. Your town may have the most recent births, but there are at least six places in Romania within fifty kilometers registering children with these characteristics."

Vaughn Collar

Dr. Shevchenko sat back to collect her thoughts. "Tell me, if you can, what is the age spread? Maybe some event caused this. If so, the oldest of these children should match the time frame."

"Yes, that seems logical." Maryia glanced at her other monitor. "Um ... I see a grouping of fourteen to twenty-two." Pausing, Maryia's eyes lost focus before returning to the screen. "That grouping ... all the mothers would have been pregnant at the same time. Just in different stages."

Dr. Shevchenko nodded. "Therefore, we should look for an event around the oldest. But what?"

"I can think of only one," Maryia stated, "but it should not be creating the physical changes we're experiencing. I find it hard to believe ..."

The children were not old enough to develop odd features just yet, but unusual things happened around them. Plants in and near the households seemed to grow faster – much faster. Pets, especially dogs, were extremely playful with the children, which saved one dog's life. He was all but uncontrollable, almost vicious. When the family's daughter was born, the dog changed to a docile, friendly pet, always near the child and highly protective of her.

There had been only one meeting between any of these children. In the village of Kam'yanka, the two families inadvertently met at a small grocery store. The children immediately gravitated toward each other. The startled parents almost hit the shelves with their carts trying to avoid the children.

"I'm so sorry!" the mother of the young girl said. "She never acts like this."

The children, a boy and a girl, were chattering away. Some of the words were clear but most were gibberish. The mothers smiled, watching. As the children played, a slow change was happening.

The Rift - *Beginnings*

The flowers in the florist section freshened. Blooms, once sagging, now spread out. The scent became stronger. People suddenly acted – peaceful, happy. A man, aggravated with the produce manager, stopped mid-sentence and apologized.

The parents looked at each other. Though they didn't know what had caused the changes, they knew their children had something to do with it. They also knew there was now a tie, a bond between the two families. They exchanged phone numbers and promised to not only keep in contact, but to let the children play together as often as possible. Maybe having a friend would ease the burden.

They had no idea that hundreds of other families were experiencing the same phenomenon, not only in Europe and the U.S., but also in Japan and Scotland.

Vaughn Collar

CHAPTER 27

Jan returned to the U.S., looking forward to his new position and a fresh start. He wasn't antisocial, far from it. But now that he was in a serious relationship with Shelly and with his new-found magical abilities, he felt no need to socialize.

I've got better things to occupy my time.

Every day, he looked forward to continuing his magic studies. Each new spell gave him the same feeling as discovering a rare item at a dig. An interesting one was the ability to breathe underwater. *Could come in handy.* Just thinking about using the spell sent shivers of anticipation all through him. He planned out a trip to nearby Lake Merriweather for the next weekend as the weather forecast was promising.

He woke Saturday to a bright sun and warm temperatures. It was only a short trip to the lake. After finding the trail, he walked far enough until he could no longer hear traffic. Stripping down to his trunks, he cast the spell and stepped in. The initial shock from the cold stopped him.

"Wish it was still summer for this!" Laughing, he walked until the water was waist deep, then dove.

The water was a little murky, limiting his visibility to about ten feet and was brown from the recent fallen leaves. He stopped,

The Rift - *Beginnings*

feeling a little apprehensive as a film surrounded him, keeping the water from touching his skin to about mid-chest. *Just do it, Laddy.* He exhaled then slowly breathed in. The film rippled in front of his face, and the air was fresh and cool. He rolled over to watch his breath rise in hundreds of tiny bubbles.

"Wow! This is cool!"

His feet touch the murky bottom and mud oozed between his toes. Looking up, the surface was just visible. A school of bream chased the diffused bubbles. A large catfish slowly swam away without fear. The surface ripples caused the sunlight to shimmer like drapes before an open window. He stood quietly, enthralled with the view. It was a new world – slower, perhaps, but no less beautiful than above.

Slowly, he became aware of a rising band of cold encircling his chest. He looked down and paused, the waterline was creeping up. *The spell is wearing off!* He swam to the surface just as the spell ended. Walking to his pack for a towel, he looked back at the lake.

"I need to try this in clearer water. Maybe the ocean?" Ian whispered.

Another interesting spell was one that would slow down time. *I could see some uses, for sure.* A quick trip into town, and in the second thrift store, he found what he was looking for – an hourglass. Returning home, he sat his new treasure on the table. Clearing his mind, he allowed the spell to dominate his thoughts. A timer was set on the stove and another next to the hourglass to track how long the spell lasted. Pulling out his pouch of components, he flipped the timepiece over and watched the first grains of sand fall.

"TEMPATE, TARDATE!"

The falling grains slowed. Each one landed on the pile, leisurely bouncing and rolling to the bottom. Sounds from outside were distorted, as if hearing them channeled through a synthesizer.

Everything seemed affected, except for him. He moved his hand and nothing changed. A fly buzzed slowly enough for him to reach out and grab it, if he so chose. Each tick of the timer echoed before the next click. The hourglass was good for five minutes but looked as if it had barely started. Then, everything sped up and normal time returned. For Ian, it had been a full five minutes. But the timer showed it to have been only twenty seconds.

"Woah! Five minutes for me, but only twenty seconds in reality." Ian's smile stretched ear to ear as a wave of exhaustion hit. He stumbled to a chair, collapsing into it.

Man, I don't know about the tired part ... but I love magic!

The Christmas holiday finally arrived. Ian was making some notes on a spell when Shelly walked in.

"Ian!" Dropping her bags in the doorway, she launched into his arms. After a passionate kiss, they pulled apart, looking into each other's eyes.

"I've missed you." Ian let go, reaching for her bags. "Here, let me bring these in. No sense in giving the neighbors an eyeful." He wiggled his 'brows at her. Both laughed.

That night, after eating out – Ian was a terrible cook, more familiar with something out of a can over an open fire – they settled in. He poured each a snifter of brandy and joined her on the couch, handing her the small glass.

"Washington keeping you busy?" he asked.

"More than I like. There are daily reports of odd things happening. Most of 'em are easily discounted. But ..." She pursed her lips.

"But ...?"

"But some of the rumors fit with ... well ... your abilities."

Ian's 'brows raised again. "You've found someone else?"

The Rift - *Beginnings*

"Oh, no, not like that. It's like ... okay ... in Japan, there are reports, *substantiated* reports, of rhesus monkeys *deliberately* starting fires. And not random ones. The fires are small and well ... controlled. Like ... campfires."

"Camp ... no shit?"

"Yeah. And Brazil has managed to shut down *all* news coming from the Amazon. Nothing in or out." She sat her glass on the table. "Ian ..." – her voice took on a sultry tone – "... I didn't come here to discuss the news. I could've stayed in Washington to do that."

Ian snorted and stood. He pulled her into his arms, kissed her passionately, and they disappeared to his bedroom.

The next two weeks were a break from their regular lives. Shelly was able to forget about Washington, and Ian showed her the newest spells in his repertoire. She especially liked the idea of breathing underwater, as she was an avid scuba diver. With it being winter, it was just too cold for swimming. They didn't spend a lot on Christmas, just being with each other was gift enough. All too soon, it was time for Shelly to return to D.C. and Ian to school.

Spring arrived and the weather was glorious with clear skies and warm temperatures. Bird songs filled the air from dawn to dusk. Crickets, frogs, and cicadas added to the cacophony of sound at night.

Ian left for the week, intent on camping in the mountains and escaping civilization. Shelly, to their disappointment, had not been able to break away from Washington.

He stood at the edge of the tree line and paused. The path led into the woods and it wouldn't take long for the sounds of the highway to disappear. Soon, he was surrounded by birds and the wind in the trees. Every once in a while, a squirrel chattered at

Vaughn Collar

him. He could see wispy clouds through the canopy of the brighter, green leaves.

Green was the predominant color. New growth was everywhere, and the filtered sunlight took on a greenish hue as it penetrated to the forest floor in beams made visible by dust in the air. Under the trees, he enjoyed the musty smell of dampness. Every so often, the trees would thin out and wild flowers would add their scent.

Ian felt refreshed, not tired, even after several hours of hiking.

A perfect, little clearing with a creek gurgling over the rocks would be his camping spot for the first night. He set up his hammock and tarp, started a fire, and settled in. Dinner tasted great, and a small shot of bourbon matched perfectly with the evening. He fell asleep, studying the constellation Cygnus.

Awakening with the dawn, he stirred the embers of the previous night's fire. After a quick breakfast and a cup of tea, he was ready for the trail. His destination was around ten miles away, or so he reckoned. Satellite imagery had shown a spot where tall cliffs towered above the creek.

He made good progress throughout the day. The undergrowth was not as heavy as he would have imagined, and he made it to his site early, which gave him more time to prepare his next camp. He planned on staying for a few days and wanted to make sure this site had everything he needed. A little digging and some rocks made his fire pit and soon he had a nice, little blaze. The exertion of the hike and the clear air made his dinner taste wonderful.

The stars were brilliant this far from the light pollution. Naming the constellations was difficult with so many stars not usually this visible. Soon though, clouds started to build and he could see lightning pulsing through, silhouetting the mountains. His last sensation was hearing the rain tapping on the tarp.

He woke to a misty morning, cool and damp. It felt like he was back in Scotland, at least until the sun burnt through the fog. His

The Rift - *Beginnings*

initial plan was to fill his water bottles at the nearby creek, but the water was cloudy from the night's rain. Then he remembered there was a smaller creek not far away. A few minutes of walking and he located the water running from the hills clear despite the rain. Filling one bottle, there was an odd impulse to take a drink. He sipped and a strange sensation crept through him.

He stood, allowing his senses to take over. Individual leaves on a tree atop the towering cliff seemed so close he could make out the actual veins. A fish surfacing for a morsel looked close enough to count the scales. There were sounds he'd never heard before – the rustling of a worm under the leaves, baby birds waking in their nests to announce their hunger, beetles clicking against each other as they fought. A hawk calling drew his attention. He spotted the birds soaring on the thermals radiating from the valley. He could smell the earthy tang of damp soil, a cedar somewhere nearby with its distinctive scent.

As suddenly as the feeling appeared, it disappeared. He contemplated the bottle of water for a moment, taking another, much longer, drink. His senses reawakened.

"Woah. This is almost ... magical?"

He returned to camp, had a bite to eat, then returned to the creek. Ian followed the water up a gentle slope. Just ahead, he could see the tops of many cattails between the trees.

Those only grow in water-logged soil. I wonder.

He increased his pace as his sense of curiosity urged him on. The sound of a waterfall drew nearer as he crested a small incline. A few more steps and a pond was visible.

The water was just as crystal clear as the creek – the surface calm, almost a mirror. No ripples flowed in or bubbled out from the ground. The water was only a few feet deep, the bottom clearly visible.

"What is it with this place?"

Vaughn Collar

Water that enhanced his senses? A pond where there shouldn't have been one? Everything looked perfect – too perfect.

The hike up the hill took all the energy he had gained from breakfast, and the cattails looked like they were perfect for gathering. The tubers were edible.

Maybe I can add a few to my dinner ...

As he reached out, a dragonfly landed. But this dragonfly was larger – much larger. He guessed it was maybe a foot in length. He leaned closer to get a better look. The wings seemed normal, except for their length. But the front legs. They bent at odd angles, and the foreclaws –

Opposable digits?

He rubbed his eyes and looked again. The foreclaws had three digits opposed by – a thumb? The shape of the claws would make grasping efficient. It wasn't only the front legs, though. The middle pair just barely reached the plant's stem.

Okay, the back legs ... wait a minute.

The back pair were not attached to the body like a regular insect. Instead, they extended out from the abdomen – which in itself seemed smaller. Well, smaller in proportion.

Another dragonfly, shaped the same, abruptly landed on a stalk next to the first. The first one tilted its head, looking at the second.

Senses still sharpened from the water, Ian watched.

Their mouths – he could swear they had a lower jaw. Even more, they seemed to be aware of his presence. Not just as something in their view, but as if they were studying him. The staring contest lasted only a few more seconds before the dragonflies flew away.

Ian stood in awe.

The heightened awareness ... self-aware dragonflies? Magic? What the hell is happening?

The Rift - *Beginnings*

Absently, he took a drink from his water bottle and he shivered. A feeling welled inside as an electrical charge ran through him. The words to a spell surfaced as if he had just read them from his spell book. Out of curiosity, he tried the words.

"Luxor," he muttered.

A ball of light appeared, much larger and brighter than anything he considered before. Incredibly, the spell didn't leave his mind. He could still remember it. On a whim, he tried to see if magic was involved.

"Rilevate magiate!"

The aura threatened to overwhelm his senses. The entire pond, the plants, the insects, even the water flowing downhill, glowed with a nebulous, orange-yellow hue.

He felt a power, more intense than he had ever felt before. He concentrated, trying to focus. A wavy ribbon was just visible, hovering over the pond. The phenomenon seemed familiar and matched with the energy wave he'd experienced from the reactor incident.

Ian reached out and gingerly tried to touch the light. A couple of small sparks from the ribbon reached out to him. The touch wasn't painful. Instead, his sense of power seemed to grow. He looked up, distracted by movement.

A luna moth alit on a small tree limb. He could easily see that the insect had changed, perhaps more than the dragonflies. All of its limbs were transformed. The eyes, though, were slightly recessed, and not as faceted as a regular moth. Amazingly, it had a mouth with an upper and lower jaw. The moth looked straight at him, then lifted one of its front legs.

Ian delicately held his hand close to the moth. With a gentle sweep of its wings, it flew off of the branch and landed on his finger. The moth positively glowed with magic – whispery, flowing

Vaughn Collar

hues of orange and yellow. With one last look at Ian, the moth spread its wings and flew away.

The magic wore off and Ian's senses returned to normal. Hours must have passed as it was becoming a little dark, the sun just barely glowing above the mountains to the west. The walk back to his camp was quiet.

So much to take in. What the hell has happened?

He made it back with the last few minutes spent walking in the dark. It wasn't long until a fire was merrily crackling, a kettle heating water for tea, and his dinner in a skillet, sizzling.

Hmmph. Magic water, giant dragonflies, and huge moths ... self-aware at that. Another ribbon, still present. Me ... this was all from the reactor incident? How?

Ian's thoughts ran rampant, flitting from idea to idea. Night had fallen, his fire low, before he was able to find that tranquil place. Stirring the embers, he heated water for another cup of tea. Once poured, he sat there long into the night, thinking.

The Rift - *Beginnings*

CHAPTER 28

The summer of 2079 was halfway over before Lucian knew it. He sometimes felt there wasn't enough hours in the day for what he wanted to do. He returned once to the monastery and uncovered only one other scroll, and a quick glance did not look promising.

He wondered if there might be anything of interest outside. The ruins rested on a mountaintop to the northeast of Petroșani. From the cliff, there was a perfect view of the town. This part of Romania was free of the rewilding efforts to the east, and Lucian knew there were no large animals to fear.

His search revealed nothing more than a great view. Though not scared of heights exactly, the sheer cliff unsettled him enough to avoid the edge. Besides, there was a large rock situated perfectly to enjoy an eagle soaring on the warm air rising from the town. Several times, Lucian watched as the eagle dove into the valley, before reappearing with a small animal in its claws. It would land in one of several trees in a small alcove not far below.

Nothing here now, except the eagle and a molding ruin of a building.

Vaughn Collar

Lucian had talked with Nadia early in the summer. The two had discussed the monastery. Lucian wanted to know if there was any lore surrounding it.

"You mean the ruins ... up there?" She had motioned toward the mountain.

"Yes. I've heard there are places near Petroșani that can trace their history back many centuries."

"Well, that is one. There are dark tales about it." She walked over to a shelf and pulled out a scroll. "This should tell you what was there."

Lucian motioned to the table. "May I?"

"Hold on." She reached under the counter and handed him a pair of thin gloves. "Use the holders, please."

He secured the scroll and unfurled it. The tale it told was of a sect of learned men trying to find ways to turn back the Mongol horde. It was dark and gory with several mentions of sacrifice and worship to ancient gods.

He looked up. "This took place up there?"

"From what I've heard, yes. Not a place to be alone."

Lucian raised his brows. *How many nights have I been there ... alone?* "Surely these beliefs are long dead."

Nadia stared at him, then sighed. "If you want to stay there, likely nothing will happen. I'm pretty certain the old *ghosts* of the past are long since gone. But ..." she shook her head and lowered her voice, adding, "... don't be too eager to announce you've visited the site." She accepted the scroll, putting it back in its place. She turned her head, looking over her shoulder at Lucian. Pursing her lips in thought, she stared at him briefly, then left the counter. She approached a shelf and selected a book. "Read this. It's compiled from many of the older legends. It should illustrate why the superstitions exist about that monastery."

The Rift - *Beginnings*

Lucian accepted the book. Reaching into his back pocket, he started to pull out a few bills.

"No, no. You've brought me many an item over the years. Keep it." She pushed his hand away.

"Thank you." He looked at Nadia, unsure of himself. It was a rare thing for someone to be ... *nice* ... especially to him. A smile crossed his face. "Thank you ... my friend."

There were a couple of more stops, before Lucian made it home. Soon enough, he sat back in a chair to read the book. It told of rituals performed, dark rituals. Many were traced prior to the time of Vlad Tepes, better known as Vlad the Impaler. Many died during these rituals.

Lucian gathered that the sacrifices were conducted to obtain human blood. Despite the warmth of the fire, he felt a little chilled. Science was not well advanced during the Dark Ages, but – sacrificing people for their blood – impaling them to hasten their *ascent* to heaven? A shiver ran down his spine at some of the stories. He placed a bookmark to return to a section about the Szekelys people and closed the book.

Something about the Szekelys' people ...

There was something familiar about it, some vague reference.

Oh well.

Having returned from his last trip with only the one scroll, Lucian dedicated himself to concentrating on the magic. Experimenting, he found he could tailor certain spells to better fit modern components. Also, with practice came an ease of casting. He retained a few spells, usually ones to change his appearance for amusement. His *push* spell was a permanent fixture, more so once he figured out how to consciously control the amount of force he applied.

As he gained power, he knew he needed a better living arrangement. He couldn't count on privacy near town and

Vaughn Collar

trekking to the monastery was not a hike he wanted to experience daily. A trip to Bucharest showed a few new areas, mostly appearing to be uninhabited. He returned to a spot he had found during an earlier trip.

A wide shoulder offered a convenient pull off. He stepped out and stretched. A gap in the low brush hinted at a dirt trail leading into the dense forest. Lucian took in a deep breath and a heavy mist reminded him of a warm, rainy day. He could hear water rushing from somewhere down in the small valley. Stepping between the trees, the light darkened, seeping around him, and the dense canopy soaked up the morning sun. Rustling announced nervous, small animals. After a quick glance at his car, he stepped deeper into the darkness.

Maybe ... let's see where this goes.

Though in good shape for his age, he needed a few breaks over the next couple of hours. There didn't seem to be much in the way of wildlife for a brown, yellow, and red canopy kept the forest floor dark and cool. The sunlight only occasionally filtered through to look as if a spotlight was shining down.

The valley flattened out where another creek was joining the one he was paralleling. Where they met, a pond had formed. Several places would have been perfect for tents. The water was crystal clear and cold. The mountaintop wasn't too far away as Lucian could see the trees thinning out at the higher elevations.

"I wonder ... does someone own this land?" he murmured aloud. "Need to check on that in town. If no one does ... this is perfect. Solitude, water ... yeah." He checked the time and figured he had an hour, maybe a little longer, before heading back to his car.

He resumed his climb and soon reached the forest edge. The summit was a large meadow barren of trees. Pockets of snow remained in shaded places. Rhododendrons formed a pink carpet

The Rift - *Beginnings*

in this alpine setting, along with blueberry bushes dotting the meadows. A perfect place to practice spells requiring open spaces.

This is getting better every second!

His spare time was up. After walking down the mountain, he made it to his car just as it was falling dark. He pulled away from the forest, making a mental note of the location. Once home, he formed a list of things to do, items he needed to buy.

Another trip to Bucharest.

The following morning, he inquired at the municipal center about the ownership of the mountain property. To his surprise and delight, it was available and for a decent price. His first offer was accepted.

"The land has been on the market for some time," the clerk told him. "The owners had thought of a ski resort but lacked the funds to develop it."

"Pays to be in the right place at the right time." Lucian was delighted with the purchase. He now owned a place where he could research on his own terms, with no one to interfere or hide from.

The next morning, he hiked to his property. His first task was to clear an area for his cabin and then a trail to the road. Over the next several days, he purchased material in several places to avoid drawing attention. Magic helped, but building the cabin was primarily hard work. The hardest task was lugging an old wood stove he had found at an auction. But he finished his one-room haven near the end of September. Just in time as the first snowflakes were falling at the higher elevations.

He brought in the last load with the snow swirling. The storm left about a foot on the ground. The little pond soon froze over and silenced the creek. At times, he sat outside, reveling in his isolation. The only sounds were the occasional scratching of animals looking for food and muffled thumps from snow falling

Vaughn Collar

out of trees. His beard and hair grew longer and shaggier. Shortly before Christmas, he noticed his reflection.

"No one would ever recognize you, Luce." He chuckled a bit and continued with his day.

After an expensive purchase of a computer, satellite dish, and solar power equipment, he was almost self-sufficient except for food and the occasional pieces of clothing. The isolation gave Lucian the time to rummage through everything he had found at the monastery. Reading one of the scrolls, he absently wondered if the monastery itself could be purchased. An email to the property clerk came back as a negative. It was not for sale.

Well, it may not be for sale, but no one ever goes there ... so there really isn't much difference.

Through the winter months, Lucian watched endless hours of world news. The howler issue in Brazil didn't attract his interest. But the stories of children with unusual characteristics around the world, especially those originating in Romania along with the border countries of Moldova and Ukraine, did. A necessary trip into town for groceries gave him a chance to purchase a large world map. He pegged the map to a wall, adding thumbtacks for each birth.

He was marking a small town in Moldova when a memory triggered – of something. Staring at the map, he realized he was looking at places where he'd seen energy spikes the day of the reactor incident.

"Wait ... there were so many! Why aren't there more events showing up?"

He tried to pull together a picture of the wave in his mind. He looked out across the snow and sunlight glittered off the crystals. Glittering sparks?

Wait. The monastery was one of those sparks!

The Rift - *Beginnings*

He thought of the amorphous ribbon and the fractal pattern on his hands that had long since faded.

"That wave ... what was it?"

The longer he studied the map, the more his curiosity grew. How many things changed all because of whatever that energy was? Even more disturbing – who *else* had been changed?

Vaughn Collar

CHAPTER 29

Despite of or maybe because Shelly's government position kept her away, Ian made their time together a high priority. Often, even if she was in Washington, they would arrange to meet for at least a meal at a central location. It was a rare treat to spend time at one of their homes.

Holidays were a special occasion. Thanksgiving arrived and so did Shelly. She had previously mentioned there were a few things she wanted to discuss. Now, he was a little concerned not knowing if it was work or – them. She arrived with a couple of bags and a huge smile.

After dinner, Ian made tea. Sitting close to her, he said, "Let's talk. I've been curious for days."

Shelly gave him a wan smirk, before staring into her mug. "There are things happening. Things I want to talk to you about."

"Bad things?"

"Mmm ... not bad ..." – Shelly swirled her tea – "... concerning."

"Washington? Or is something to do with ... Scotland?"

"Both, but mostly Scotland ... and the explosion."

"Among other changes?"

"That's part of it. There's more ... quite a bit more. And ... part of this is you."

The Rift - *Beginnings*

Ian felt the blood leave his face. "Wait ... what? Me?"

Shelly reacted to his expression. She reached out and touched his cheek. "Oh, no. Not that! Never that. No, your abilities."

He drew a slow breath, feeling relieved. "Okay, my abilities. What else?"

She stood and paced the room. "You know about the howlers in Brazil. Then ... there's you ... the monitor lizards in Africa ... DNA changes in the Appalachians ..."

"There's more?"

"A ranch in Montana, a few horses."

"Horses? What's happening with the horses?" He rose to pour another cup of tea. Motioning at her cup, Shelly handed it to him for a refill.

"A few are different. All white, larger, more intelligent."

"More intelligent? Anything else?"

"Seems there's a troop of rhesus in Japan that are showing signs of reasoning." She glanced at Ian. "Crafting tools. Improving where they live."

"Nothing like a little renovation ..."

She glared at him momentarily before giggling.

"Okay, I'll be serious. Crafting tools. Now that *is* new."

She set her cup on the table. "A couple were witnessed deliberately striking rocks together. Like they're trying to start a fire."

"Woah! Creating fire?" Ian stood a little straighter, no longer feeling amused.

"There's more ... mosquitoes in British Columbia are five to six times larger than they should be. And ... we've received reports of children in Scotland, Romania, Ukraine ... among others ... with the same changes as the kids in Virginia."

Ian walked over, reaching for her hands. "I haven't said anything, mostly because I know how intense your job is. But ... I

Vaughn Collar

can add to your list." He guided her back to the couch and they sat. "I found a small area in the mountains with fascinating changes. Altered plants, insects, and ..." He stepped over to his fridge and withdrew a bottle. "Take a sip."

Shelly gave him a guarded look but took a small taste.

Ian watched as her expression transformed from wary to a look of wonder.

"Oh my," she said. "It's like all of my senses are better ... magnified." Her eyes widened, taking in everything. "I can hear a bee on that flower out there." She pointed at the neighbor's window. "What's in that bottle?"

"Water from a stream. In the area I just told you about." He watched, fascinated, as Shelly took in the sensations.

"It's gone!" She frowned. "Like someone just flipped a switch."

Ian gasped. "Already? It lasts about ten minutes for me." He placed the container back in the fridge. "The children in other countries ... is the news about them getting out?"

She stared at the fridge longingly for a another sip. "No. Some countries are a little better at silencing the media. Most of the news is actually filtering through the scientific community. Same changes we're having here. Eye and hair coloring, altered genetic markers. The oldest showing heightened cognitive reasoning at a very young age."

"There's more?"

She nodded. "What I'm about to tell you is just coming out. A child here in Virginia and a couple overseas born the same week are showing a faint bluish-tint to their skin, mostly in their hands." She glared at him. "So, how are things with you?"

He studied her, not sensing anything behind her question other than caring. His nagging feelings about her being snared within the government bureaucracy somewhat faded. Therefore, he decided it was time to take her to the pond. *How to answer her*

The Rift - *Beginnings*

question ... ah. He spotted the bottle of wine he purchased earlier. *Perfect!*

Muttering a spell, he focused on the bottle. It rose slowly and hovered. After a subtle hand motion, the bottle glided effortlessly to the coffee table, gently setting itself down. Another glance into the kitchen and two wine glasses made the same trip. Then one last look for the corkscrew. His concentration broke when Shelly clapped her hands.

"Ian, that's great!"

He smiled. "I've been practicing. A lot! Those glasses are probably the eighth or ninth set." He pulled out the cork, pouring them each a glass. "Does this answer your question?"

"It does." She paused for a moment. Then an impish grin creased her face. "Is that all you can do?"

They arrived at his well-used campsite shortly after noon. For late fall, the weather was gorgeous - clear and cool - comfortable for a good walk. Ian took the bottle from her pack and knelt at the water flowing from the woods.

"This is the creek?" Shelly asked.

"Yes. Just in case, I marked it." He made an intricate gesture at a nearby oak. A large *"A"* was carved into the trunk of a tree. "I used an alpha symbol to mark my spot ... my ... *sanctuary* would be a better word." He motioned back at the water. "This far down, it's diluted a little. Should be refreshing without the interesting side effects."

They followed the faint foot trail and soon arrived at the pond. Under the shade of the trees, it was cool enough that both shivered a little.

Vaughn Collar

"I should be tired, but ..." – she shook her water bottle – "... it's like you said. Refreshed." She stood, clearly taking in the view.

Ian felt a familiar sensation, an awareness of an awakened life force. "Do you feel anything?"

She shrugged. "I do, but I don't know what." She glanced around. "Ian! These flowers ... they shouldn't be in bloom. Not in late November." Her brow furrowed. "How high are we?"

"Not sure. Maybe thirty-five-hundred feet or so. Why?"

"There should have been several nights of frost. Maybe even a little snow."

"Honestly, I think it's part of the magic. Everything grows ... bigger, larger, stronger." He felt the force approaching and gently touched her arm. "Don't move. Just follow my lead. There's something you need to see."

He slowly motioned for her to look up as a bald eagle soared in just above the outstretched cattails. It landed on a thick branch in a nearby tree, staring down at Ian as he made a soft whistle. The eagle cocked its head to one side, and with a single flap of its huge wings, landed on his outstretched arm.

Shelly's eyes were large, reflecting her amazement. She took a couple of steps back.

The eagle moved a little farther up Ian's arm, lowering its head and rubbing its beak against his cheek.

"Say hello to my new friend." Ian gently scratched the bird's neck. "She won't bite."

"She?"

"Yes."

The eagle issued a soft two-tone chirp.

Ian nodded.

"You can ... communicate?"

"Mmm, in a way. More like I can *feel* what she wants."

The Rift - *Beginnings*

Another soft sound from the eagle.

"Come closer. She wants to greet you."

Shelly held out her hand.

The bird uttered another chirp before gently touching Shelly's hand with her beak.

Ian whispered something and the bird hopped to the ground. "Kneel down, Shelly."

Shelly hesitated then knelt.

The bird, more at home in the air, was a little awkward on the soft dirt. It took a strange hopping-step closer to Shelly. Slowly, it stretched out its wings and embraced her.

Shelly's eyes teared. "It's hugging me," she whispered. Shelly gently lifted her hands, caressing the bird.

The bird tilted its head to momentarily rest it in her hand, eyes closed. Hopping back, it pulled in its wings and uttered a loud cry before taking off. It circled once, making the same cry as it soared toward the distant ridge.

They stood, arms around each other, watching as the bird disappeared into the whispery clouds.

"What is this place?" Shelly's smile lit like a beacon, tears still trickling down her face.

Ian gently wiped them away. "This valley is special. A haven away from the world. Every time I come here, I leave believing I can conquer anything."

"And it stays warm? How's that?"

"I'm going to guess it's the magic. If I concentrate, and I mean *really* concentrate, I can see an energy wave hanging over the pond." He gently smiled. "There's nothing to worry about. I just wanted you to see for yourself."

She nodded. Cuddling deeper into his arms, she whispered, "Only way I would have believed you. It still feels like a dream."

Vaughn Collar

He held her tighter, loving her. He looked out at the horizon, and the sun was just touching the distant mountains.

"There's one more reason I wanted to come here with you."

"Oh?"

Ian knelt, taking Shelly's hand in his.

She looked down just as he revealed the ring. Her tears fell as she whispered, "Ye ... ye ... ye ... yes!"

The Rift - *Beginnings*

CHAPTER 30

Between grading papers, wedding plans, and finding a new home, Christmas arrived before they were ready. Several weeks of wonderment and excitement left them closer than ever. Unfortunately and all too soon, Shelly had to return to work, which left Ian with time to contemplate their future.

Finding a house took on a whole new meaning once they figured in his abilities. No neighbors would be ideal. What they found was even better. In Charlottesville, they located a house on five-acres bordering a state park. The location was about as perfect as they could hope, and Ian was only an hour from work, Shelly two.

Though their new home was in a great location, Shelly kept her apartment in Washington. She could commute most days. However, her work was unpredictable, and frequently, her meetings lasted long into the evening. Keeping the apartment just made sense.

They walked the property several times before deciding on it. On the second inspection, Ian found a small hut that the former owner had used as a tool and storage shed. He would, however, convert it into a lab.

Vaughn Collar

"Way out here?" Shelly questioned. "Why? You gonna walk through snow or rain?"

Ian chuckled. "I'm thinking it'll be safer. You wouldn't want me to accidently blow up our new house ... would you?"

Shelly sighed, knowing he was right. However, she did not particularly like it. But she changed her mind once Ian discovered a *move earth* spell, allowing him to tunnel underground. Once finished, he could practice to his heart's content and no one would know.

Shelly was able to convince the right people to set up an office for her at home. Security measures demanded her computer to not be connected to the internet. Therefore, a team from Washington installed a satellite antenna. Nominally, this was for Shelly to monitor news from around the world. While true, the feed would also alert her if someone had a line on Ian. She was well aware of what would happen should his abilities be discovered – especially by people in Washington.

With a secure place to work, Ian spent his free time filling in his spell book. As he worked on deciphering more of the staves, one spell proved to be troublesome, mostly for material. Most bats were on the endangered lists, and the few places they were found were off-limits to the public.

So how am I going to get my hands on bat guano ... or is that really what it says?

He took a long second look. The words still didn't translate clearly, but – gunpowder?

Hmm, that's even worse. It's illegal. Better yet, how do I get my hands on gunpowder? A college prof with a gun? Hah!

He followed the weather, waiting for the right moment. There was a spell he had recently deciphered and was eager to try. A late

The Rift - *Beginnings*

spring thunderstorm was in the forecast. On his way home, he could see the clouds rapidly darkening. He waited until the storm was directly overhead. Rain pelted in slanted sheets, soaking him. He stared at the pouch with his components and smiled. This was exactly what he wanted. He pointed at the dark clouds with the copper rod.

"*F*ULMENATE*!*"

A long, jagged bolt streamed up from his hand and into the storm. The noise was deafening as the force drove him to one knee, vivid stars swimming in his vision.

"Yes!!"

The power coursing through him could become addictive. His senses, not just the normal five, were more intense. His magic power had just increased. Now, he could feel others' moods, and occasionally, their fleeting thoughts. He often exercised his ability when eating lunch in the common area. The stronger their desires, the deeper he could delve. He honed his ability to ignore distractions. Even so, it was rare to sense anything without concentration.

On a warm Saturday afternoon, he and Shelly took a trip to Roanoke. There were a few second-hand stores Shelly wanted to visit, and Ian could always find a book covering local history. They walked oblivious to others passing by. A quaint, little deli beckoned them, offering sweet baked goods, fresh-made sandwiches, and a wide selection of teas.

They picked seats outside to enjoy the warm sunshine. Ian lifted his cup to take a drink and a dark, intense emotion drew his attention. The hatred he felt was as if a black sheet had just been thrown over him. He glanced around and spotted the source, a man sitting at the edge of the patio.

Vaughn Collar

"Ian, what is it?" Shelly asked.

He tapped his ear, letting Shelly know he was *hearing* something. He focused on the individual. Beyond the surface thoughts about his meal, the man was furious. Ian could *sense* another person in the man's thoughts.

That asshole! The man's mood intensified. So strong were his feelings, Ian felt nauseous.

What is with this guy? Ian reached into his mind, casting his telepathy spell. The thoughts of everyone around him threatened to flood his mind with a cacophony of sound. He focused and singled into the man's thoughts. He felt the man comforted by –

Oh shit! He has a gun!

Ian scribbled 911 on a napkin and slid it to Shelly. She looked at him with wide eyes. Ian motioned at the man and formed a gun with his hand. Shelly paled as she left her seat for a quieter spot to make the call.

Ian reached into a small pouch of spell components. Finding a smaller bag, he carefully poured the contents into his hand.

The man stood, reaching into his pocket. The sense of violence growing deeper into his soul with a hard and sharp emotion.

Ian swept his hand at the man, and the sand sprinkling across the patio. "DORMINATE," he whispered.

The man with the gun fell. Unfortunately, so did two others. A couple not far away stumbled and stretched with profound yawns. The three on the ground snored loud enough that Ian could hear them some twenty feet away. He chuckled and listened as another man nearby laughed.

Shelly sat, her shoulders shaking with laughter.

Sirens screamed and a police car arrived. Two officers hurried to check on the fallen. As one officer knelt to check for a pulse, the sleeping person moved just a little before resuming to snore. The other officer looked on with incredulity.

The Rift - *Beginnings*

"They're asleep?" the standing officer asked. "How ... how the hell does someone just fall asleep?"

The kneeling officer was looking intently at the man Ian had targeted. "Recognize him?"

"Nope." The standing officer knelt and rummaged through the man's jacket. "Woah. Gun!"

The officer's eyes narrowed. "I'll be damned. It's the Snake. Looks like we've got a little parole violation here ..." He motioned at the gun.

"Uh, wake him or just shove him in the car?"

The first officer laughed.

Ian reached for Shelly's hand. They sat back and watched the show.

"Ian?" she whispered. "Was that ..." – she slightly motioned with one hand – "... you?"

He nodded. "Yep. I felt the guy's mood and searched a little deeper."

"Felt his mood? What?"

Ian lowered his voice enough that Shelly had to lean closer. "I can sometimes *sense* things. Like strong emotions. If I concentrate, I can get a word or a thought, here and there."

Shelly raised a single 'brow, then made a motion to keep talking.

"It has to be pretty strong. He positively radiated *anger*. I cast a spell to dig deeper. He was on his way to a killing, or at least, preparing for one."

Their desire for window shopping had faded, and they decided to return home. Ian now felt more confident about his abilities. Being able to use them for good felt – good. So many of the spells were offensive in nature, with the *lightning* spell being the most dangerous.

Vaughn Collar

But, Ian reflected, *the world was still a dangerous place.* At least the global war had ended. The radioactive wastelands of India and China constantly reminded everyone of the dangers of nuclear war. Now, though, small scale clashes remained. Many of the larger cities were in the grip of more-or-less constant gang warfare. Chicago, Los Angeles, and Detroit were no different than Rome, Moscow, and Baghdad.

Hmm ... maybe I should keep a couple of offensive spells around after all. Having to use spells like this in a city as small as Roanoke is a little disturbing.

"Shel ... how bad is Washington?" Ian ruffled through his student's paper. The assignment was to compare modern domestic issues with ancient Rome.

"Bad?" Shelly turned after checking a pot on the stove.

"You know ... gangs?"

Her mouth twisted into a frown. "Not good. We have to make provisions in budgets ... in pretty much all departments for security. Why?"

"Well, umm ... because of what I can do."

"Can do?" she asked. "Some of your spells are ... dangerous?"

Ian chuckled. "Oh, yeah. Uh ... given time to refresh, I could probably take out, oh ... a battalion or so."

Her eyes widened. "That's a thousand ... really?"

Ian grew serious. "Yes, really. I haven't deciphered a tenth of what's on those staves. If there are spells that are as dangerous as what I've already cast ... I don't know."

Shelly pulled out the bread and closed the fridge. "Like what?"

Ian leaned back. "Um, let's see. There's a lightning bolt I can create. A few spells allow me to create and manipulate fire. Some

The Rift - *Beginnings*

are subtle, but ..." An impish grin crossed his face and he whispered a few words.

Shelly screamed as she was lifted a foot off the floor. "Wha ... eeeh! Ian! Warn me next time!" She glared at him.

"I would never hurt you. I was just showing off, but ... take that spell and, oh ... watch what happens when I lift a howitzer ... or two or three. Which brings me to my next point. Have you heard of anyone else like me?"

"No, not at all. But then, we really haven't been looking. I've been trying to keep the search away from ... people doing *strange* things."

"Fair enough and thanks. I'd rather not become a human guinea pig."

"Me either!" She paused. "Promise me something."

"Okay. What am I promising?"

"Never use your powers in public. NSA would be on you faster than a gossip columnist on a rumor in Hollywood."

They looked at each other before busting out in laughter.

When he could finally string words together, he said, "Nice analogy! Can I keep that?"

"No way! That's all mine!"

Vaughn Collar

CHAPTER 31

Christmas was never meaningful for Lucian as he had nothing to celebrate. His early childhood memories were of cold nights and hungry days. Romania was recovering from the incompetence of a totalitarian government, along with the destruction brought by the war. As such, it remained a backwater country in Europe. Petroșani, his hometown, was moving forward. Continued global warming had shut down the only real industry the town had – coal mining. As jobs disappeared, so did the people. Tourism was now the main source of income.

Lucian realized he was somewhat better off than most of his peers. He had known and lived with his parents – at least until his teen years. His father died in 2036 to government protestors, his mother soon after to AIDS. Lucian was left homeless at fifteen. A kind principal allowed him to finish school even though he lived on the streets. His grades were among the best in his class, and he applied for a scholarship mostly as a dare. To his intense surprise, he was awarded a full ride at a nearby college.

Advancing far in life was both luck and a testament to his academic abilities. Since most of his existence was a personal hardship, his ability to feel empathy had faded. Now alone, he felt rewarded and fulfilled for maybe the first time in his life.

The Rift - *Beginnings*

His small cabin provided him with all the comforts he needed. The only addition was a lab and more importantly, space. Using mostly magic and hard labor, he dug and created an underground workshop. Part of the room was an airtight alcove for storing ancient scrolls and tomes.

The first use of his lab was to create something to preserve the scrolls. It took about a week and when finished, the scrolls were protected inside a glass case. They were also protected from fire as he accidentally discovered by carelessly shoving a mixing bowl onto a burner. Nothing happened to the bowl and it wasn't even hot to the touch. But applying the mixture to the scrolls would make them fireproof.

Hmm, that could come in handy ... yeah!

The mountaintops were perfect for practicing spells requiring large, open areas. He was a little concerned about satellite coverage. Not that a satellite would be able to see him directly, but a bright flash from something like one of his fire spells could possibly trigger sensors to target his mountain a little more intensely.

What I need to do is determine when the satellites' windows occur.

Between buying lab equipment from three different suppliers and finding information about satellite coverage, he stayed a little under a week in Bucharest. He obtained the orbital windows for the satellites that could potentially detect his spell work. As the winter months passed, Lucian worked his way through his collected material. His progress was slow, very slow. Several times, he spent a week or more on a single spell, figuring out how to use it in multiple scenarios. The snow fell, piling high enough to hide the cabin from casual inspection – though he didn't expect visitors. Not on this mountainside.

His spell repertoire steadily increased as did his overall knowledge of magic. Most of the month of January, he remained

Vaughn Collar

busy studying a tome that showed how to imbue magic into items – such as rings.

Ah, yes! The ring from the monastery.

Rummaging through a couple of trunks, he found the ring. Turning it over, he checked for inscriptions or markings.

Nothing ... good. Okay, what spell then? Maybe one I need quick ... ah yeah. Disguise.

The spell altered his appearance and his clothes. He could appear a foot shorter or taller, gain or lose half his body weight, even look female.

Good one, Luce. Should help that I've worked on some different personas.

The first spell he cast prepared the ring for accepting a spell. A quick touch verified it was successful. He could see the aura from the ring. Carefully, he cast the alteration spell, concentrating on every word of the transference of power. A small pulse of light signified the spell was successful. The ring now radiated with magic.

Donning the ring, Lucian concentrated – *long, blonde hair, gain a few kilos and a few centimeters –*

He held out his arms to watch as his dark skin changed to light. A glance at a mirror showed him exactly who he was thinking of. His wavy, blonde hair now rested on his shoulders.

"Yes!" He almost yelled. "It works."

Lucian uttered the reversal command and his appearance reverted to normal. As he changed back, he felt the power in the ring vanish.

What did I do wrong?

He double checked the tome and a footnote on the next page told of another spell that had to be used at the same time. He riffled through the pages and found it. The spell would make the magic cast on an item permanent until released.

The Rift - *Beginnings*

Too fast, Luce. Slow down.

The materials needed would require another trip to Bucharest. Just the thought of trudging through the snow and navigating the many curves and steep slopes made him tired.

No ... not until winter is over. This can wait.

Lucian's former life receded in his memories as he mastered his magic skills. He might teach again, someday. But it would be on his terms – and only his terms. For now, refining his skills and increasing his power was what drove him. Sometimes, this drive was all-encompassing to the point of forgetting to eat or sleep.

By spring, Lucian had learned such difficult and exotic spells that he was amazed by what he could do. After weeks of heavy concentration, the shifting seasons and dripping water grabbed his attention. He sat in his favorite chair and watched as a beam of bright sunshine flowed through the barren trees, reflecting off the white snow. A soft whoosh echoed as snow fell hitting the ground. He stood and peered outside.

Maybe a little fresh air would feel good.

He walked outside for the first time in over a month. The temperature was above freezing, and the warm sun felt good. He stayed outside for a while, enjoying the change of season.

And weather ... hmm. Good time to try the spell from the night before last.

The spell was capable of controlling the environment – to a small degree. He stepped inside to memorize the spell. An icicle hanging from his roof would provide the material component.

After locking it in his mind, he walked back outside. His target was a group of trees dripping with melting snow. He cast the spell, attempting to lower the temperature. The dripping stopped almost

Vaughn Collar

immediately as the snow hardened into ice. One tree split from the water that had accumulated in a hollow.

Whoops! Okay, the effect is immediate. Something to remember.

Over the next few days, Lucian experimented with the spell, finding its limits for temperature control and wind speeds. He could even cause small clouds to dissipate or form in the sky. Something for him to remember.

Another spell that appealed to him as a history teacher was transforming flesh to stone or stone to flesh. The description cautioned the use of changing a living creature.

But ... flesh to stone? Wait a minute. The Medusa stories? I wonder ... maybe there was a little truth there. And if so ... what other myths have truth in their foundations?

He reflected, thinking it could make for several other avenues to explore. The main thing the winter had taught him was to make sure he had plenty of spell components. There were several times he had deciphered a spell, only to discover he couldn't cast it. Spiderwebs and such weren't difficult to find. Gemstones, however, were an entirely different matter. Lucian was fairly well off, but a profligate use of items like diamonds, rubies, and other gems would quickly run through his funds.

Finally, he had to leave for town. His pantry was rather bare, and so were the easily replaceable spell components. Oddly enough, when he thought about the trip, he couldn't keep one thought out of his mind. His favorite café would be open – and he could almost smell the aroma of a freshly grilled hamburger. Arming himself with a few components, including the ring, he left his cabin to find his car. The trip in was easy with the snow largely melted at lower elevations and only a little ice where sunlight could not yet reach the valley floor.

Leaving a small market, Lucian headed for the hotel. He planned on one more day in town before returning home. Still, it

The Rift - *Beginnings*

was a nice day, and the walk in town felt good. He passed a jewelry store, paused, and returned to the display window.

I wonder how much it would be to purchase raw gemstones?

His train of thought was interrupted. An elderly lady also stopped to look inside. Lucian doubted she could afford anything but didn't blame her for stopping. There were a few really nice necklaces on display.

A car pulled up and a man jumped out, walking swiftly to the store. He was paying attention to his phone and not where he was going. The elderly lady turned and her cane tapped an odd staccato. The man looked up at the last possible second and stumbled when he tried to avoid her.

"Watch where you're going, old woman!" he yelled.

"Oh ... I'm so sorry," she stammered.

The man's voice raised, thick with curse words.

The lady was almost in tears as the man raised his hand as if to strike her. Lucian had seen and heard enough.

"Nemernic!" he muttered under his breath, his push spell rising in his mind. "Ventilabrum!" Unintentionally, Lucian channeled his anger through the magic, adding strength.

The man screamed as he was launched from where he stood straight into the display window. The sound of shattering glass echoed off the surrounding buildings. The owner of the business rushed out, eyes opened wide as he took in the scene. Kneeling, he felt the man's neck. His face fell white.

"*Crina!* Call an ambulance!" he yelled at someone in the store.

The elderly lady was beside herself. Tears dripped as she sobbed. Lucian felt stunned but retained his composure.

"Ma'am, let me help you." Lucian let her hold onto his arm as he guided her to a bench on the sidewalk.

She sat, patting Lucian's hand.

Vaughn Collar

Seeing that the lady was merely winded and not actually hurt, Lucian left for his hotel. He walked quickly around the corner before using the spell in the ring to transform his appearance. A police car passed, not paying the least attention to the lone old man shuffling along. Lucian snuck a quick glance at the police and smiled.

Arriving at his hotel, Lucian used the cover of a large bush to resume his normal appearance. Once in his room, he opened a bottle of wine he'd purchased earlier.

What did I do wrong? That spell is only supposed to provide a small push. Maybe enough to make someone trip, but not launch someone a couple of meters!

Sipping on his wine, he thought long into the night, reviewing the scene several times. He wasn't the slightest bit concerned over the dead man. No, his concern was with the uncontrolled magic. If this simple spell could be that powerful, what could a truly damaging one do?

Tossing back the last of the small bottle, Lucian glanced at his watch. He really needed to get some sleep. A soft bed, along with the wine, relaxed him and he was soon asleep.

The Rift - *Beginnings*

CHAPTER 32

The rest of the spring semester flew by for Ian. Busy as his life was, he was still distantly troubled by the conversation with Shelly, wondering if there was someone else like him out there. *But how to find him ... or her?*

Looking through all of his material yielded no success. Sure, he had a spell to figure out if there was magic nearby, but this had a very limited range, about the size of a basketball court. The target also had to be in his line of sight.

No, that won't work.

Late one night at his school lab, Ian was working on material brought in from a nearby dig. Though North America wasn't his specialty – history was still history. And these specimens were fairly interesting, dating Native Americans to their arrival in North America, in this case from a site in Kentucky. Reaching for the next artifact shard, his hand landed on an empty table. Looking around, he spotted the set of slides on the next table over. A quick glance verified he was alone. He pulled out his pouch and stared at it.

"Viverrat."

Vaughn Collar

The set of slides rose into the air and floated across the room, and a clicking sound startled him. He grabbed the slides and looked for the source. A Geiger counter a few feet away was clicking softly.

"Students," he muttered. "How many times do I have to tell them to turn things ... wait a minute."

Ian waved the slides at the Geiger counter – silence.

Okay, not that. What else did I d ... no. "Really? PERVELLON."

The counter faintly clicked. A more powerful spell generated a quick but loud buzz. The gauge moved enough to register a count of 0.15 milliSeivert. He had to look it up. The amount was somewhat less than an average chest X-ray.

What about stronger spells? Could they actually be dangerous to cast?

He set aside the concern about self-harm with the realization he may have found a way to detect magic – with modern equipment.

"Now, if I were to set counters ... lengthen their range ... how to use this?"

Ian was a historian and archeologist not an engineer. But – he knew just who to talk to about it.

It was a rare event for Shelly to beat him home. But the fragrance of Chinese food was the first sensation registering as he walked through the door. "Hey you!" He snuck up from behind and wrapped his arms around her waist. She rewarded him with a smile, leaning against him.

"You're home late. Something happen?" Shelly started dishing food onto the plates.

"You could say that. Remember us talking about how to find another person able to use magic?"

"Yes. Why?"

"I think I have a solution. I was in my lab and used a levitation spell. When I did, a Geiger counter started clicking."

The Rift - *Beginnings*

Shelly stopped with her fork almost at her mouth. "A Geiger counter? What made you think of that?"

"I'm guessing a student left it on."

"And it clicked when you cast a spell?"

"Yes. I tried a weak one. It clicked, barely. I tried a much stronger one. It registered almost as much as a chest X-ray."

Shelly absently pushed the food around on her plate. "Magic can be detected? Damn."

Ian had to talk around a bite. "Yeah, that's what I thought. I'm guessing there's some kind of radiation emitted." He paused long enough to take a sip to wash it down. "So, got a question for you. Do we have satellites that can pick up radiation on the ground?"

Shelly looked out the window. "No, not right now. I'm not in that field, but it has come up before. Looking into monitoring old fission reactors." She took a sip of soda. "But, if you're correct ..."

They let the subject rest for the night. Though there didn't seem to be any dedicated technology for monitoring radiation – and possibly magic – it still concerned him. With the possibility of detection, he needed to be even more circumspect while casting spells.

They planned a three-day weekend in Asheville. Both had an extra day off and looked forward to relaxing and enjoying their time away from work. They left early, wanting to arrive in time for a nice dinner. Passing through a small community named Hayden, Ian felt an odd sensation. Similar to what he'd felt near the pond in the mountains. The normal background buzz, usually well below any level of sensing, increased dramatically. He felt it through his body and in his mind.

He must have made an odd noise, for Shelly sounded concerned. "Ian, you okay?"

Vaughn Collar

"I am." He closed his eyes, trying to isolate the sensation. "There's a source of magic fairly close."

"What? Are you sure?"

"Definitely. It's getting stronger."

"I just remembered." Shelly's eyes opened wide. "This is where the first child was documented with the altered DNA. There were at least four more since." She glanced at Ian. "It isn't advertised. Um, could you hand me the phone from the glove box? It's buried and behind a little latch."

Ian rummaged through the compartment until he felt a small latch under the top. Pushing it aside, a phone dropped into his hand. "Got it. And yeah, I understand about the secrecy."

She took the next exit and found a strip mall. An empty spot well away from the road was perfect.

Ian handed her the phone. "Um ... Shel? Do you think it would be possible to meet one of these children?"

She glanced at him before her face fell blank, and Ian understood that she was probably deep in thought. A smile creased her face. "Yeah, we can do that. The press doesn't really know who I am or anything about my new position." She placed a call.

Ian sat back to listen. No cars were parked near them. But the sensation of magic was growing stronger.

"Hello, Pam?"

Ian could hear a female voice, but not what she was saying.

"It's Shelly Kirk. My fiancé and I are passing through, and ... well, I haven't seen you in a while. Mind if we stop by?"

More indistinct words.

"Not for long. We're headed to Asheville for the weekend. Traffic's been light, and we're ahead of schedule."

The voice lowered somewhat.

The Rift - *Beginnings*

"No, he's trustworthy." Shelly winked at Ian. "I wouldn't have asked if he wasn't." A pause. "Great! We will be there in, oh ... ten minutes?" Another short pause. "Okay, thanks. See you in a bit."

She dug into her purse, pulling out a slender pick and something else. She opened the phone, tapped out the sim card, and replaced it with another. She handed it to Ian.

"We have replacement cards for our phones."

Ian cocked his head, 'brows raised.

"Keeps nosy people from tracking specific numbers."

Ian laughed, replacing the phone to the hidden compartment. "I guess government employment has its reasons for paranoia."

Shelly laughed. Before pulling back on the road, she entered an address into the GPS.

"Wait a minute," Ian said. "Shelly ... Kirk?"

Shelly glanced over. "The families down here know me by that name. Just a little more *paranoia* from your friendly federal employee."

They pulled into a small neighborhood and had to wait for children playing hopscotch to move before turning onto a street where the houses looked worn and the yards were less maintained. The driveway was one of the few not cluttered with a bicycle, tricycle, or outside toys.

The house was maybe the most worn for this block, but not by much. The backyard seemed small, but it was not clear where the yard ended and the dense woods began. Ian's senses were now buzzing loudly. Intense magic was close – very close.

Shelly paused and whispered, "Just follow my lead." She rang the doorbell.

A woman, maybe thirty by appearance, glanced through the drapes – noise from the locks and the door opened.

"Ms. Kirk! Come on in."

Vaughn Collar

They entered and Ian looked around. The furniture was old, the rug in the living room frayed at the edges. But everything was neat and clean. Finger paintings dominated one wall, clearly made by someone young. A baseball glove hanging from a chair was the only hint of perhaps another child.

A giggle caused Ian to look down. A little girl peeked around her mother's legs, curiosity brightening her face. Deep, purple eyes stared back at Ian in wonderment.

"Momma, who is this?" she asked, pointing at Ian. Her high-pitched voice sounded like bells chiming or birds chirping.

Ian knelt. "My name is Ian. Who might you be?"

The little girl giggled. "I'm Hope."

Ian took her slender hand in his and gently shook it. "Pleased to meet you, Hope."

His senses were fully alert. He had never felt such a strong concentration of magic. Looking at her was like watching a sunrise, so bright and powerful was her aura.

Shyly, she ducked back around her mother's legs, still giggling.

Pam looked down. "I've never seen her act like this. Usually, she waits on the couch or runs to her room."

"She's grown so much," Shelly remarked. "Especially her hair."

Ian studied her more intently. Her hair fell to the small of her back, a deep, glossy black. When she moved, it resembled silk drapes flowing in a breeze. The tips of her fingers had a faint bluish tint – almost not visible. So too were her cheeks with just the faintest tinge of blue instead of the normal pink.

Ian glanced at Shelly.

She was smiling at the way Hope was taking to Ian. Meeting his eyes, Shelly winked as if to say *you're doing good.*

Ian nodded. He could feel his senses reacting to Hope's presence – the magic in his system almost boiling.

The Rift - *Beginnings*

"Can I get you something to drink? Water ... a soda?" Pam asked.

"Water would be fine," Shelly replied. "Ian?"

"Um, yeah water would be great. Thank you."

Hope spoke up. "Momma, can I sit with Mr. Ian?"

"Why don't you ask him?"

Hope turned her deep purple eyes to Ian. He held out his hand and helped her onto the couch to sit beside him. Pam returned with full glasses.

"I swear," Pam said. "I've never seen her like this."

Shelly and Ian exchanged a glance.

"Pam ... there's another reason we stopped by. Ian?"

Ian smiled. "This might explain her reaction." He turned to Hope. "Watch this." He whispered a few words and held out his hand. One by one, a string of colored lights puffed out. Trailing a finger in a circling motion, the lights formed a ring, floating in a circle above his hand. He brought the lights down to Hope, gently taking her hand, allowing the lights to form a circle above hers.

Hope's eyes brightened. She giggled.

Suddenly, the lights disappeared.

"Where'd they go?" Hope asked.

"Pam, this is our secret. Ian has gained abilities just like Hope. He can sense things."

"Things?" Pam asked.

Shelly nodded. "Yes. Like Hope ... and her magic."

Ian chimed in. "We were on the highway when I felt the sensation. It grew stronger the closer we got. I asked Shelly if there was something special around here and she remembered Hope."

Hope tugged on Ian's arm.

Ian cast another simple light spell.

Pam silently cried. The tears ran down her face, tracing along the lines formed by her smile. "I'm so sorry ..." She wiped them

Vaughn Collar

away the best she could. "This is so much to take in. Lance and I knew she was special, but ... not like this."

Hope saw her mother's tears, hopped off the couch, and ran to her. "Momma, are you all right?"

"Yes, sweetie. Maybe never better." She reached down, picking her up in a big hug. Wiping her eyes, she looked back at Ian. "What is it you sensed?"

Ian smiled. "Magic. Strong, intense magic."

Pam straightened a bit. "If I hadn't seen it for myself, I'd be throwing you out. But ... you've confirmed what Lance and I have been thinking. Hope, show Mr. Ian."

Hope's eyes grew large. "Really?! Okay." Hope sat quietly with a look of intense concentration. One small light and then another appeared in front of her. She reached out her hand, and the two lights slowly merged into one before landing on the table. "Look, Momma!"

The light swayed for a couple of seconds before blinking out.

Hope yawned. "Tired, Momma." The little girl was asleep within seconds.

"It tires her out," Pam whispered.

Ian nodded. He gently reached out to brush a lock of hair away from Hope's eyes. Just for a moment, he stared. Looking at Pam, he nodded and placed a finger to his lips.

The three talked for a few minutes with Ian promising to return.

At the door, Shelly turned to Pam. "I didn't ask. Where's Lance?"

"At work," Pam replied. "Things are a little tight, so he's working two jobs. If Hope was like other children ... well, maybe she could attend daycare. But ... we're doing okay."

Shelly and Ian read each other's thoughts as they agreed to do what they could to help.

The Rift - *Beginnings*

"When I get back to Washington," Shelly whispered, hugging Pam, "I'll see if I can do something."

Pam's eyes filled with tears.

"We have ways to help. Hope will be safe, trust me." Shelly reached for Ian's hand.

He added, "If you ever need anything, anything at all, please call me." He handed Pam a business card.

They sat in the car, looking back to see Pam waving. The remainder of the trip remained quiet, and they arrived in Asheville in time for dinner. They were strangely silent during their meal, both lost in thought. Once alone in their room, Ian broke their trance.

"Shel, did you get a good look at Hope? You know ... besides her eyes and hair?"

She frowned. "No ... why? Did I miss something?"

Ian chuckled. "I noticed something, but not sure if Pam wanted anyone to see."

"And ...?"

"Hope's ears."

"Ears? What's wrong with her ears?"

Ian took a long, slow breath. This wasn't going to be easy. "Her ears, well ... they come to a fairly sharp point." He touched the top of his own.

Shelly looked puzzled. "Okay. And this is important ... because?"

"Let's talk a little about mythology."

Shelly blinked. "What does mythology have to do with Hope?"

"All ancient mythologies have some similarities. Magic is one. We've told ourselves for years that magic isn't real." He shook his head with a slight smirk. "We know better ... don't we?"

Shelly nodded.

Vaughn Collar

"Many of these mythologies have legends of magical creatures. Fey creatures ... such as faeries. I'd swear some of the insects in my little glade are turning into faeries."

Shelly looked frustrated. "Ian, get to the point. Hope's ears?"

"What creature do you think about when you think of a creature with strangely colored eyes, an affinity for magic, and pointed ears?"

Shelly held a blank stare for only a moment, then her eyes flared. "Elves? Oh my god!"

"Yeah ... elves. It fits with everything that's going on, doesn't it? We have insects that are turning into faeries. Magic seems to be returning. And now we have children that will live for a couple hundred years and resemble elves. Evolution is going crazy."

Shelly sat back and Ian could almost see her mind racing. His thoughts were running also. Just then, he had a horrifying thought. He stood and paced the floor. "I just thought about something. The howlers, in Brazil? They're changing too."

Shelly nodded.

"There's another race of beings existing in pretty much all of western mythos. Goblins or ogres or whatever you want to call them. It fits, think about it. Those monkeys are showing traits of cruelty. Not just aggression to protect the troop. No, they are showing aggression as if they're enjoying it. And at least one is displaying signs of awareness of death and spirit. Remember the one that looked at the head of the older one they killed? He stared at it before closing the eyes."

"I remember. This is so much more than we thought. I think I need to get back to Washington. Tomorrow."

"Yeah, I know ... dammit. So much for the weekend." He stopped pacing and sat on the arm of her chair. "If someone starts connecting these dots ... there will be a stampede to control."

The Rift - *Beginnings*

She wrapped an arm around his. "Ian, it's not just the events. I have *you* to protect. I'm not losing you ... no way." She stood and they embraced.

Ian pulled back just enough to look into her eyes. "Shelly, this definitely connects to the reactor incident. However, I haven't the foggiest about what actually happened. But the results are plain. Whatever I can do to help, let me. I'm an integral part of this now."

They stood, holding each other. It was a long time before they went to bed.

Vaughn Collar

CHAPTER 33

Richard Coleman lived peacefully in his ordinary world. Never noticed anything unusual. Never asked to volunteer. He wanted nothing to do with others. Never expended more energy than what was absolutely necessary. He felt all was right with his little world, just another analyst at the CIA, lost amid the galaxy of other analysts. His job was to find nuggets of useful information. He sometimes wondered if he had ever found anything worthwhile. He reasoned that he must have found something – something worth keeping his paychecks coming.

This day, he happened to be in the right place at the right time and be the right person to understand what he found. Taking a sip of his second cup of tea, he wistfully remembered coffee. Forced to switch when coffee became more expensive than caviar, he found green tea was sufficient. Not great, but sufficient. It had caffeine, his fuel to push through the day.

He sifted through mountains of information, looking for items and events around the world deemed strange and unusual. With the patience of a monk, and about the same personality, along with a touch of OCD, he was perfect for the position. Eight hours daily, he added to a database filled with words. He sorted the data by

The Rift - *Beginnings*

dates to see if strings of events would connect. Rarely did he find those strings.

Over the past month, however, the data was starting to show some similarities between events seemingly unrelated. He briefly scanned reports of howler monkey activities in Brazil and odd sightings of huge mosquitoes in British Columbia. Individually, neither generated significant interest. Today, however, two more stories crossed his path. One was of strange incidents with rhesus monkeys in Japan, another about a rapid decrease in monitor lizards in Africa.

"Oh yeah, more unsubstantiated rumors," he thought out loud.

Sequestered in his small office, he often vocalized his thoughts. As he added these reports to his database, he was struck by the sudden appearance of other odd events that he couldn't quite trace back in time in order to *connect the dots*. The only thing he could tie together was that none were more than three to four years old. Absently, he picked up his cup of tea.

"Gah, cold!"

Richard was assigned to an Eastern European section. With its economy back on track, Russia was becoming a growing concern. Since his particular assignment was watching for unusual events, he often heard others call his area *Creeps and Critters*. Now, an event in Petroşani had him wondering if unrest was hitting Romania again.

The report had noted that a man was tossed through a storefront window, killing him instantly. There were no suspects. Only an elderly woman was questioned and only briefly. One look at her was enough to cure any suspicions about her involvement. She looked like she would have trouble lifting a gallon of milk, much less tossing a full-grown man through a pane of glass. But the truly unusual event was captured on a traffic camera. The feed showed the man catapulting off the sidewalk without being touched.

His phone rang. "Hello?"

"Mr. Coleman, we need you in a meeting in ten minutes ... the main conference room."

"Very well, I acknowledge. Ten minutes."

The call ended abruptly.

"Great ... just great."

The next morning, Richard was back at his desk. The café was serving cinnamon rolls, and he had stopped to grab one on his way. Wiping his fingers, he pulled up his database. The Petroşani incident had been bugging him all night. Running through the incident several times, he was unable to discern anything unusual.

"But ... how could a ...?" No matter how many times he watched the video, he could not understand how a man was launched through a storefront.

"I wonder."

He set the system to scan for similar stories. After a few minutes, he berated himself for the loose parameters. Several hundred worldwide events remained unexplained. Far too many for an initial workload.

Okay, set the time for five years, and ...

This search cut the numbers to less than a hundred.

Still too many, but manageable.

After reviewing just a few, he tried a new *tack*. He removed any events that looked staged or resembled a prank. A strange incident in Boston grabbed his attention. Two men had become entangled in a web – a gigantic spiderweb. They were unable to free themselves and were fearful of what had made it. That is, until the web dissolved. A spiderweb in and of itself was not unusual.

The Rift - *Beginnings*

However, one strong enough to entangle two grown men and then vanish? This definitely fit his parameters.

Okay, what else is in here?

Two more events popped up. One was in – Petroşani? Then another – in Boston? Both involved someone stepping on something slippery. The one in Boston was investigated by police who never found anything *slippery*. Both incidents occurred within a week of each other.

He leaned back in his chair, thinking. Prior to the reactor explosion, he had not seen anything more than isolated incidents anywhere in the world. *But – after?* He charted the hits. Following the happenings in Scotland, a quick uptick in these unexplained events was definitive. Bizarre accidents, animals across the world – *changing?*

"What the hell does a reactor incident and these events have in common?"

He wasn't able to pursue his train of thought before the office called yet another meeting. Richard was needed for his ability to string together random events. And an unexplained, large number of events happening in Eastern Europe required his attention. Richard was one of several tasked with organizing the news to see if a clearer picture could be drawn. It would be well over a week before he was able to return to his regular desk.

When he finally walked the familiar halls of his floor, not that anything had changed, but still – the lame artwork on the walls were comforting. Arriving at his office, he sat at his computer and pulled up his programs. About a hundred new hits of strange events were logged.

"Gonna be a long day ... at least it's not terrorism."

Multiple reports of DNA analyses were tagged from routine amniocentesis procedures with the same results. And all traced back to – the reactor incident? He double checked. The women

Vaughn Collar

were pregnant and all within a small geographical area – the Appalachian range of Virginia and North Carolina.

He stood to pace and think. Making a cup of tea, he stared out his window that overlooked the parking garage. He may have been high enough up the food chain to have an office with a window, but not far enough to have a view of anything interesting. Today was worse than normal, as a cold front was passing with lots of rain. The world outside was nothing more than a blur of grays and blacks.

My, my ... aren't you cheerful today!

Laughing at himself, he picked up his cup and sat back at his desk. He stared at the screen, willing it to make sense.

Nope.

With a soft snort of derision, he pulled up a data acquisition request. The files were protected, requiring a special requisition form. Well within his security clearance, he did not expect any troubles. A second form popped up, requiring a city and the name of the clinic in question, along with the gender of the person who was the target and when the incident happened. After entering the information, he submitted the form and settled back

A loud buzzing startled him. He turned and look at his screen. It was frozen momentarily, before a highlighted warning appeared.

<u>WARNING</u>
<u>Access Denied</u>
<u>Security Level Violation</u>

He stared at the screen, confused.

Security level violation? What? For a DNA report?

Scratching his beard absently, he pulled down another tab. A quick check on his security clearance found it had not changed.

The Rift - *Beginnings*

Shaking his head, he re-entered the data and sent the requisition through again. The same message popped up.

"What? Since when are OB-GYN records ... classified?"

As he finished asking the question, the monitor fell blank.

"No, no, no! I didn't save! Dammit!" He punched in the command to reboot. Nothing happened. *Okay, try this, dammit!* He spun in his chair, reaching for the plug. He pulled it, waited a few seconds, then plugged his computer back in. Still nothing.

"What the h ..." His phone rang. "Yes?!" he answered a little too loudly.

"Mr. Coleman!" The voice didn't sound pleased.

"Yes, this is Richard Coleman," he replied, glancing at the number, which was not familiar.

"You have attempted to access information above your level. Please wait in your office. You will be debriefed." The line fell silent.

Part of him panicked. *Ten years down the fucking drain. For what? DNA records? OB-GYN shit?*

A knock on his door, loud and pre-emptory, and the door opened. A large man stood, nodding. "Mr. Coleman? Please, come with us."

Richard stood and walked out. Another man was in the hallway. Neither one struck him as being conversational. The three walked in silence to the elevators. The first man pulled out a card, inserting it into a slot above the floor selector.

Seventh floor? Oh ... what have I done? Now Richard was scared. Seventh floor was the top brass. Curiosity and fear were making a hash of his emotional state. He could feel a cold sweat forming. The elevator stopped. He was gently pushed into the hall. They turned left – Richard had expected right.

Wait, what? I'm not going to Intelligence?

Vaughn Collar

Another turn, then they stopped. The office was unmarked. The first man opened the door. "Mr. Coleman?" he asked as he motioned for him to enter.

A woman looked up from her work. "Mr. Richard Coleman?"

"Yes." Still more alarmed than anything, he sat on the lone chair in the small office.

"You can go in now. You're expected." The woman motioned to a doorway before turning back to her work.

Richard entered the room. A woman sat behind a large desk cluttered with various papers and folders. Most of the folders had stripes on one side, signifying the level of clearance needed to read them. He wasn't surprised in the slightest to see one or two marked *secret*, the rest *top secret* or higher. The woman looked to be in her early thirties. She could easily have passed as a movie star.

"Mr. Coleman," the woman said, "please, take a seat."

He sank onto a plush couch.

The woman touched a button on her desk. Within a few moments, the assistant walked in, bearing two cups of ... coffee? She handed one to the woman, the other to him. The aroma of the freshly brewed relaxed him.

"Thank you, Melissa. That will be all." She took a sip from her cup. "My name is Shelly Lang. I'm kinda new to the hierarchy here. So ... I'm curious. Why were you attempting to access my database?"

Richard's 'brows shot up. "*Your* ... database? Have I done something wrong?"

Shelly smiled. "No, not really. The database was out there to see if anyone had the, oh ... fortitude to connect the dots ... to get to it. You have done that. So ... why were you looking up that particular subject?"

"For my research. I'm tasked with searching for abnormal or unusual events. Once found, I try to figure out the who, what, when, and why. As you put it, I try to *connect the dots*. The DNA

The Rift - *Beginnings*

reports certainly fit my parameters." He took a sip of the coffee. It'd been years since his last cup.

Shelly sipped on hers then placed the cup down. "Well, I'll hand it to you. You're the only one to get as far as you have. We've been watching for people like you. Your work is fairly impressive." She turned her monitor around.

Richard saw his personal spreadsheet. His relaxed feelings vanished.

The woman sat up straighter. "Mr. Coleman ... or if you'd prefer, Richard ... I've got a proposition for you." She paused, looking like she just remembered something. "Sorry, I'm getting ahead of myself. You've already stumbled onto a few things that are entirely unknown to the general public. We'd like to keep it that way as long as we can. Toward that end, a new department was formed. I'm the director."

Richard tried to take it all in. With her words, he realized the government already knew about the strange events and likely a lot more.

Shelly continued. "Your work was brought to my attention. Thus ... the Eastern European assignment. They really didn't need you. But, it gave me time to scan through your work without blocking you out."

Richard felt a little angry at her last statement. *Purposely pushing him out of the way?*

"If you're feeling a little betrayed ... well, I'd like to say I'm sorry, but ... there are numerous security issues here. Would you rather be grilled for hours on end?" Shelly gave him a strong stare.

There's some iron behind that smile. Watch it, Richard. This lady holds your future in her hands. "I see your point ... and no, I'd rather not be grilled."

"Good. Like I was saying, your work is impressive. It is now deemed *top secret*. I know what your security clearances are. So,

Vaughn Collar

here's the offer. You transfer to my department. It will mean ... a nice pay raise, a little promotion commensurate with the raise, and oh, working one floor down from here. You'll have a nicer office ... one with a better view. Also an agency car."

Richard sat back. He never dreamed of getting to the level Shelly was offering, at least not for several years. "Okay, it all sounds great. One question."

"Yes?"

"What is so secretive about OB-GYN records?"

Richard leaned back in his chair and looked around his new office. He couldn't help but wonder at his luck. A real wood desk, not some featureless, cold metal. The warm sunshine was filtering in through the drapes, and the smell of fresh coffee brewing was – *wait, what?* A small machine sat on the counter, steam and the wonderful aroma of a fresh brew filling the room. A basket decorated his desk with a bag of pods clearly visible, along with a note.

Richard, knowing you will need the caffeine ... and congratulations on the new position. It was signed – *Shelly Lang.*

He had the same computer, though. He didn't mind, he was used to the keyboard and his database was something he had created, down to the encryption. He had just signed on when a soft knock diverted his attention.

"Uh ... come in?"

"Good morning, Mr. Coleman." Shelly held a cup of something steaming.

"Please ... Richard."

"Richard, then." She nodded. "I see you've made it through the briefing?"

He smiled. "Yes."

The Rift - *Beginnings*

She motioned at one of the chairs on the other side of his desk. He nodded.

She sat and placed her cup on a coaster. "I know this may seem fast, and this is your first day, but ... I'd like to go over your assignment."

He opened a drawer, looking for pen and paper.

"I think you'll find all the notes you need in the file. For now, let's just discuss things."

Shelly's eyes told him everything. It was time for him to earn his new pay. He set his cup down, leaning back a little in his chair.

"There are some changes happening around the world. You came across some of them in your searches."

His 'brows narrowed a little. "You mean the OB-GYN stuff?"

Shelly nodded. "Among others. You've also noted the changed mosquitoes and the hyper-aggressive howlers in Brazil." She leaned back, taking a sip. "Your search patterns show just how thorough you've been. Tracing the timelines back to the reactor sets off the first alarms. The DNA find cemented it. Now, I will explain the high security requirements." She paused, giving him a flat look.

"I understand completely. Nothing past that door," he said, motioning.

Shelly smiled. "Okay, this should fill you in a little more." She walked over to a large viewing screen. She grabbed a remote. A picture showed the Earth seen from orbit above Europe. "Note the date and time."

Richard looked and it was dated May 2, 2076. *The date of the reactor explosion?*

Shelly pressed *Play*.

A few seconds passed, and a bright light filled the sky above Scotland. A light shot from the ground directly into space, receding so fast that it disappeared.

Vaughn Collar

"Let me start it over and slow it down. I keep forgetting the light distraction. Focus on the ground, please." She restarted the video.

Richard kept his attention on the ground. Soon after the explosion, nebulous bands of light expanded out with the shockwave. Shelly zoomed in, and a phenomena creating violent changes in pressure soared through Scotland. She refreshed the screen and the compression, sudden and violent, increased in density, spreading out in various directions. Richard watched as the wave, speeding almost faster than light, increased in amplitude, blinking into existence across Europe – Asia – North and South America. The colored ribbons fascinated him.

"That all came from the reactor explosion?"

"Unknown," Shelly answered. "But that is one of your goals ... determine what happened. Your primary task, though, is this ... find out what changes, if any, have been created from those ribbons of light." She froze the screen and turned to face him. "Including humans, by the way."

He stared at the screen with the view stopped at the height of the light show. Points were visible on every continent.

Most in areas sparsely inhabited, if at all. Richard wondered about this. One last look before Shelly turned off the viewer.

"Humans?" he repeated, then remembered the OB-GYN records. "Oh my god!"

"Yes, DNA changes. You noticed the numerous small ribbons in the southern Appalachians? I don't find it just a coincidence. Those DNA changes correspond with those lights." She walked back to the chair and sat. "Your place in this, well, we need you to continue your strange and unusual database construction. You know ... your *Creeps and Critters*." She giggled. "Aptly named!"

Richard felt his cheeks flush. "It wasn't my idea ... but it seems to fit."

The Rift - *Beginnings*

"Indeed it does." She adjusted her skirt, leaning back. "We need to track changes globally. We also need to keep this as black as possible. Your promotion isn't officially noted. Right now, the media has no idea who you are. We want to keep it that way."

Richard nodded. He knew of several people in the agency who didn't *exist*. Just another way to hide information.

Shelly continued, "So, tell me. What have you uncovered so far?"

Richard logged in and opened his database. The incident in Romania seemed to be news to her. It took him a good hour to go over everything. Shelly proved to be a good listener, only interrupting a couple of times, asking him to repeat a point or two. Richard finished with his research into the enlarged mosquitoes.

"You now have access to my database with the children's DNA results. I'll let you go over it in detail by yourself, but for now ..." – she managed a slight shrug – "... the genes controlling the aging process have been altered. We estimate these children will have a life span of up to two hundred years."

Richard's jaw dropped. "T-t-t-two hundred?" Eyes wide, he absently looked around his office, then back at Shelly. "Now I understand the ultra-high classification."

"Can you imagine the storm if news of this leaked? There would be stories that the government was withholding an anti-aging serum."

Though his mind still reverberated with shock, Richard felt a few dots connect. "These fit within the time frame." He explained his findings about the spiderweb and the old lady in Petroșani. "I haven't been able to find a correlation between the two, but they definitely fit into the classification of unusual."

"Most definitely. Richard, I think you'll do just fine here." She glanced outside with a thoughtful look.

Vaughn Collar

Richard watched as her expression changed. Clearly, she had just made a decision.

"You need something let me know. The budget isn't unlimited, but it's a lot higher than it was." She stood and held out her hand.

Richard stood, taking her hand in his. "I won't let you down."

Shelly entered her office and locked the door. She placed her hands flat on her desk, willing them to stop shaking. She knew hiring Richard was a good move. She just hadn't expected him to uncover evidence about Ian – or someone else able to wield magic. *At least, not this soon.* She slid a chip into her phone, converting it to a secured line. She dialed Ian. He picked up on the second ring.

"Ian, I may have found another magic user."

The Rift - *Beginnings*

Chapter 34

"Yhel, think about it. What would the odds be? I'm the only one affected ... out of a few billion people? I'm only surprised it took this long."

Shelly nodded and continued to chop the onions.

Ian read over a student's papers. A couple of suspicious sniffs echoed out from the kitchen. *Onions ... oh well.* "You know, the potential for abuse is incredible. I mean, invisibility? Telekinesis? Illusions made to look real? I can just see the police report from a jewelry shop. 'Well, sir, the video shows the cases opening by themselves, merchandise floating across the room, before disappearing.'" Ian snorted a derisive laugh. "Yeah, I don't see it."

Shelly let out a chuckle. Using a towel to wipe her eyes, she answered, "I don't either. I'm glad it feels like there is only one other."

Ian looked up. "And he or she is a real winner. Falling through a window? That looks like the receiving end of a serious *push* spell. And there was no one in the camera feed except for the elderly lady."

"Ian ... can *you* do any of that?"

Vaughn Collar

"A *push* spell is easy. The rest ... just depends on what spells I memorized for the day. And the more I'm able to decipher from the staves, the wider my repertoire. Both in terms of numbers and power." He paused. "And speaking of power, whoever used that spell has some serious energy. *Push* spells are only supposed to apply a little force."

As Shelly poured the chopped onions into a skillet, they stopped talking until the sizzle died down.

"This is not good," she said.

"No, it isn't. Some of the spells I can use are pretty dangerous." He paused, a thought wavering just at the edge. "Ah ... do you still have the video?"

"Of the man flying through the window? Yeah, its on my phone ... in the outer pocket of my purse."

Ian pulled her purse off the chair and found her phone. He handed it to her and she started the video. Ian watched it several times before becoming distracted by the wonderful aroma of Shelly's goulash.

"Looks like there're a few spells involved. That's if our mystery mage is close by." He watched another run through. "Could be someone not in view. Do you have access to all the street cameras?"

"I do. Give me a second." She dried her hands before logging onto her laptop. They watched as Shelly cycled through various views of the different street angles. One showed a man staring straight at the victim and woman in question. He made an odd hand motion along with saying something. As he did, the victim was launched through the window.

"That was a spell! Guaranteed. I *know* that motion." He looked at Shelly. "That's him! That's our missing magic user. Shame we can't get a better visual."

The Rift - *Beginnings*

"Hey, at least we know." The stove beeped, letting her know dinner was ready. "Ian, write down the time. I'll see if I can get someone on my staff to enhance the image."

After dinner, Ian and Shelly spent several hours trying to figure out how to have Geiger counters installed in Petroșani. Especially without alerting anyone.

The spring semester of 2080 was a blur for Ian. He volunteered to assist at a dig in Kentucky, though it meant putting off Scotland for another year. He and Shelly felt it would be best if he kept a low profile and not travel overseas.

Shelly had her own problems to work around. The oppositional party seemed like they could win the next election, though with the economy improving, a little wind was taken out of their sails. She had no idea if they'd been briefed on her new department, or if so, what their intentions were.

While in Kentucky, Ian found very few opportunities to use magic. He brought with him only one spell book that held less powerful spells that might prove handy. By now, he was able to cast to find magic without anyone knowing, which so far had not detected anything. His calls to Shelly sounded so lonely, she made a special trip to lift his spirits.

Saturday dawned bright and sunny and humid, too humid to remain outdoors. They chose to visit the Cumberland Museum instead. Ian held up his dig pass, entering for free. Holding hands, they walked into the entry hall.

"This looks like a new building," Shelly said. The angel mural on the ceiling took her breath away.

"It is. I think the original was flooded. Not really sure."

Vaughn Collar

The animal display was fascinating. Aside from odd creatures, such as the platypus, it paid particular attention to recently extinct species.

"A Scottish Wildcat!" Shelly placed her face closer to the glass. "Such a shame. They tried so hard to keep the species around. He's beautiful."

"He?"

"Alright, maybe a she."

Ian draped his arm around her, feeling her sad mood.

The museum had been expanded recently. One of the additions was a room dedicated to artifacts from the Middle East. They meandered through the area until Ian spotted a large display of crucifixes. The majority were found in digs focused on the Crusades. Glancing around, Ian figured he could satisfy his curiosity and cast a spell to detect magic. Much to his surprise, one of the crucifixes glowed.

Ian tapped Shelly on the shoulder. "Shel, look at that cross."

"Which one?"

Ian chided himself. *Of course, she can't see it.* "Third from the left, top row. It's glowing."

"Glowing? I don't see any ..." She turned to give Ian a hard look. "Magic?" she whispered.

"Yes."

"Ian, are you nuts? Casting a spell in here?"

"I was careful. Nobody could've heard anything, and the spell doesn't require an elaborate hand motion."

One last, hard stare, then her excitement took over. "Can you tell what kind of magic it is?"

"No. I'd have to lay hands on it, run a few more tests."

A card noted the crucifix was dated back to the third century A.D. and recovered from a dig close to Konya, Turkey.

The Rift - *Beginnings*

Ian thought about it. "That ... may have been lost by a traveler. Turkey used to be the major land route from Europe to the Holy Land. Especially for members of the clergy ..."

Shelly turned to Ian. He was quiet, his eyes not focused. She glanced back at the cross, then to Ian, waiting.

His face came alive. "Eastern Europe!" he whispered. "Romania isn't that far from the old route from Greece ..." He paused while processing his train of thought. "Hmm, we need more information about Romania. Think about it."

"Petroşani is in Romania!" She laughed. "Where the other magic-user is located. You're right, we do need more information."

Ian nodded, still focused on the crosses.

"So, how do we get Geiger counters installed around Petroşani?" she whispered.

Ian shrugged. He knew they weren't going to answer that question easily. But what about that cross? *I wonder ... maybe my credentials will get me a direct look?* "Let's see if the curator will allow access."

The curator shook his head. "The atmosphere in that case is pure nitrogen and pressurized to keep the air out. I'm sorry." He ran his fingers across his mustache. "Tell you what, Professor McGregor, we periodically inspect for leaks and whatnot. Leave me your contact info, and I'll let you know ahead of time."

Ian handed over his card. "I would be in your debt. Thank you!"

Ian and Shelly toured the remainder of the museum. No additional discoveries happened along the way. Over dinner, they discussed Petroşani and how they could pinpoint who the mystery man was and how to locate him.

Vaughn Collar

The remainder of Ian's summer remained busy. The dig was funded largely due to tales of an old settlement mentioned in the Shawnee legends. Near the end of the month, traces of burnt wood in stone circles and wooden pegs with notches, along with a few pottery shards were discovered. Ian, even with magic dominating such a prominent part of his life, was still a historian at heart. Working an ancient village was exciting. He was able to put aside his magic and concentrate on the dig for the remainder of the summer.

Shelly flew back to Washington. She had some ideas in mind about Petroșani, along with potential solutions. A series of meetings led to purchasing time on an old satellite with a name from operations.

Her department combed the surface of the globe for anomalies and found a few interesting developments in Eastern Europe. Enough to justify her flying over for a face-to-face meeting.

Shortly after arriving in Vienna, she made contact with the station chief and arranged to meet for dinner. She had some time to kill, and after several charges and burdened with shopping bags, she went back to her hotel to freshen up. The restaurant was only a block away.

"Reservation for Mr. Leitner and friend," she told the maître d.

He looked at the list, nodded, and showed her to a table. She was early and was looking at the wine list when Mr. Leitner arrived.

"I hope I haven't kept you waiting," he said with a smile.

"Oh, no. I just arrived myself."

He pulled back a chair and sat.

"I don't know what Washington told you, but ... let me start with this ..." She passed him a card on which was written the initials *R.M.*

The Rift - *Beginnings*

His eyes widened momentarily. "Good to see you again, Ms. Kirk." Though they had never met, the charade had to be played out.

"You too, Karl." She reached out to shake hands.

He grabbed hers and bent to kiss it. He smiled. "It has been ... what ... three years, maybe four?" The numbers were code for *how important is this?*

"Has it been that long? Four, I believe."

"So, what brings you to Vienna?"

"A short vacation. Might want to come back, use Vienna as a starting point for traveling."

The waiter arrived to take their orders. Karl ordered for both. The waiter gave him a look, then pointed down with one hand. Karl smiled at this. "We can kill the code. He's ..." – indicating the waiter – "... one of my agents."

Shelly allowed herself to relax. Being an operative was causing anxiety. Still, this meeting was too sensitive to her personal life to trust with just anyone. "Thank you ... I've always loved this city. I came here, oh, five years ago." A sip of water. "I need your help."

He raised one 'brow. "I'm listening. Important?"

"Could be. I need to place someone in Petroşani ... quietly."

He lifted his wine glass. "I need a little more than that."

"We need to install Geiger counters throughout the town. Without publicity."

"Geiger counters? Is there a risk of radiation?"

"No risks, no. More of a detection for faint sources ... sources we are interested in locating."

"You'll need to be more specific. Petroşani was a coal town. The mines still give off a little background radiation. Not enough to be harmful. But ... enough to detect. The counters will need to be particle specific." He paused. "Is there someone trying to circumvent the European treaty on coal mining?"

"No. But ... I think you just gave me my cover. We could hide them as traffic cameras. The city ... doesn't need to know."

Karl nodded and replied, "I believe I could make that happen. Let me reach out to my contacts. In the meantime, I see our food is coming."

"How much coverage are we talking about from the satellites?" Ian asked.

"Around two, maybe three hours monthly," Shelly answered, pulling clothes from her suitcases. "I know it's not much, but any more would bring questions I can't answer."

Ian laughed. "True enough." He handed her a few hangers from the closet. "And the idea of placing someone in town was brilliant. Can you trust him?"

"I believe so. He's been a valuable asset. An operation like this shouldn't tax him or his people."

"Ah ... yeah, okay. And how many counters?"

"At least six. The highest traffic areas and several other sites with potential."

"Sounds good." He thought for a moment. "I hate that we have to wait on this other person to act. No one else needs to be injured or ... killed. I just don't see any other way."

They talked long into the night until Shelly fell asleep in Ian's arms. His dreams were littered with images of the man in Petroşani being thrown through the window.

Ian woke early. The time on the dig had reverted him to his on-site routine of working before the day's warmth kicked in. Just as well, classes were starting soon.

Careful to not disturb Shelly, he reached for his watch and turned off the alarm. He slowly rolled out of bed and padded his

The Rift - *Beginnings*

way to the kitchen. Reaching for a bowl, a slight noise startled him, accompanied by a giggle.

Shelly sat at the table, laughing, a twinkle in her eyes.

"Oh, very funny. You're on alert now? Payback's a bitch." His smile took the threat out of his statement.

He turned to the cabinets and froze. An electric sensation coursed through his soul, driving him to his knees. He could hear the faintest of sounds, feel the slightest disturbance in the air. The lights were blinding. Every one of his senses felt amplified. He looked down at his arms, his hair standing up straight. He turned to Shelly, and her eyes widened.

"Shel, what's ..."

Ian fell, pulling his knees to his chest as the pain grew. He gasped. It felt as if his soul had just been hit with a cattle prod. He screamed.

"Ian!!" Shelly lunged out of her chair, gathering him in her arms.

The sensation eased with her touch – then ceased. He sat up, shaking from the overwhelming, electrical surge. Only a distant sensation of warmth remained. Familiar – but he couldn't quite place it.

"Ian? What's happening?" Her voice trembled as tears welled in her eyes.

He reached up and wiped her cheek. "Help me up," Ian said, motioning to a nearby chair. With her help, he sat. The last vestiges of nausea slowly dissipated. "I have no idea." He took in a deep breaths. "I don't have anything to compare it to. It was like ... like my soul was being jerked around." An image of a waving ribbon of light surfaced from his memories, as did the feeling of power he had felt with the copper rod and storm and with the young child. "Remember how I was able to *feel* when we were close to Hope? The young girl in Abingdon?"

Vaughn Collar

"Yes, why?"

"That's what it felt like ... magic ... pure, strong magic. Everywhere." He shook his head, trying to ease the remaining dizziness.

Shelly stood and glanced at her laptop. "Ian, look at this."

Site after site streamed across the screen. Reports of bright lights and static, electrical charges from across the globe glowed. Power outages dotted the eastern U.S., far too many to attribute to anything natural.

"Can you get satellite data from here?" Ian asked. "Something more than the news?"

"Hold on, give me ... Ian! Your hands!"

"What?" Glowing fractal patterns were spreading across his hands and up his arms. Just like – before. "Shel, I could be wrong, but ... I think another wave just hit. Look at the globe. Bright lights lasting only a few seconds. Some up to a minute. And my hands. Even my heightened senses." He stood and walked over to a window. Nothing seemed out of place. Birds were singing, including the mockingbird in a nest just outside the window.

Shelly stood quietly, her hand on his shoulder. "I believe you. But ... what now?"

He sat with a frown, deep in thought.

Shelly proceeded to make some tea. When done, she brought him a cup.

He glanced up and smiled. "Thanks," he whispered. "My guess is, any creatures affected before likely felt this again. And if that's the case, you probably need to get your guy in Romania to work double-time installing those counters."

Her phone buzzed, startling them. "Oh shit," she cursed. "It's the president."

Ian burst out laughing. "I've never heard you say *that* before!"

The Rift - *Beginnings*

She glared at him, then laughed. "I've got to go. I'll shower at my apartment in D.C."

Ian stood and gave her a hug. "I love you. Drive safe."

She smiled and gave him a long kiss. "Love you too."

Vaughn Collar

CHAPTER 35

Lucian sat in a chair outside his cabin, watching sunbeams on the forest floor as the light pierced through the clouds ahead of a storm front. Even though it was August, a little dusting of snow on the mountaintops would not be a surprise. A good day for deep thoughts. A squirrel stopped and stared.

"No, little one. You're safe," Lucian quietly said. *But what about people?*

His conscience somewhat troubled him. Not so much about the actual killing, but why he didn't feel anything, especially remorse. He was, though, a little peeved about the rashness of his actions.

"Next time, Luce ... make sure no one can see anything."

He was sure there was no way to link the man's death to him. *After all, no one can detect magic.* With that thought, he pushed the matter aside.

"One less arrogant asshole in the world."

Justice was served, as far as he cared. The darkened path he now traveled didn't concern him. His life had been one of hardship and only rarely had he been happy. Those infrequent times were exactly that – infrequent. Losing his mother to AIDS – Ursel to the earthquake – both left deep scars. And that

The Rift - *Beginnings*

Russian vrăjitoare, that witch, Natalya - he opened up just enough to feel the bitter sting of betrayal puncture him yet again.

No, never again. Never.

The majority of his time was now spent in his lab. After building most of his equipment, he still had several boxes in one corner. A series of burners rested on a table, a new centrifuge on another with its base still needing to be mounted. Even with his workshop in pieces, he'd made good progress on a few items.

The first task was mostly a proof of ability to create a wand. Early in the summer, he'd made a trip to the foot of the mountain, searching for the perfect willow twig. Once found, he infused the twig with a spell to find magic. It took him a few tries but soon he had made his first wand. The next step was embedding the ring to hold two spells to alter his appearance anywhere from slightly to becoming a completely different person. Prepping the silver to be receptive to magic turned out to be a laborious process.

Though he considered himself to be a patient man, taking a month to make one of the potions was a little more than he wanted to spend. Even the simplest of potions required a week. An image of laboratories from various films came to mind, with bubbling liquids and multiple beakers filled with substances.

"They don't know how close to the truth they were," he mumbled and laughed.

Lucian stood at the edge of the cliff overlooking Petroşani. The small town had been his home for most of his life. His childhood memories were spent on its streets. He was luckier than most, at least he had known his mother. But he left when she died, leaving him with the horrors of his teen years in Bucharest. Now he was back, hopefully to stay. Even this high up, he could smell the

Vaughn Collar

aroma from the various restaurants, promising a good meal when he returned.

He turned back to the monastery as a wispy smile spread across his face. The old building felt welcoming, despite the decay. Here was where he had discovered magic. Here was where his future would be determined. He walked around the building, moving aside a rock or uprooting a vine that covered most of the ruins. The stonework showed the craftsmanship of long-ago builders as the structure remained upright. Only a few places were damaged, where centuries of wind and frost had cracked the bricks or caved in a wall. His hand ran across the brickwork, as if to feel the effort poured into this ancient site.

He stopped at what had once been the entrance. One pillar still stood, supporting the ceiling above the stairs. The other had long since collapsed, taking half of the roof with it. Staring into the dimly lit chamber, he recalled where he had already searched.

"I wonder," he thought aloud, "if I found everything."

He ran through the spells, including ones he hadn't memorized but knew what they were.

"Ah ... *hidden doors*. Just what I need."

He dug into his pack and removed a small notebook. Perusing the pages, he found the words he wanted.

Hmm, I need an amethyst.

He dug into a pouch hidden inside his jacket. Dumping the contents into his hand, a finely cut amethyst spilled out. Holding the jewel tightly, he went over the spell until it locked in his mind. Once he felt the familiar *click*, he walked inside. Facing the north wall, he held out the amethyst.

"OSTI ABSCONDITATE REVELITE MIHI!"

A purple beam shone from the gem, dully lighting the wall. Lucian slowly turned, holding out the gem. He shown the beam directly at the site and an outline appeared on the floor. It looked

The Rift - *Beginnings*

large enough to allow an adult to pass through. Lucian knelt and brushed away the dirt to reveal a hidden entrance. The spell expired as he traced the last turn.

"Just in time!" he softly exclaimed.

The hidden door was now clearly visible. He returned to his pack and retrieved a couple of pry bars. He had also brought a lantern, thinking to reserve his illumination spell. The lantern's light reflected against the dusty line, but Lucian could see no way to open the door – no latches, no obvious hinges. Not even a gap. Whatever was down there, the builders wanted it kept secret.

Should I open it at all?

He knelt and ran a finger along the trail, feeling only the vaguest hint of a depression. Using his fingers, he slowly traced the outline deeper in the dirt. Around a corner, the crack stopped.

"What the ...?" he whispered.

After marking where he was with a stone, he grabbed his backpack.

No telling what I'm going to need for this.

He selected a brush and returned to the stone. After sweeping away more dirt, he noticed that the crack ran along several bricks. A few more minutes passed until he had cleared one side. Lucian stood to relieve the pain in his knees. Looking at the path, he noticed how there was no mortar around one edge. A *hinge!* Ignoring his protesting knees, he knelt and cleared away the rest of the dirt. He ran his fingers lightly along the edge opposite the hinge. It took three attempts until he found a slight depression. The underlying brick was worn smooth from years of people pushing on it.

Wait a minute. The hinge doesn't allow it to open in that direction.

He searched the hinge side in the same manner. Knowing what to look for, it didn't take long until he found a worn surface the

Vaughn Collar

size of his palm. He pushed hard on the door and was rewarded with a puff of dust from the other side.

Must be jammed ... damn. Back to work, Luce.

He sat back to wipe the sweat from his 'brows. Only then did he consciously notice the changed light. A glance outside revealed it was close to sunset. Hours of work and he had only opened the door an inch or so. His sweat had turned dust to mud in a couple of places. His fingers were sore and one fingernail was half torn, the blood from the injury clogged by dirt. Resting for a few minutes, he caught his breath, giving his heart and lungs a break. An energy bar helped, providing a little boost.

"You're going to give yourself a heart attack," he murmured. A long exhale, then he whispered, "One more try, Luce ... one more."

Feeling re-energized from the break, he returned to the hatch. Choosing a slender pry bar, he ran it along the opening. A small stone was stuck in the crack. Tapping on the pry bar, he managed to loosen the stone. This gave him room to push the bar in and lift the hatch a millimeter. A second wedge fit just above the first. He pushed his weight on the two bar, ignoring the blood flowing down his fingers. A grinding noise echoed. A second push moved the hatch a little more. There was now room for a larger pry bar. With his remaining energy, he pushed with all his weight. A grating, rasping noise sounded in the chamber and one of the pry bars slipped into the crack. A gust of air whistled past Lucian and into the chamber.

"No wonder! The hatch was vacuum sealed." He gasped.

Nervous excitement coursed through him, wiping out his exhaustion and pain. He was able to lift the stone door fairly easily now. The old hinges suddenly worked as if they were brand new. Only a faint poof where dust and gravel were sucked in. He placed

The Rift - *Beginnings*

a few bricks to keep the door from closing. Once secure, he grabbed the lantern and looked in.

A spiral staircase led down into the gloom. The stairs appeared to have been chiseled directly from the hard rock. The steps were worn smooth by years of use. The wall was similarly smooth, from people bracing themselves for the steep descent.

Lucian could still feel a faint breeze as the air pressure equalized. The flow was reversed, with air now coming out of the room. With it came a horrid, fetid stench. There was a metallic tang to the odor that he couldn't immediately place. The image of a butcher shop came to mind.

"*Vas* ... that's blood. What the hell have I found?"

He cast a light spell, wanting to see more of what he was entering. All he could see were more stairs. Holding the spell steady in front of him, he slowly descended. The faint echo of his footsteps followed. He had come full circle when he reached the floor.

He moved the light higher. A large room was revealed, tables and benches lining one side. The craftsmanship of the door had prevented anything from entering the room. No spiders, no vermin of any sort could be seen or heard. There was hardly any dust.

Behind the tables were a series of arches with a corridor beyond. Shelves were chiseled into the stone on a far wall. The floor was smooth, almost polished from wear. An odd-looking table was in the center. He stepped closer, intrigued by its shape – a cross. Long grooves were carved into each end.

Almost as if someone ... oh my god! Lucian felt an intense urge to run, evil chilling in his veins.

He looked closer. There were slots carved into the stone where straps could be placed to hold a person down.

This is a sacrificial table!

Vaughn Collar

The stone was stained dark from countless amounts of blood running into containers below the table. One of the containers was still there, a faint coppery odor present. He knelt and held the lantern closer. A dark crust lined the inside, the reek of aged blood much stronger.

He stood and scanned the chamber. The nearest wall had slots similar to the table. One slot had something hanging from it. He stepped closer. It was leather wrapped over metal cords. Gingerly, he reached out and touched the strap, before lifting it. It was quite heavy, the leather preserved. He gently pulled and nothing happened. He tried again with more force. Again, nothing.

They didn't mean to have anyone escape this. What have I discovered?

Over the years, he had found evidence of sacrifices, but nothing like this. This place was tugging at his very soul. He could imagine the scene of people strapped to the table, their throats cut, blood running into the containers. People strapped to the walls, screaming in horror. A shiver ran down his spine. Steeling himself against the repulsive scene, Lucian pushed himself to remain calm. He had to close his eyes momentarily to block out the sight of this horrid chamber.

As he did, a curious sense of familiarity hit. He could feel, very faintly, magic. He touched his pouch and whispered, "Rivelate Magiate!"

The spell led him to a blank wall. Whatever the source was, it lay behind the brick. He grabbed a nearby stone to make a mark. A long look around the chamber showed this was the only spot where he could feel the pull. It took him only a minute or so to climb the stairs and grab his tools.

He returned to the spot and lit another lantern. Now with two lights blaring, the room was fully in view. More importantly, the light revealed the faint outline of a door or passageway. Wear in the stone at the base suggested the door opened into the room.

The Rift - *Beginnings*

Applying some force with a pair of pry bars, the door swung open fairly easily with only a faint grinding sound. A small hallway was revealed. Two doors were visible, one to each side. The sense of magic was coming from the door to his right. A slight push and it opened.

His senses felt the presence of various items. Several scrolls beckoned him. He unrolled one and was instantly on his knees after only a couple of words, the feeling of a thousand daggers stabbing his head from the inside. The spells were way beyond his abilities. He sat, waiting for the sensation to subside. He had not felt anything that powerful before.

"Mark these for later ... much later," he ruefully observed.

Further searching found a ring, ornately carved silver with an inset emerald. He set the scrolls and ring gently aside.

Several books didn't radiate magic but appeared old. He thanked the long-dead builders of this underground chamber. The almost air-tight construction had preserved the books and kept insects and mice away. A few utensils nearby looked interesting and joined the scrolls.

"I'm going to need to make a couple of trips," he muttered aloud.

For a find of this magnitude, he didn't begrudge the anticipated effort. This find alone would keep him busy for another year. Maybe two, if the magic in the scrolls was any indication.

Another look around didn't show anything else, either magical or of particular interest. The room on the other side of the hallway was just like the first, the wooden door swinging open with only a light push. The room was a disappointment in comparison. A few desiccated furs hung against a nearby wall. A bag on the floor tore when he tried to open it. Some coins fell out, not much more than

Vaughn Collar

a handful. Lucian placed them into a small storage pouch. Another glance around revealed nothing but an old tapestry.

But something about the tapestry bugged him. The longer he stared at it, the more one edge seemed out of place. He lightly ran a finger along the surface. The material felt smooth until he was close to the end. Very slightly, he felt a small crack under his finger. Tracing this outline revealed a small, wooden door.

He pushed – nothing. The outline crack wasn't large enough to insert even the smallest of his pry bars. He stepped back, examining every square inch. Nothing on the door itself. Then he saw a small opening to one side. The opening was shaped oddly, like a special key would be used. He searched the room and found nothing even remotely resembling a key.

"Alright, if I was the creator, the key wouldn't be far ..."

He kept looking at the hanging tapestry. If they used it to hide the entrance – *I wonder*. He reached to the top, working his way down. About a third of the way, he felt something hard woven into the fabric. Shining his light closer, he chuckled. The key. Without feeling for it, the key looked like a piece of the fabric.

"Clever, very clever. I'm impressed!"

He pulled out the key and inserted it into the lock. The lock was a bit stiff from the years but a little effort opened the small latch. Two books were inside along with a leather bag. Neither showed the glow of magic. Lucian carefully opened one and recognized the language. Some of the words looked Latin, but changed by centuries of being adapted into local dialects. After scanning down a couple of paragraphs, Lucian remembered where he had seen this dialect. It was the court language used at the time of Vlad Tepes!

He sat, his knees feeling weak. Very little had survived from that time. This was a find of incredible value. Looking more carefully, Lucian was able to pick out a word here and there. His

The Rift - *Beginnings*

blood chilled as he continued to read. The passage seemed to be describing the sacrifices of captives for their blood.

He left the room but glanced back at the table. He read a little more, then thought better of it. He didn't want to be near this place any longer. The sense of dread, of evil, was almost physical in strength. For anyone else, the sensation would likely have caused them to run. Lucian was very uncomfortable, but not fearful.

He wrapped the two books before placing them into his pack. He reached for the old leather bag next. Age had made the thin leather stiff and brittle, and it fell apart as he grabbed it. Stones fell out – red, green, purple, some clear, scattering across the floor. He picked up the closest one. Though not finished, he knew he was holding an emerald. The other stones – rubies, amethysts, opals – even diamonds. The wealth pouring out of the bag astonished him. *I can practically buy Petroşani with this!* He gathered everything, missing none of the stones.

"This solves the material issue with some of those spells."

Despite the chill and the surroundings, Lucian was smiling as wide as he'd ever smiled. Pleasant thoughts of furthering his magic abilities filled his head. He left the monastery without looking back.

Had he looked back when he climbed the stairs, he would not have had such pleasant thoughts. As the light from both lanterns and his spell receded, a swirl of dust lifted, taking on a corporeal form of a human before darkness closed in around it.

He had to be careful on his way down from the monastery. A light rain was falling, making for slippery footing in the decaying leaves and exposed rocks. Diminishing light made for an adventure he really didn't care for. The extra weight he was carrying didn't help either. What was normally an hour hike turned into a three

Vaughn Collar

hour slip, fall, and stop journey down the mountainside. He was thoroughly soaked by the time he reached his vehicle, along with harboring a fresh collection of bruises. Once back at his cabin, a hot bath felt great, but the exertion of the day was still with him.

Luce, you're not thirty anymore ... or even forty.

Laughing at himself a little, he sat to rest. He awoke in the darkness, feeling disoriented. Fumbling for the switch, he turned on a nearby lamp. It was just after two in the morning.

"Must have been a lot more tired than I thought."

He made his way to his bed and fell asleep. Birds chirping greeted him when he woke. Feeling stiff from exertion, he shuffled for a quick breakfast. The finger with the torn nail made handling anything painful.

"This is going to be a long day." He sighed.

He gathered up his bag and made his way to his lab. Setting everything out, he wondered where he needed to start. The bag of gems could wait. He knew next to nothing about their values, but they weren't going anywhere.

The book with the script from the court of Vlad Tepes beckoned him. Though not especially superstitious, he felt reading this book would be best outside – not in a small, confined room.

With his joints creaking, he set down his tea and settled into a chair on his porch. Only a few pages in, he reached a description of the rooms he had found. The words written made his decision to be in daylight more comforting. The paragraphs outlined a horrific scene where men were restrained and force fed the blood from the sacrificed. Spells were described to accompany the feedings. The end result left him speechless.

Men were turned into monsters with superhuman strength. Although they looked somewhat normal, their eyes glowed a bright red, and they grew fangs similar to a large snake. Their bodies became firm and likely invulnerable to weapons of that age. An

The Rift - *Beginnings*

overwhelming hunger for flesh and blood grew as if it were nourishment. It was necessary to cast spells to control and keep them weak until ready to throw at an enemy.

"Wait a minute. I've always thought the Huns were incorporated into the populace."

The book he held said something else. The newly created monsters were used to fight or attack small settlements of Huns. The practices described were dark, very dark. So dark, in fact, they eventually were forbidden. Some of the monsters continued to roam the countryside, looking for victims to feed on. Their horrific behaviors were already infamous by the time of Vlad Tepes.

"So, this is how the vampire stories started. There was a little truth behind the fables?"

Lucian kept reading until he came across a name – Stefano. A man returning to the area with an artifact to control the monsters. A ring to control the thirst for blood. Lucian put down the book and went back to his lab. He found the ring that radiated magic. But what kind of spells were infused in it?

It took Lucian several hours to figure it out. Casting them took all of his control and knowledge. Spells to determine what kind of magic, then determine if it was control or casting. Suffering from a blinding headache and clutching his component pouch, Lucian cast the last spell.

"QUID TIBI ELEMENTATE CONTROLLST!"

The ring glowed a reddish-purple hue and turned ice cold. Intricate markings around the central ruby materialized, the glyphs indicative of blood and control.

It controls the desire to taste blood? This was the ring spoken of in the story! That would make this ring ... almost two thousand years old, at least.

He was stunned. His research over the years had uncovered numerous legends of magic. He had always scoffed at these legends, believing them to be just the explanations of unknown chemical reactions or something similar. But now – now, he *knew* that magic existed. And was present long ago. Those legends would need to be examined – again.

By the end of the summer, Lucian knew he would likely have to start working again. His savings were still plentiful, but they wouldn't last forever. He couldn't go around cashing in valuable gems either. People would ask questions – awkward questions.

He landed a position teaching at the local college. They hired him to instruct an adult education course in history. On reflection, he felt this could prove to be rewarding. The people taking the course were there because they wanted to be there, not because of some degree requirement. Maybe a little time with students might not be so bad. He had almost completely withdrawn from society with his home off the grid.

One more weekend and he would have to become presentable to society again. His day was pretty much normal thus far – breakfast, a shower, study magic until lunch. He was sitting outside and enjoying the warmth of a late summer day. The warmth would not last much longer. The cold, soggy rains of autumn were less than a month away, and soon snow would fall in the alpine meadows high on his mountain.

The trees burst into a blinding light as birds took flight. The air became stiff and oppressive. Lucian felt a static charge.

Wha ...?

As the thought took form, a sensation passed through him. It strengthened, becoming almost a physical pull. It felt all too familiar, yet – different. Painful and nauseating at the same time. He staggered to his feet and looked into the forest.

The Rift - *Beginnings*

A ribbon of light flared across his little valley. The light becoming a jagged bolt, with a static charge shooting off in all directions. Where they landed, small fires sprung up in the leaves and pine needles. One small bolt lanced across the grass, enveloping him.

It wasn't the pleasant sensation of the light from four years ago. Searing pain radiated throughout his body. His chest grew tight as his heart raced. Driven to his knees, he curled up on the porch, the searing pain devouring his entire being. Screaming, Lucian's soul twisted. Yet – a whispery sound penetrated his yelps and surrounded him with a rhythm that felt as if someone – or something were speaking.

Not you ... not you, in a voice both soft and grating.

Then it passed.

He struggled back to his knees, gasping for air. A foul stench filled his senses, increasing his nausea. He managed to clear his porch as he lost his breakfast. He crawled and sat, leaning against his cabin, his head in his hands.

The feeling receded and the world slowly stopped spinning. He took a deeper breath and glanced around. Except for a few small, smoldering spots, everything looked normal, as if nothing had happened.

He knew better. Another rift had opened. This time, it *tasted* different, more spiritual, more powerful. Another fundamental change had happened. What – and where – he needed to know.

Time to see if his professor status could be useful to find the information he wanted.

Vaughn Collar

CHAPTER 36

The second wave, in its very nature, was significantly different from the first. It was less violent, not as dramatic. But changes wrought would not take as long to be observed. The first wave had brought massive casualties and damage across the globe. This time, however, there was only one direct fatality.

A rancher in Wyoming woke early to the sound of his cattle. He saddled a horse to investigate. He brought a rifle just in case it was a wolf pack or a bear.

He rode over a small rise and noticed his herd milling around one of the water ponds. The lead bull was positioned to charge at something out of view. With a bellow, the bull ran and disappeared behind a berm. A loud, crackling noise echoed across the field and the bull's call abruptly ceased. A breeze brought the odor of burnt flesh to the rancher, spurring him to move.

"What the hell ...?"

As he rode up, the area was lit by a slow-moving ribbon of electricity, sparks flying out in all directions. He hadn't noticed it initially, the sunrise diffused by the fog. He dismounted and approached on foot, mud squelching around his boots from the trampled ground. Walking past the large tree, the rancher was stunned by the scene.

The Rift - *Beginnings*

The bull lay on the ground, smoke rising from his corpse. The aroma of burnt flesh and hair filled the air, gagging him. The front half of the bull was gone. The exposed flesh cauterized by the intense heat.

"Oh my lord," the rancher exclaimed. Looking up, the shifting column of electricity had moved closer. "And what in the hell is that?"

One of the sparks flashed directly at the rancher, the entire flare following. It hit. The rancher stared at the hole in his chest, collapsing to the ground. Smoke from his body joined what was left of the bull. The herd milled around the two corpses for a bit before returning to grazing as this event receded to the background of their bovine minds.

His family did not discover his body until late in the afternoon. No one else had seen the event, marking his death as a mystery.

Life continued for most of the world. People had their lives to lead. Countries were busy rebuilding from the almost-constant civil unrest over the past few decades. Nature slowly took back what was hers, restoring forests and plains, allowing waterways to run clean. Only a few years had passed since the first wave. Now, with a second, new species were affected and some previously affected had changed more swiftly.

The howler monkey population was declining as the second generation of the changed species approached adulthood. The changes were no longer subtle. Most were taller, up to four-and-a-half feet, with smaller tails. Dwelling on the ground and walking upright meant the monkeys no longer needed prehensile tails. A social animal to begin with, the males now formed hunting packs. Meat was an increasingly larger portion of their diet. Sexual

Vaughn Collar

dimorphism was even more readily apparent, with the males significantly larger than the females. They were much more dangerous as a pack, as several jaguars had been killed. The leader of one pack wore the skin of a jaguar as a trophy. As for the unchanged howler monkeys, the changed members treated them with disdain, pushing them aside.

 The group of rhesus in Japan had similar, though lesser, growth than the howlers in Brazil. Their cognitive abilities had progressed even further. Several individuals in each group had mastered the use of simple tools. Rocks were used to crack open nuts. Long sticks were used to knock down fruits from slender limbs. A couple had learned not only about using rocks to create sparks, but exactly which rocks to use.

 One female was knocking stones together when a small piece flaked off. Curious, she picked it up. In doing so, she accidentally cut her finger. She dropped the sharp piece, sucking at her wound. A couple of days later, a juvenile member of the troop started screeching. It was stuck to a tree, the flowing sap mixing into its fur. The group gathered around, trying to help but not knowing what to do except to screech along with it. The female stopped, looked, and ran over to where she had dropped the flake. She picked it up and returned to the juvenile. Having an adult female close comforted it enough to calm it down. The female looked at the flake, then at the juvenile's fur. Haltingly, she initially tried to use the dull side to move the sap away. She turned the rock around, and with the sharp side, cut the juvenile away from the tree. It ran to its mother, seeking comfort. The female with the flake sat, staring at it. A male stepped up, and a glance passed between them. A new mental connection had formed. A new tool, a tool used to cut.

The Rift - *Beginnings*

The researchers assigned to the area reported one other important change. The monkeys, already a fairly vocal species, were using new sounds. Some of the sounds, the researchers were able to observe as repeated and were used to identify a certain tree or a certain nut. Not true words – not yet.

Hope Asher was the first born of the children with DNA changes. Her parents kept her at home, free from ridicule and publicity. For one, Hope was physically lagging behind other children her age. She looked younger than she truly was. Mentally and emotionally, however, she was far more advanced. She was reading books most second graders read, and she had a grasp on rudimentary math.

One startling change was her voice. Her regular speech was almost melodic. But when she sang, which was frequent, the very air itself seemed charged with positive energy. Plants around her visibly brightened. Birds would accompany her singing. The family dog acted like a puppy, not the nine year old she was.

Other changes were just becoming apparent as each child aged. Those like Hope, with black hair and purple eyes, were starting to acquire the faintest of blue tints to their cheeks and fingers. The children with golden hair were showing very faint tints of gold. And all had pointed ears.

The sun rose lazily over the dusty plains of the Serengeti. Before the noon heat reflected off the scorched dirt, animals started their day to avoid activity under the searing glare of the noon sun. The sky was a clear, pale blue with no visible clouds. Monsoon season remained many months away. A few watering holes spotted the landscape, but in most places the ground was cracking apart from the intense heat. Animals sought out shade to

Vaughn Collar

rest in cooler places. The temperature rose with the advancing afternoon and dust simooms spun from the dry clay of old creeks and ponds.

A small mound above the plain, nestled just under an acacia bush. It was positioned to absorb heat from the day and warm a clutch of buried eggs. A silvery ribbon of light appeared with small electric sparks. Through winding movements, the ribbon slowly advanced, flowing over the mound. It remained for a moment before wafting away.

The mound burst apart close to the base and several eggs rolled out. A few opened with the hatchlings literally cooked inside the shell. Several more died soon after, their bodies not fully formed. Parts of the dead were slightly larger than usual and the remainder at least twice as large. The stench of burnt flesh was thick. Entrails spilled out from the deformed carcasses.

Three eggs survived. The shells tore open and the young crawled out. A few moments rest as the sun dried their skin. Glancing around, the males attacked each other. Skin flew as razor-sharp teeth dug into the flesh. The sound of the struggle echoed across the plain, attracting the attention of a nearby serval. Within moments, one of the young was dead, its body torn apart, already attracting flies. The other two faced each other and the frills around the back of their heads flared with different colors. The male possessed a gaudy frill, the female rather plain as it blended with the dry clay of the area. Both backed off from confrontation. Instinctively, they recognized each other as the opposite sex.

The serval attacked from behind as it hurtled its body at the male. The male straightened its legs and expanded its frill. Behind its front shoulders, two spikes rose. A loud, guttural hiss sounded. The serval froze, unsure of its attack. The lizard hissed again, bright teeth shining with deadly incisors.

The Rift - *Beginnings*

The cat paced and growled. Hunger was vying with caution. The female had circled behind the mound and attacked from the side. The serval sprang out of the way but landed too close to the male. The male rushed in, closing its jaw around the cat's neck. Blood splattered across the dirt. The cat yowled, desperately trying to free itself. The male hung on tight, using its body to pin the prey down. The female slashed with her sharp claws, tearing the belly open. The death throes of the cat ceased.

The male released its hold and walked over the carcass as it climbed the mound. The eyes of the two lizards met and they made a guttural grunt. Rearing up on hind legs, the male spread it vestigial wings, issuing a sound never before heard in the barren Serengeti plains.

The cry was somewhat between a hiss and a roar. The male repeated the call several times before the female mimicked the sound. The male dropped to all fours. The vestigial wings spread wider than before with the evolved flexible joints. One last hiss and the male closed his jaws, a thin trail of smoke curling up and out of its nose.

Vaughn Collar

The Rift - *Beginnings*

Vaughn Collar

is a busy actor, appearing in *God's Not Dead: A Light in Darkness* and several student films, along with appearances in *Preacher Six* and *Life's Masquerade*. The Rift is his debut novel. He's spent hours researching the history of Vlad Tepes, weaving history and ancient Roman culture into an intriguing tale of *what if's?*

He's married, very happily so, to Linda, and has one daughter, Morgan. He calls Little Rock, AR and Vancouver, B.C. his hometowns, after spending twelve years in British Columbia during his teens and early adult years.

Vaughn Collar

The Rift - *Beginnings*

The Rift - *New Paradigm*

Ian and Lucian return as their magic grows in both power and strength. But were they the first? Were they the only humans affected?

New Paradigm, the second book in *The Rift,* shakes the world as another wave hits. A wave that sends others into that dark void known as *magic*.

As more animals and insects change, what are they changing into? Are legends just legends or are past myths our new reality?

Shelly searches for these wielders of lost magic, while asking the harsh question ... 'are they good or evil?'

New Paradigm, scheduled release – spring of 2025

Vaughn Collar

The Rift - *Beginnings*

Vaughn Collar

Printed in the USA
CPSIA information can be obtained
at www.ICGtesting.com
LVHW040612210624
783604LV00017B/39/J